The Cosy Seaside Chocolate Shop

Caroline Roberts lives in the wonderful Northumberland countryside with her husband and credits the sandy beaches, castles and rolling hills around her as inspiration for her writing. She enjoys writing about relationships; stories of love, loss and family, which explore how beautiful and sometimes complex love can be. A slice of cake, glass of bubbly and a cup of tea would make her day – preferably served with friends! She believes in striving for your dreams, which led her to a publishing deal after many years of writing. *The Cosy Seaside Chocolate Shop* is her sixth novel.

If you'd like to find out more about Caroline, visit her on Twitter, Facebook and her blog – she'd love to hear from you!

🐦 @_caroroberts
📘 /CarolineRobertsAuthor
carolinerobertswriter.blogspot.co.uk

Also by Caroline Roberts

The Desperate Wife
The Cosy Teashop in the Castle
The Cosy Christmas Teashop
My Summer of Magic Moments
The Cosy Christmas Chocolate Shop

Caroline Roberts

The Cosy Seaside Chocolate Shop

Harper*Impulse* an imprint of
HarperCollins*Publishers*
1 London Bridge Street
London SE1 9GF

www.harpercollins.co.uk

First published by HarperCollins*Publishers* 2018
1

A catalogue record for this book
is available from the British Library

ISBN: 978-0-00-829554-7

Set in Minion Pro 12/15.25 pt by Palimpsest Book Production Limited, Falkirk, Stirlingshire

Printed and bound in the UK by CPI Group (UK) Ltd, Croydon CR0 4YY

MIX
Paper from
responsible sources
FSC™ C007454

This book is produced from independently certified FSC™ paper
to ensure responsible forest management.

For more information visit: www.harpercollins.co.uk/green

For Julie and Kathryn –
onwards and upwards

'There is nothing better than a friend,
Unless it is a friend with chocolate.'

Linda Grayson

1

'Is it ready yet?' The young man stood at the counter smiling, a hint of nervous anticipation in his blue eyes.

'Yes, of course. I added the final touches to it this morning,' Emma answered.

'I can't wait to see it. And did it fit in okay?'

'Yep, no problem at all. I used one of the little cellophane bags I usually put the truffles in to protect it – didn't want any chocolate smears to spoil the box. It looks great, honestly. I'm sure she'll be happy with it. Anyway, I'll go and fetch it from the crafting kitchen, where I've kept it safe for you, then you can see for yourself.'

It had been an unusual and rather lovely request: to place an engagement ring inside a hand-crafted chocolate Easter egg. Emma had been asked to design several creations, or add special messages to gifts, over the eight years since she had opened The Chocolate Shop by the Sea, but never this. She'd thought it wise to keep the ring in its jeweller's box, so the lucky girl in question didn't spoil the moment of revelation by eating it accidentally and ending up in A&E!

Emma had spent many hours designing and crafting the delicate, filigree-inspired sugar-paste design of hearts and flowers that adorned its moulded dark chocolate sides (dark chocolate being the fiancée-to-be's favourite). With some trepidation, and not wanting any breakages at the last moment, she carried it carefully through to the shop, praying that it would be everything that Mark, the young man waiting at the counter, was hoping for.

'Wow, that's *amazing*.' The young man's jaw dropped.

Emma felt her shoulders relax as she placed the very special chocolate egg on the counter-top.

He smiled ecstatically at her. 'The design is just stunning. She'll love it, I'm sure. Let's hope she loves what's inside too.'

'She'd better,' Emma grinned. 'If someone had made that much effort for me, well . . .' She let the words trail. Someone had, once, many years ago. Just the memories and the love she still felt for that wonderful person took her back – and still, after all these years, it had the power to make her feel raw, bruised.

'Well, best of luck,' Emma rallied, not wanting her own past to tarnish someone else's bright, shiny future. 'Here, let me pack it up for you. I have a box and bubble wrap to make it as safe as I can.'

'I'll drive home steadily, I promise.'

And a few minutes later, the young man was setting

off with his 'engagement egg' safely stowed in his arms, along with a heart full of hopes and dreams.

Emma stood at the counter, waving a cheery goodbye to him, but he could only manage a small nod in reply for fear of dropping his precious cargo, although he was smiling broadly.

Emma sighed happily. She loved this job so much. Well, it was more than a job to be honest – it was her own business, with her gorgeous little flat above the shop that was compact but cosy. 'The Chocolate Shop by the Sea' had been her refuge all those years ago, and now it was her joy. Coming down in the mornings to the scent of cocoa and vanilla, and sometimes warming whisky or orange, depending on what she'd been crafting the night before. The flavours and smells changed by the seasons, as did the colourful displays in the shop. Now, it was spring with wraps, boxes, ribbons and tags in Easter-bright yellows, pinks, blues and greens.

She looked around her. The shop, with its café, was fairly small, having been someone's front room once upon a time. It had a traditional wooden floor and the original stone cottage walls and there were two round tables set in the window-seat area that overlooked the quaint village street. The counter area had a refrigerated unit to store the cream-based truffles and ganaches safely and wooden shelves for her fabulous displays of chocolate, including a quirky boat-hull-styled unit that she kept filled with pretty packs of truffles, fudge and hand-crafted chocolate bars.

She had re-styled the shop to echo the pretty harbour location, with new sky-blue seat pads for the window seats and stripy cushions in blues, cream and greys. Even the chocolates on the counter featured puffins, shells, anchors and boats.

Holly, her seventeen-year-old assistant, was due in any minute. She usually started at ten o'clock on a Saturday. Holly, a bubbly, pretty girl with a mass of wavy brown hair was in her final year at the local Sixth Form and worked for Emma at weekends and holidays. Emma knew she would likely lose her after the summer, when university or a college course beckoned. They had chatted about it recently after closing one day, both perched on stools with hot chocolates at the counter. The young girl would be a real miss at the shop, with her sunny nature and diligent attitude, though of course Emma wished her well for her future. They had worked hard together this last year, turning the business around and making its new coffee shop a success. There had been much fun and laughter along the way too.

Em spotted Holly's dark curls bouncing by the front window.

'Hi, Em.' Holly was grinning happily as she came into the shop.

'Morning, Holly.'

She was followed by a smart-looking lady in her sixties, who approached the counter with a friendly smile.

'Hello, I'm looking to buy three chocolate eggs for my

grandchildren. Something a bit different for each. Any ideas?'

'Boys? Girls? Any hobbies?' Emma asked.

'Well then, Laura's seven and into football, having just got into the school team.'

'Ooh, well done to her.'

'Her little sister is just a toddler who adores all things pink. And my grandson's nine and mad about all those Xbox games and cricket.'

'Okay, I have some suggestions.' And with that, Emma brought forward some examples to the counter. 'So, I do have a football egg, and believe it or not an Xbox-controller-shaped egg. It's been popular, I can tell you. Or I can personalise a traditional egg with a name and a message, and there are large chocolate Easter bunnies and chicks, with varying ribbons and decorations. I can certainly go large on a fancy pink ribbon for the toddler with any of those. There are also hamper-style gifts with a selection of things in.'

'Hmm, I can see I'm spoilt for choice. These all look fabulous. I'm so glad the young man at our hotel told me to call down here.'

Holly was now standing beside Em, with her stripy blue apron on. Em felt her positively glow. The young man in question being her boyfriend, Adam, who worked as the assistant manager of The Seaview Hotel at the top of the village.

'I'll go with the football egg and two of the bunnies,

please,' the lady continued. 'Can I have one with a pink ribbon and the other with a green spotty bow tie?'

'Of course. Let me pop them into bags for you. Can I help with anything else?'

'Hmm, yes,' The woman scanned the glass window of the refrigerated section. 'Maybe a box of whisky truffles for my husband.'

After that, being the day before Easter Sunday, the customers kept piling in, and the café was buzzing all morning. The mini egg bags had run out by lunchtime, but there were plenty of other options. It was a fine balance, ensuring there was plenty of choice for those special occasion days, but also that you weren't left with too much. Emma and Holly didn't stop. Thank goodness Emma's close friend, Bev, had agreed to help this afternoon too; she usually worked for a couple of days in the week.

The Chocolate Shop was in full swing right up to the close of business – an hour later than normal at six o'clock. Emma saw the last gentleman out with his huge fancy marbled milk-and-white egg filled with truffles, checked the street for any last-minute stragglers and seeing there were just a couple of tourists heading down the hill towards the harbour, she shut the door, turning the painted wooden sign to *Closed*. Wow! That was some day – feet throbbing, hands sore from all the wrapping and tying of bows, and a till hopefully laden with cash ready to pay next month's rent.

'Thanks for all your hard work, ladies.' Emma turned to Bev and Holly.

'You're welcome,' Bev replied.

'No worries.' Holly smiled at her boss. 'I'm going home to get ready to go out with Adam. I think he's taking me for a meal.'

'Ooh, lovely. *And*, hang on, I have a gift for you both. You can't be working in a chocolate shop and not be getting any perks.' Em trotted off to the back kitchen to fetch the two chocolate eggs she had hand-crafted especially for her staff. Both had their names carefully written in white chocolate across them. Holly's was milk with white chocolate spots all over it and Bev's was dark with hand-crafted flowers in white and dark chocolate, both filled with their favourites: Eton Mess truffles with meringue and strawberry pieces for Bev, and Baileys truffles plus some salted caramels for Holly.

'Oh my, that is amaze-balls.' Holly beamed. 'It's almost too good to eat.'

'That is *so* pretty,' Bev added. 'Mind you, I'll have no trouble tucking into mine. It looks divine. Thanks so much.' She gave Em a hug.

'You only love me for my chocolate,' Emma jested as they pulled away.

'Absolutely.' Bev grinned.

'Right, well, time to get yourselves home then. We've already run well over time, so thank you. I'll do the last bit of tidying here.'

'You sure?' Holly checked; she'd quite gladly help for a while longer.

'I'm fine, honest. Go get your glad rags on, young lady, and enjoy your evening. Tomorrow's a day off for me too. *Yee-es.*' Em was more than ready for it, the run-up to Easter being particularly hectic. It was one of the few Sundays of the year when she closed.

The perfect antidote to a hectic day in the shop was a walk along the beach. After her staff had gone home, Emma nipped upstairs, took off her work apron, and found the lead for Alfie, her much-loved springer spaniel. He leapt out of his bed in her upstairs kitchen and was soon bouncing around her ankles.

'Come on then, boy. Time for the beach.'

He knew the routine off by heart and didn't need asking twice; he bounded off down the stairs then sat waiting, tail wagging eagerly, by the back door. They left by the courtyard, a lovely stone-flagged area to the rear of the shop, turned out through the side alley to join the main village street of quaint stone cottages, and headed down the hill to the harbour, past the grocer's store and the new arts-and-crafts shop. It was breezy but mild, and a few fishing boats bobbed alongside the harbour wall; two of the traditional cobles had been brought up to the shoreline and rested amongst lobster pots, colourful buoys and thick-corded ropes. Emma said 'hello' to a group of tourists she passed, and gave a wave to Danny, her friend from the pub. The Fisherman's Arms was set on top of the slope that rose gently to the right of the harbour and Danny happened to be out in the front car park, chatting to some guests.

Within five minutes she and Alfie were walking along the sandy track through the dunes, coming out upon a golden sweep of crescent-curved beach. Emma let Alfie off the lead and he ran joyfully down to the water's edge, where rolling waves foamed in from the pewter-grey North Sea. It was beautiful there and strolling along the soft sands calmed her instantly. The hush of the waves, the breeze on her face, Alfie in his element – Warkton-by-the-Sea, with its beach, harbour, village of stone cottages and warm local hearts – this was home. This was her happy place – at last.

She walked the length of the bay to where the rock pools gathered before the low cliffs. The evening was beginning to creep in, the sky gently fading to a peachy-grey before night came. She'd get back; she needed to get ready to see Max anyhow. It wasn't only Holly who had a date night to look forward to. Emma's boyfriend would be with her in an hour or so. Wow, she could still hardly believe all that had happened in the past year. She never imagined she could fall in love again – after the pains of the past she could hardly bear to think about – yet here she was – *they* were – still in the early, tentative, but oh-so-sweet-and-sexy days of their relationship. Another love.

2

Emma woke the next morning to find Max asleep beside her. It was rather wonderful, but it still took a little getting used to. He'd arrived a little later than expected last night, so they had had a chilled-out evening in the flat above the shop, catching up on their week apart over a supper of chicken and salad.

The morning light glowed on his face, which was framed by short, mid-brown hair. She studied the dark lashes on his closed lids, the shallow lines on his forehead, deeper laughter lines around his eyes that she knew were hazel-green, the sensual curve of his lip, the cropped beard. It was a handsome face, a little lived-in and rather gorgeous. Watching him made her melt and then spin inside. It was hard to pin down these new emotions. She had been self-contained for so many years; a case of necessity. And day by day she felt her heart unravelling just a little more. It felt beautiful . . . and somewhat scary.

She reached to gently touch his shoulder which was

bare above the covers. He was well-built, the muscles defined. There was the small scar where he had injured it just before Christmas. He still had to be careful, the dislocation to his shoulder making it likely that it might happen again. She loved him for his scars, his hurts, as well as his bloody sexy body. And hey, there were worse things to get used to than waking up to a strong, caring guy who looked a bit like Gerard Butler.

His eyes blinked open. 'Morning, beautiful.' His just-awake smile was warm in his voice.

'Hello, gorgeous.' Their morning greeting had become their 'thing' as they welcomed another day. It started off as a cheesy joke but had stuck and it never failed to make her smile. 'Oh, hang on,' she added, 'Happy Easter.'

'Happy Easter, Em. Now then, I haven't got you a chocolate egg – thought you might be all chocolated-out by now. But I did get you this . . .' He got out of bed, totally starkers, and wandered across to the chair where he had placed his clothes and overnight bag. She loved that he was happy in his own skin, uninhibited. He lifted out a small gift from his luggage. 'For you.'

He climbed back into bed, as she opened the gift bag to reveal a very cute soft toy rabbit.

'Well, you seem to be the one doing all the Easter-egg making and delivering around here, so I thought your very own Easter Bunny might be quite fitting.'

'Aw, how sweet. He's really lovely.' The toy was gorgeous, all soft beige fur, with a white fluffy bib area and a yellow-spotted bow tie. 'Thanks.'

With that, she leaned down to find her gift for him where she'd hidden it under the bed. 'And this . . . is not your average Easter egg, by the way.'

'Oh, I can't wait.' Max opened the medium-sized cardboard box, unwrapping layers of tissue paper to find a set of chocolate tools: spanner, hammer, nuts and bolts, and a screwdriver with screws.

'Hah, this is brilliant!'

'All edible,' Emma announced. She had seen the moulds online and knew that was *just* the thing for Max, who owned his own building company. It had taken a while to get the silver-metallic finish just right, but she was pleased with the end result.

'Wow, I've never seen anything like this. It's so cool. I'm gonna have to show the lads at work. Thank you.' He beamed at her. 'I love it.'

'You're welcome.'

He leant across to give her the most tender kiss – an embrace that promised so much more.

'We have no rush this morning,' she hinted. 'I'm not opening the shop today.' After three weeks of manic build-up, creating chocolate eggs of all shapes and sizes, filled chocolate bonnets, moulded Easter chicks and bunnies, she was more than ready for a day off – a rare treat. Running your own business meant long hours, and busy days.

'Hmmn, no rush at all then. *So*, I'm going to make love to you very, very slowly indeed.'

Em felt her whole body tingle just at the thought of it.

'And . . . I might even find a use for that chocolate spanner,' he added jokingly, with such a wickedly naughty grin on his face, that the pair of them dissolved into laughter.

Making love in the morning left you with a warm glow for the rest of the day. There had been no rush for Emma and Max to be out early, but there were two special chocolate Easter eggs she had yet to deliver to her twin nieces who lived nearby. They arrived late morning at her brother James's house, which was in a small hamlet in the countryside outside the market town of Alnwick, a twenty-minute drive away through pretty country lanes.

After the annual Easter egg trail in the back garden for the girls, which had now become a bit of a tradition (and who better to bring the most delicious chocolate eggs than Auntie Emma?), they were chatting in the family kitchen over tea and simnel cake, with Easter 'nests' the girls had made themselves with lots of chocolate, cereal and mini eggs.

'Uncle Max, do you like my chick?' Lucy asked.

Emma had lovingly crafted two large and very cute chocolate Easter chicks, which had been the grand finale of the trail. They even had bow ties on – one red and spotty, the other yellow-striped.

'He's rather fabulous, isn't he? Do you think it is a he?' Max asked, noting with a smile that there was a large chunk of chocolate missing already from the back of his head.

13

'Oh, yes. Of course.'

'Mine's a girl,' Olivia piped up. 'I'm going to call her Flick.'

'Flick, the chick. That's a cool name,' Max said, grinning.

Max was a natural with the children, so at ease chatting away with them, despite having no nieces or nephews of his own. Lucy had started calling him Uncle Max soon after Christmas, when Emma had only been seeing him for a few months, and it had stuck. He seemed very much a part of Emma's family already.

'So, how's the shop going, Em?' Chloe, her sister-in-law, asked.

'It's been really hectic in the run-up to Easter, but that's good. And I'm managing to keep up with the rent payments okay for now, so that's a bit of a relief.' There had been issues with a huge rent hike the year before, but Emma was managing to keep the wolf of a landlord from the door at the moment. The new café area was proving popular and her Chocolate Shop by the Sea was doing well; it certainly kept her busy.

'That's good news, Em. Glad to hear it. Anyone for a top-up?' Chloe got up from the table where she'd been sitting with Emma and busied herself with the kettle and teapot.

The two men were standing chatting by the French windows that led to the garden. They were talking work too.

'The accountancy practice has been full on lately,'

James, her brother, was saying, 'what with the end of the financial year coming up. You?'

'Yeah, lots on for me at the moment,' Max replied. 'Things have really picked up in the building industry again. New houses going up, conversions, all sorts. In fact, I've just been offered a great project down in Leeds.'

Emma's ears pricked up – it was the first she'd heard of this.

'Converting a warehouse into apartments, right by the side of one of the canals. The job's worth a lot of money and sounds really interesting. I like working with original buildings, but then that has its problems too, and it'll mean I'll be travelling and being away quite a bit. Gotta go where the business is, though.'

'Too right.'

Well, thanks for letting me know about this, Emma mused, feeling a little disgruntled that he hadn't thought to tell her first. It was hard enough finding time to spend together as it was, with both of them running their own businesses.

'Uncle Max, can you come and play dens with us?' Lucy interrupted.

The girls had a Wendy house all set up in the lounge.

'Yes, Uncle Max.' Olivia was on the case too.

'Okay, okay. Just give me five minutes to finish my tea.'

'O-kay.'

It always made Emma laugh seeing him trying to squeeze his well-built frame into the tiny tent-like play zone. He was often the 'giant' in whatever scene they were playing. And off he went, escorted by two five-year-olds to the play den, one holding each hand. He gave a mock look of horror to Emma, but she knew he didn't mind. Hah, they might even get to paint his fingernails again. They had once before, in alternate colours of pink and silver, and he had begged Em to go to the village grocer's for some remover, before he set off to work the next day. 'I look like Eddie Izzard or something,' he'd muttered. 'I'll never survive the ribbing from the lads if I don't get rid.'

Em chatted with James and Chloe, catching up on her brother's recent visit to her parents – she hadn't had a chance to call across herself with the shop being so busy lately – whilst Max kept the girls happily occupied. She peeked into the lounge at one point to find them putting hair clips in his hair, which was a challenge with it being so short. They stayed for another half hour or so after Max managed to escape the den, chatting over a glass of wine, and then set off back to Warkton-by-the-Sea.

'Max . . .' Emma said in her car on the way home, 'I couldn't help but hear you and James talking earlier. Why hadn't you told me about the job in Leeds?' It had been simmering away in her mind. She concentrated on her steering as she reached a sharp bend in the country lane. Her fingers tensed.

'I was going to – it just didn't seem right last night when I'd only just got there. I wanted to relax and have a nice evening. I would have said something tonight.'

'Oh. Well, with you away more, will I still get to see

16

you?' They only managed to snatch days together at the weekends as it was.

She sounded needy, she knew, and hated that. But she was just getting used to being in a relationship again, had only just let someone back into her heart. It felt odd, like a loss of independence, life had been a lot simpler for all those years on her own.

Simpler, but rather lonely, something inside reminded her.

Ah, relationships, they made you feel out of control, fuzzy at the edges somehow. Hah, that's when they didn't rip you apart.

To be fair on Max, working six days a week herself and also a Sunday afternoon at busy times, didn't help matters. It was hard for both of them, with their homes an hour apart, leading different and hectic working lives. It was sometimes a miracle they had time to meet up at all. But the alternative, no Max, she didn't like to think of that.

'Sorry, I didn't mean for you to find out like that.' His green eyes gazing across the car at her were caring, his gentle smile honest.

How could she stay cross with him? 'Ah, it's okay.' Her tone softened. Through the windscreen, the metallic blue of the sea came into view as they approached her village. She was more annoyed at herself for beginning to rely on him being there. She knew he had to be back at work early tomorrow, leaving her bed in the early hours and she didn't want to spoil this evening. She had plans for them to walk on the beach with Alfie, before a cosy supper, a seat for two on the sofa by the fire, then hopefully making love once more. Having Max in her life was *so* much better than having him out of it.

3

'How's sexy lover boy, then?'

'Morning, Bev.' Thank goodness there were no customers in as yet. Em felt her cheeks tingle with a blush.

'So,' her friend continued angling, 'good weekend?'

'Yes, thanks . . . very good. And yes, Max did come up.'

Bev's eyebrows arched cheekily. 'Hmm,' was all she uttered with a daft grin on her face.

'. . . *to stay.*' Emma completed the phrase, shaking her head.

'Ah, if only I wasn't already married!' Bev was still grinning away. She loved teasing Emma. 'Now I know why you were all ice maiden for six years: I think I would have been too if I knew that was the prize at the end of it.'

'O-kay, enough!' Yes, so Max was pretty good-looking, but really, despite being her best friend ever since her arrival in Warkton-by-the-Sea, Bev could sometimes take things a little too far. But still, the conversation *had* made her smile, she conceded.

'Right, what do you need help with this morning, boss?' Bev asked cheerily.

'Well, I'd like to crack on in the kitchen with making some more ganaches and truffles. It'll be a nice change from Easter eggs and that'll replenish the stocks for the refrigerated counter. I fancy doing some Irish Cream truffles and trying out some new Red Velvet ones. I thought I might experiment with that flavour.'

'Ooh, they sound nice. I am prepared to sacrifice my waistline to test any new chocolates out, you know.'

'That's no surprise. So, if you can just keep an eye on the shop and café whilst I'm in the back kitchen, I promise to bring through a couple to try once they are made.'

'Can't wait. We can test them out with morning coffee.'

'Perfect.'

'Oh, Em. I've brought in some miniature daffodils from my garden for the posy vases on the tables.'

'Aw, thanks. That'll cheer things up in here.' It was a grey old day outside, the April sky heavy with cloud and the threat of rain. But hey-ho, it might just make a cosy chocolate shop café even more appealing to the tourists on their Easter holiday break.

The shelves behind Bev were stacked with chocolate bars in many flavours, packs of chocolate-dipped fudge, a counter with truffles and melt-in-your-mouth ganaches, moulded lollipops with puffins and teddy bears on, a few remaining Easter chicks and bunnies, and lots more.

Emma loved the chance to change the selections by season and special holidays. Now the displays were brightly coloured for spring and Easter, with gift boxes in gold and white, and pretty cellophane packs with curls of ribbons in pinks, blues, greens and yellows.

Despite the grey skies outside, spring was very much in the air. The season of hope, new life and second chances.

There was a lull just after eleven and Emma made coffee for herself and Bev.

'Coffee time,' she called, bringing through a tray with a cafetière of coffee on, as well as a small plate with a selection of choc-chip shortbread, the new Red Velvet ganaches, and a couple of other chocolates to try.

'Oh my, I think I'm actually going to drool.' Bev's eyes lit up. 'How did I get so lucky as to work in a chocolate shop, with my bestie, no less?' The novelty of helping out at The Chocolate Shop still delighted Bev. She also worked a couple of mornings as a receptionist at the doctors' surgery in the next village, which had been her job for many years, but now she was also helping her friend, and this didn't feel like work at all.

They settled themselves on stools to the side of the counter.

'Now these are lemon meringue cups, and the new red velvet, and there's a strawberries-and-cream bar in white chocolate that I've broken up to try. I'll put some out as tasters on the counter shortly.'

Bev dived straight in, taking a bite of a lemon cup. 'Oh wow, delicious!'

Em poured out the coffee, its rich aroma filling the shop.

'I've been thinking . . .' Bev started.

'Now that could be dangerous!'

'Hah.' Bev looked indignant.

'Go on.'

'Well, you remember what a success your launch night for the chocolate café was? With all the chocolate and bubbly we had. And you're always looking for ways to improve the shop, and bring in more money, of course . . .'

'Ye-es.' Em wondered where this might be going.

'Well, what about prosecco-and-chocolate nights? Girlie nights, celebrations, that type of thing.'

'Hmm.' Emma sipped her coffee. 'You might just be on to something there.'

'Well, *I'd* love to go to something like that, so would lots of my friends, I'm sure. Something a bit different from going out into town or to the local pubs and clubs, getting pushed about in a crowd, your toes stood on and lager spilled down your back. Yes, chocolate nights in.'

'Interesting . . . I know there's all sorts of legal implications to consider for being licenced to serve alcohol for the prosecco, but I might just look into it. In fact, I think it could work well.' Emma was always open to new ways to expand the business and protect her Chocolate Shop's future. 'Yes, I can picture it now. Hen do's, small parties, birthdays. Maybe we could do a hands-on truffle-making session too, as part of the party.' Her mind was on a roll now. 'My cocktail-based ones might work well. The Pimm's chocolate cups I did last summer, or the Pina Colada or Mojito truffles.'

'Ooh, yes. Sounds brilliant. Of course, being my idea, it will be.'

Emma took a sip of coffee. 'Hmm, I'm liking it, Mrs Walker. You might well be on to something. I'll do some research. An extra string to The Chocolate Shop's bow can only be a good thing. Whilst we're going along nice and steady at the moment, who knows what's around the corner?' She remembered only too well the rent hike of last year, and her greedy landlord, Mr Neil, was always waiting in the wings. But more than that, it sounded a really lovely thing to do.

With that, the shop door chimed, and in came old Mrs Clark, one of their regulars. The elderly lady was well wrapped up in her coat and scarf, but she looked a little more stooped lately, and her face a little paler than usual.

Emma stood up to greet her. 'Morning, Mrs C, and how are you today?'

'Not so bad, Emma, not so bad.' It was as though she was trying to convince herself. 'Mind, that hill up's a bit of a bugger. Gets steeper every time.' Mrs Clark loved the 'B' word and used it prolifically. It always made Emma smile.

'Well, come and have a seat, Mrs C. What can we get for you? The usual coffee? We have some nice chocolate cake, freshly made too, if you fancy?'

'Just a cup of coffee, pet. That'll be grand. And how are you two ladies?' Mrs Clark settled herself into one of the window seats, placing her large handbag beside her and removing her woollen coat and patterned head scarf.

'Good thanks,' answered Bev. 'We're planning prosecco parties.'

'My, that sounds fun. That's what you young ones should be doing, having fun. Life's too short not to enjoy it. We had some good parties in our time. I remember the old tea dances down at the village hall. Me and my Jim, back when we were courting – those were the days.' Her grey-green eyes seemed to light up with the memories, then she smiled and sighed all at once.

'Go on, tell me about it back then, Mrs C,' Bev took up.

'I'll just go and fetch your coffee, Mrs Clark. Won't be a minute,' said Emma, knowing the story would still be in full flow on her return.

'Thanks, pet.'

'Well then, I do remember one of the tea dances in particular. I wasn't supposed to be going out that night at all as my dad was still cross. You see, I'd been out with Jim to the pictures in Alnwick two days before, and somehow we'd missed the eight-fifteen bus home.'

Bev was nodding, enjoying the story. She liked to hear about the village in the old days.

'Well,' Mrs C continued, 'if truth be told, I think we'd spent far too long kissing round the back of the picture house after the film. Lost track of time. Of course, there were no mobile phones, not even many telephone boxes back then, to let my parents know. Well, my dad was all burnt up with anger when I got back.'

'Ah, he was probably just worried.'

'Yes, but you don't think the same when you're young and in love. That was it, he said I wasn't allowed out for another week. And warned me never to be late again.'

Emma returned with a cafetière of fresh coffee that gave off a gorgeous aroma. She'd popped a mini chocolate brownie on the side of Mrs C's coffee cup for good measure.

'Well then, my Jim had other plans. Little did I know he'd been planning a special night. He'd gone to call on my dad without me knowing – one, to apologise and two, to ask for something else.'

'Ooh, and what was that?'

'Suddenly, it all changed and I was allowed to go, my mother making a big fuss over my dress choice, which wasn't like her at all. Well . . .' The old lady grinned, her eyes twinkly at the memory. 'He only went down on one knee in the middle of the dance floor. Oh, I still remember that so well, the band were playing Buddy Holly's "True Love Ways". Jim had asked for it specially, it was one of my favourites. I said "yes" straight away, of course.'

'Aw, that's such a lovely story,' Em smiled.

'True love, hey, Mrs C,' Bev added.

'Ay, those were the days.'

4

Even when you fall in love with someone new, you never stop loving and thinking of that first person – not when they had died only a few months before you were due to be married.

There was a phone call that Emma had been meaning to make for a few days now. That Monday evening she picked up her mobile and dialled.

'Angela, hello. It's Emma.'

'Oh Emma, how lovely to hear from you. How are you, darling?'

It had been a month since she had spoken to Angela. She was Luke's mum – Luke, Emma's fiancé, who at only twenty-six had been knocked off his bicycle by a lorry and killed instantly. Luke, whose photo still sat on Emma's dressing table.

'I'm fine, thank you.'

'And are you still with your young man?' Angela asked.

'Yes, I am. It's going well.'

'That's good. I'm pleased for you, Emma. Really.'

It must be hard for her to say that when they both knew that it should have been her son's place next to Emma in the world. And yet, here was a mother, generous with her love and good wishes, despite all the pain and the might-have-beens.

'Thank you.' Emma's voice had quietened. Although she had fallen in love with Max only recently, and Luke was no longer here, it still felt a little like a betrayal.

'And how has The Chocolate Shop been doing, and the new café? You must tell me all about it.'

And so the conversation moved on to easier topics, chatting away about chocolate and village life. Emma asked after Luke's father, John, and the family.

'Oh, the lovely news is that Nathan is coming back home for a while. Finished his travelling, as far as we know, and is looking for work back in England.'

'That's good. Send him my love, won't you?'

'Of course.'

Nathan was Luke's younger brother. It had hit him extremely hard, losing his sibling in such a sudden, horrendous way. Just a month after the funeral he had upped and left his job and set off with a backpack and a few possessions. He'd been travelling and working his way around the world ever since, with just the odd visit home, but he'd never settled. Every now and again, Emma would spot a new Facebook status with some amazing scenery or mention of a hostel with newfound friends in another foreign country.

'Aw, it'll be lovely to have him home again,' said Emma, suddenly realising that for Angela, in a way, it must have felt that she had lost both her sons that year, and all those years since.

'Yes.'

'Well, you take care, Angela.'

'You too. And you know you are always welcome if you ever want to come and stay.'

'Thank you.'

'So lovely to hear from you, Emma.'

'Yes, it's been good to chat. Lots of love.'

They still felt like family. Just speaking to Angela brought back so many memories, happy times and the saddest of times too. After putting the phone down, Emma realised she had tears in her eyes, but the best antidote for sadness was work, Emma had found. So she was soon in the shop's kitchen, making buttery flaky pastry ready to turn into chocolate croissants that would be just-baked and still warm for the arrival of her customers in the morning. Another day with customers to serve and chat with, chocolates to craft, bills to pay, a spaniel to walk, and a heart to keep healing.

5

With Easter now over, it was time to change The Chocolate Shop's window display. Emma loved the changing of the seasons, seeing it as a new chance to be creative – with the chocolates she made, the drinks and cakes she served, and the styling of the shop itself. For this summer she had decided on a harbourside, coastal theme for her window extravaganza, reflecting the beautiful setting of their village, which would hopefully help to draw in the summer customers.

Holly loved getting involved with the window displays too. She had agreed to come in on Tuesday afternoon, straight from the Sixth Form bus, to give her a hand. A while ago, Emma had found a scrap of blue fishing net on the beach, which she'd taken home and washed thoroughly. She'd known it might come in handy one day, and this was now set out at the base of the window. She carefully placed some pieces of driftwood, smoothed and weathered to a bleached grey, on top of it and an old-fashioned indigo glass float. From the craft shop halfway down the hill she had bought a wonderful model coble boat and intended filling the hull with chocolate truffles, and she also had three small, very cute wood-painted puffins. Along with a selection of her moulded chocolates shapes – seashells, anchors, starfish, and packs of chocolate puffins and seals – it would look delightful (hopefully!).

Holly had helped her place all the items carefully and was now standing outside, judging the final effect and getting Emma to tweak the positions so it all looked just right. There was lots of nodding, pointing and thumbs-up signs going on.

'Your turn now. Go on out for the final approval,' Holly said to Em with a grin, as she walked back in.

Emma was soon standing outside. 'Hmm, pretty good. Just up a bit with that puffin there, yes. Perfect. Yep, I'm pleased with that.' Emma gave a final thumbs-up sign to Holly through the glass.

Just then, Adam came past. 'Looking good!' he exclaimed.

'The window display or Holly?' Emma grinned, as Holly was inside beaming out at the unexpected sight of her tall, sandy-haired boyfriend.

'Both,' he announced wisely with a grin. 'See you later, Holly,' he called out. 'Can't stop. I'm on a super-speedy mission for gluten-free bread. I'm hoping Sheila's got some left in stock. Got a hotel customer with dietary needs they hadn't specified before arrival.'

'See you,' Emma said as he strode on by.

'By-ee!' Holly was waving animatedly from the other side of the window.

Em walked back inside, 'Hey, look at you, grinning like a Cheshire cat. So how are things going with you two? I don't suppose I really need to ask, looking at that beam of a smile,' Emma said, grinning.

'Great. He is just *lush*, Em, and we are getting on *so* well.' There was virtually a swoon going on. If they were back in the Victorian days the old smelling salts would be coming out right now.

'Well that's brilliant. I'm happy for you, Hols. Now then, let's get back to work.'

Just after closing time the phone rang.

'Hi Em, it's a lovely evening. Pete's got one of his golf committee meetings and I wondered if you fancy coming down to The Fisherman's Arms? We could sit outside with a drink and watch the sun go down. What do you think?' It was Bev.

'Sounds perfect, yes.' It had been a busy day – one of the ones when Bev worked at the surgery, so Em had been multitasking. A chilled-out evening might be just what she needed.

'I could ask Ali too. It's been a little while since the three of us have had a catch-up.'

'Great. What time?' Em glanced at her watch; just after six. She had closed the shop an hour ago and had been thinking of making some more chocolate-shaped puffins and seals, but she had felt tired and ended up reading her book for a while instead.

'In about half an hour so we can sit out while it's still warm?'

'Yep, I'll meet you there, shall I?'

'Yes, great. I love it when a plan comes together. I'll ring Ali straight away.'

Emma had made some lovely friends since arriving at Warkton-by-the-Sea, having known no one at all in the village at the start of her Chocolate Shop venture seven years ago and at her darkest of times, her friends and her family had become a bit of a life-support system, especially Bev.

The three ladies were soon installed at a wooden picnic bench in the back garden of The Fisherman's Arms, the village pub, which stood proudly on the rise of land to one side of the harbour, nestled by old stone fishermen's cottages. There was an area of grass to the rear of the pub, and a little gate that led out to the coastal footpath on one side, and some steps that led down to the harbour on the other. She often let her mind stray to times gone by, to when the fishing fleet would be bringing in their catch of herring or the like, ready to take to the smokehouses on the other side of the street, all but one now converted into a restaurant and cottages. It must have been a hard life, with the North Sea always cold, at times treacherous, the women left at home mending the nets, nursing hungry children. They would have known grief and loves lost, for sure.

'So, been busy today, Em?' Bev brought her back to the here and now.

'Yeah, it has actually. Even though the schools' Easter holidays are over, there're still plenty of tourists about. I think the fine weather has drawn them out.'

'Ah, yes. The village is pretty busy. I had trouble getting parked today.'

'Been up to much, Ali?' Em asked.

'Head down at work too. An outbreak of the norovirus has kept us pretty hectic, hasn't it Bev?' Ali worked with Bev at the doctors' surgery.

'Yeah, it's been like D & V city. Oh, the joys.'

'D & V?' Emma quizzed, then wished she hadn't.

'Diarrhoea and vomiting,' answered Bev matter-of-factly.

'Ah, I see.'

'Though,' Ali continued, 'me and Dan are planning a breakaway soon. Got a cottage booked for a long weekend down in the Yorkshire Dales.'

'Ooh, sounds nice.' Em couldn't remember the last time she'd taken a holiday. It just hadn't been on her agenda – building her business and keeping the shop running had kept her busy enough. And where would she have gone on a holiday on her own, anyhow? Looking out across the harbour with the soft peachy-grey shades of a late-spring evening settling over sea and sky, a few boats bobbing about and the graceful swoop of a tern nearby, this was a lovely place to be anyhow.

'Fabulous,' agreed Bev. 'Though I hope there's a nice pub or takeaway nearby. You're not out hiking all

weekend with packed lunches in backpacks, are you?'
Dan was well known for his love of outdoor pursuits.

'Hah, well there will definitely be some hiking involved, but I have checked out the local village online and it has a Chinese takeaway and a good pub by the looks of it.'

'Good girl.' Bev smiled.

Their glasses were nearly empty.

'Right then.' Emma stood up. 'I'll go in and fetch the next round of drinks. Same again, girls?'

'Ooh, yes. Thanks, Em.'

She entered the back door of the pub from the beer garden. It took a few seconds for her eyes to adjust with it being so much darker inside. It was fairly busy in there. Sounds of chatter filling the air with people making the most of a pleasant spring evening, and holidaymakers out for their supper and enjoying the atmosphere of a traditional English pub. The Fisherman's Arms had been here at the harbourside for centuries, heard and seen the tales of the local fisherfolk, witnessed hard times, and good times.

There was a guy at the bar and Emma stopped in her tracks. She felt goose bumps all over her body. *Luke!* Memories flooded her mind. That same dark-blond hair, something about the curve of the back of his neck. The clothes were a bit more casual than he might have worn but . . . yes, Luke. Oh my God. She felt giddy, strange. Dropped her purse, as her hands began to tremble, bent down to see where it had fallen. Damn, it had gone right under a chair at someone's table.

'Sorry,' she apologised to the couple sitting there, as she fumbled for it on the floor.

When she stood back up, she looked towards the bar again. He'd gone.

She scanned the room. No sign. It was as if he'd never been there. Was she hallucinating? Was it just wishful thinking? But for a split second it felt like Luke was really there. It was probably just some tourist who looked a bit like him. But blimey, it was like seeing a ghost.

There was a part of her that wanted to run out, check if he really was there, if he might be walking around the village right now. But she knew that was just plain crazy. She had seen Luke laid out, kissed his cold, scarred forehead on that mortuary slab. It was a doppelganger tourist at best, and a figment of her imagination at worst. She must have been working harder than she'd thought – she was overtired or something.

Emma headed for the bar, still feeling a prickly sensation just heading to the space where he had been. But yes, all was okay, she told herself, she needed to just chill out with a half pint of cider and her friends.

'Hi Danny, can I have a G&T, a half of Fosters and a cider, please.'

'You certainly can.' He stopped for a second and looked at her. 'You okay, Em? You look like you've . . .'

Seen a ghost, Em finished in her mind.

'Well, you look a bit pale,' he continued.

'Yeah, I'm fine, Danny. You?' she asked, neatly deflecting the question.

'Great. The good news is that the pub's up for an award – best coastal pub in the North East. We're on the shortlist.'

'Cool. Well done. You deserve it. It's lovely here. Fingers crossed for you.'

'Cheers.' Danny busied himself getting their drinks ready.

Em scanned the bar area and tables. No one at all that looked like Luke. She must have been having a 'moment'.

The landlord Dave appeared next to Danny. 'Evening, Em.'

'Hello. Well done on the short-listing for the award, by the way, that's great news. Well, so far so good, anyhow.'

'Yeah, it's fantastic, isn't it.'

'You'll be putting Warkton-by-the-Sea on the map.'

'Hopefully.'

And hopefully people would find a gorgeous chocolate shop while they were there too! Emma mused. She was genuinely pleased for the pub. It was great that local businesses were doing well and it was such a nice place to come and chill out; log fires in the winter and the pretty beer garden overlooking the harbour in summer. Fish and chips and their scrummy crab sandwiches, no wonder it was popular there. In fact, 'Danny, can I put in an order for two lots of crab sandwiches and a large bowl of chips too, please.' She hadn't had any supper as yet, and just the thought of them with freshly made, crispy chips was making her tummy rumble.

'I'm on to it.' He jotted the order down on his pad and handed it to the waitress to take to the kitchen for him.

'Thanks.'

Emma paid, then made her way back out with their drinks. She couldn't resist a scan of the harbourside and the pavement that led away from the pub but there was no one there who looked the least bit like Luke. Of course there wasn't . . .

She placed the drinks before her friends at the picnic bench. 'There you go, ladies.'

'Cheers, Em.'

'Thanks.'

She wouldn't even mention the incident in the bar or her 'sighting' for fear of sounding slightly loopy. Instead, she needed to relax and make the most of a chilled-out evening. Still, it had left her with an odd prickly feeling at the back of her neck.

6

'Oh, bloody hell, guess who's sliming his way across the street?' Holly was pulling a face.

Emma looked up from the counter to see her landlord, Mr Neil, outside. Her blood went cold. It was never good news when he turned up out of the blue. She tried to stay calm and smile as he entered the door, managing a polite 'Hello.'

'Good morning, Emma. How's business?'

It always seemed to be a bit of a leading question from him.

'Fine,' she answered, keeping her reply purposefully vague. If she sounded too positive, he might decide to put up the rent again. Who knew what schemes were going on in that greasy little head of his? 'Would you like a coffee?' Better keep him sweet. This place was her life and soul, and he held her future in his hands.

'Yes, thank you, I will.'

'I'll make it,' Holly offered. Em thought she might just

38

be looking for a way to escape the room. The guy certainly had a knack of sucking the air of the place. Or maybe her young assistant was thinking of putting salt in it or something. Em gave her a stern glance just in case she had any such antics in mind. It wouldn't do to annoy him.

'The café seems to be doing well.' He was perusing the room. The window-seat tables were taken up with two families.

'Yes, I'm pleased with how it's going.'

'Hmm, it's a good new addition.'

'Yes,' she agreed. And yes, *she'd* been the one to put in all the hard work and the finances to fund the conversion. He'd be the one gaining from it in the long run. Despite being the landlord, he didn't do a lot for the upkeep of the property. One time, when the boiler had gone down, it had taken him five days to get an engineer out to repair it. The shop and her flat were freezing all the while. She'd had to borrow a fan heater to keep the shop warm enough during the day, and she and Alfie had had to move across to sleep at Bev's for a couple of nights.

'Here you go.' Holly popped a cup of coffee on to a table which was set to the side of the café.

Mr Neil took up the chair beside it. He then took out some paperwork from his black leather briefcase and leafed through A4 sheets. At least Emma didn't have to stand making conversation with him for now, as he looked otherwise engaged.

Holly raised an eyebrow and gave a pretend shudder.

Emma held on to her fake smile, then a customer came in asking for suggestions for his mother's birthday. Em was all too happy to help, though she was still aware that she and her shop were under scrutiny from the side table.

Once the customer had left, she observed her landlord taking several photos on his mobile phone of the interior of the shop. He was definitely up to something.

After clearing one of the window tables as one group had left and tidying the counter area which was already tidy to start with, she saw him make a move. He filed back his papers, then brought his empty coffee cup over to her.

'About the rent. I've decided I'm not going to put it up further at this point.'

Wow! Emma felt huge relief; last year had been such a struggle. Well, this sounded very positive. Had he had a personality transplant or something? She stared at his slicked-back black hair (he must use lashings of Brylcreem or some such product) and found herself waiting for the *but*.

There was a second or two when he stared back. 'But . . .'

Argh, there it was.

'I won't be renewing your contract for the full year. Instead, I'll be reviewing it on a month-by-month basis.'

'Oh.' She was a bit shocked. Why was he doing that? In fact, could he just go ahead and do that? There must be laws on all this. But then, he was the landlord. 'Can I ask why?'

'Just keeping my options open.' He gave a thin smile. 'I'll get the formal paperwork on that to you shortly. Good day.' He turned on his well-polished heel.

It was obvious further questions were not going to get her anywhere.

Emma felt her heart sink as he left. Holly started doing a mock throwing-up gesture behind the counter.

'Ugh, can't stand the man. He is *such* an eel.' Holly's nickname had stuck. 'Makes my skin crawl. Can't we ban him?'

'Hah, don't think so as he *owns* the place, Holly.'

'Well, that's a bloody shame.'

7

News of the monthly contract was spinning around in Emma's mind all day after that. Max was away all this week through to Saturday evening, getting the new project in Leeds off the ground but as soon as the shop was closed and Holly had gone home, Emma knew she needed someone to chat it over with. She found herself sitting on a stool in the back kitchen, surrounded by large bags of chocolate callets and moulds ready to fill, but she knew she couldn't settle to crafting yet. She picked up her mobile and dialled Max.

'Hey,' he answered in soothing tones.

It was lovely just to hear his voice.

'Hi.'

'Something up?'

How could he tell that from just one word? But over the past months, they had grown closer and were getting to know each other well.

'Yeah . . .' Her voice gave a little waver. 'Oh, Max, Mr Neil's been in. You know, the landlord of the shop.'

'Ah, yes.'

'There's definitely something going on. He's changing the contract for the shop to a month-by-month lease only. So, I don't even know if I'll get to stay here for the whole of this year. Do you think he's planning on selling or something?' Emma felt sick just thinking about that possibility.

'Hmm, I don't like to say it, but it sounds likely, Em. Or at least he's keeping his options open to do that. He might also have a new rental in mind, where he intends charging a lot more. Sorry, Em. What a bummer for you.'

'I know. I've been feeling dreadful ever since he was in this morning, worrying about it all.' She felt fragile, vulnerable. How could she lose her Chocolate Shop? It was more than just a business, it was her home, her life. It had kept her going through the hardest of times, given her a purpose in life again.

'Ah, Jeez. I'm sorry I'm so far away right now, Em.'

'I know. Me too. I miss you.' It was at times like this that she wished he didn't have to travel miles away for work, that he lived nearer and could just pop in. Boy, she could do with his big strong arms around her right now.

'There's a virtual hug coming down the phone.'

Aw, he knew exactly how she was feeling. 'Thanks, Max . . . but somehow it's not quite the same.'

'I know, babe. I'll be back with you soon. Saturday night.'

'Yeah.' A few more days to get through. She'd been on her own and got along fine for years. Weird that after meeting and getting to know Max, just days could seem such a long time.

'I can take you out for some supper then – or maybe a night in with a takeaway would be better. Me, you, Alfie, a bottle of wine and fish and chips from the pub. What do you think?'

'Oh, yes. I can't wait.' A cosy night in together sounded perfect.

'Look, I'm sorry Em, but I'd better go. We're just trying to get wrapped up here on site for this evening.'

'Me too. I have a stack of chocolates to make.' Flavoured choc bars, lemon-meringue truffles and dark chocolate coffee cups were awaiting her attention.

'I love you.' Max said.

Aw. 'Love you too,' she answered.

It was good knowing that she had Max for support, even if he was miles away right now.

As she put down the phone, she knew she needed to think practically and to plan for the worst. What if she really did have to leave these premises? She'd have to start keeping an eye out for other properties, but where might be suitable? Warkton-by-the-Sea was a small village so she knew there was nothing else vacant like her shop. It was so ideal here, and all the renovations and work she'd had done just last year . . . She let out a long, slow sigh. All her plans for this season, the prosecco parties, the summer ahead . . . She couldn't begin to imagine leaving this place.

'Right, Emma Carter. These chocolates will not make themselves. Get to work,' she rallied herself. She began to pour dark chocolate callets into a stainless steel bowl ready for tempering. She'd craft by hand tonight, leave the tempering machine which she used at busy times sleeping, it'd keep her active and take her mind off her troubles.

The next morning, after a troubled sleep, Emma was up early. It was a bright and sunny late-April day. She took a large mug of coffee and a warm chocolate croissant that she'd just made and went to sit outside in the back-yard area behind the shop. Alfie lay down beside her feet, hoping to catch a crumb or two.

It was pretty there, a walled courtyard with cream flagstones as a patio. She had a little table and two chairs set up and there were flower pots of varying sizes, now full of bold pink and yellow tulips and the last of the spring daffodils, and a rambling rose took up the side of one wall. In summer the rose was a mass of ballerina-pink delicate blooms. The sun was just peeping over the wall, lighting her corner of the yard, but the whole area caught the sunshine through the afternoon. It was such a nice place to sit, to relax.

A thought began forming in her mind: *maybe her customers would like that too.* A sunny space to serve her café customers during the spring and summer. A courtyard café, full of chocolate cake, milkshakes, ice creams and more. But then, after her landlord's ominous visit, would she still be here? Would Mr Neil have his way and hand in her notice on the lease at any time? But she couldn't just give in and give up on a maybe. And she'd need every penny she could get if the rent was about to go up again, because she might be competing with some other party interested in taking over her shop. If she was going to go down, she'd go down bloody fighting.

Yes, it should be fairly easy to get some more outdoor furniture. She could look around a few house clearances, car boot sales, ask around. So, she couldn't afford new, but with a splash of paint, and some TLC . . . She began to feel the stirrings of hope. She needed to believe there was still a future for her here. The alternative was just too horrid.

She finished her croissant, giving Alfie the last buttery corner and a pat on the head.

'It might just work, Alfie. What do you think?'

They just had time to take a walk down to the beach before opening. Emma grabbed Alfie's lead and popped a couple of dog biscuits in her pocket. It was a beautiful morning, a day not to be wasted, and her head had been so full of *stuff* last night, it might help settle her mood. The future of the shop in the balance, Mr Neil's visit, that strange tourist who may or may not have looked like Luke – she'd never find out now – and these new thoughts of making a courtyard café area: it was all spinning about in her mind like a kaleidoscope.

They headed out through the back gate, around to the main street of quaint stone cottages, down the hill to the small harbour where a few fishing boats bobbed on a gentle sea and a couple of seagulls swooped in the morning sky. It was still quite early, so apart from a delivery van and its driver who gave her a friendly nod outside the grocer's, she didn't see anyone she knew. The harbour was quiet nowadays, the fishing fleet down to just five boats – so different from the tales of 'back in the day' from old Mrs Clark when she was a little girl, when there had apparently been up to twenty, most of them going out to catch the herring, the 'silver darlings' as the older generation of villagers had called them, that they brought back to smoke and make into kippers in the smokehouses.

Emma would sometimes let her mind wander to the harsh realities of the Warkton-by-the-Sea fisherfolk and theirs lives onshore and at sea decades ago. The men having to leave their wives and children back home to head out on perilous seas. The women mending the nets and trying to keep warm, holding it all together to keep a family fed. Emma enjoyed Mrs Clark's tales, and was often drawn in by the sepia photos of village life that still lined the walls of The Fisherman's Arms. The sea was as much a part of this place as the land.

The fishing boats still brought in some herring and there were crabs, scallops and occasionally langoustines and in the summer season the lobster pots would be set out on their lines. Today, a couple of the cobles had been pulled up on the shore with their colourful nets and lobster pots beside them. The hull of an old rowing boat had been made into a lovely flower display down by the harbour too. It was such a pretty spot.

Emma and Alfie carried on towards the dunes. They soon emerged from the sandy track on to the crescent-shaped bay where the colours of sand and sea were a wash of blues, greys and ochre and the sky still held a blush of early-morning pink and peach. The sun was beginning to warm and waves frothed to shore, the surf gentle today in a light late-spring breeze. She picked up a driftwood stick and launched it for Alfie, who dived after it into the breakers. Being a spaniel, he loved the water, and was a good swimmer. He soon returned with the stick in his jaws to shake an arc of salty droplets around him, spraying her lightly, which made her smile. It was calming down there on the beach – a leveller. Whatever worries you had didn't seem quite so bad somehow, diminished as they were against the vastness of sky and sea, the soothing sounds of the waves rolling in in a hush.

Emma sat on a rock for a while, taking in the sights and sounds of the bay, breathing in the fresh salty air. Whatever concerns she had today about the shop were nothing to what she had been through, what she had learnt to cope with in her past. She was a survivor. She'd be okay.

'Come on Alfie. We'd better get back. I have a Chocolate Shop to open up.'

And so they made their way back up the dunes, back up the hill to The Chocolate Shop by the Sea that was home.

Emma was working on her own today, which had kept her occupied and her mind off all those other things. It was nearly four o'clock when a familiar face popped around the front door: Holly.

'Hi, Em. I thought I'd call in and see how you are after yesterday.' She didn't say any more, as there were a couple of tourists sitting in the window seat, finishing off their pot of tea.

Emma appreciated her assistant's discretion; they both knew she was referring to the landlord's visit.

'Aw, thanks. I'm okay – just wondering what the nasty devil's scheming,' Em added in a whisper. 'But I'm fine. I just need to concentrate on making The Chocolate Shop the best it can be. That's all I can do.'

'Yeah, absolutely. It's already fab here anyway. Mind you, I do like the sound of the prosecco parties idea. Bev mentioned it to me when I bumped into her; she's planning a trial run, you know.'

'Is she now?' Bev hadn't mentioned anything to Em about that as yet.

'Oops, wasn't I meant to say anything? I thought you'd agreed.'

'First I've heard of it.' Em gave a wry grin.

'Ah, well Bev said it was going to take a while for the licensing to go through.'

Yes, there had been a lot more to it, when Emma had looked into it with the local council; she'd need to do a licensing course and then apply to the local authority for a licence after that.

'So, Bev thought we could give it a practice run. We'd all bring the prosecco and you'd . . .'

'Supply the chocolates,' Em finished for her.

'Exactly. So, you're not cross I let it slip?'

'No, it's not your fault. But Bev should have asked me first. I assume we're meant to be holding it here?' Her friend did tend to leap into things. 'I'll be having words when I see her next, never fear.'

'Sorry, Em.'

'Ah, it's all right. But honestly, that woman – any excuse for a party!' Emma was smiling now. 'Hey, don't worry, Hols. In fact, after yesterday I need a bit of cheering up. It sounds fun, *and* we can test out how it might go for the real parties once I get licensed and we have paying guests.'

A customer came in then, a lady who looked to be in her forties, who started browsing the artisan chocolate bars section.

'I can recommend the dark choc-orange or the summer fruits on white, but they're all lovely, to be honest.' Holly couldn't help herself praising the shop's goods. 'Right, I'd better go Em. I'll be in again tomorrow. See you then.'

'Yep, see you then. Thanks for your help with the display the other day too. And I'll phone Bev and let you know about the party that I'm holding!!' she added ironically.

'Hah, yes!'

'Thanks for dropping by, Hols.'

'You're welcome. It's hard to keep me away. I just love this place.'

It was time now for Emma to check on her other assistant's plans.

'Hi, Bev. *So*, can you tell me when I'm having this party then?'

'Ah, I was going to call you about that.'

'Ye-ah, is that before or after you've invited half the village?'

'Soz, I got a bit carried away with the idea. But the good news is that everyone thinks it sounds like a brilliant idea, so surely that bodes well for the business angle? And all the girls will bring along a bottle of prosecco so all you need to provide is . . .'

'The chocolates. Yes, I guessed that. And the venue, of course.'

'Naturally. So, it's okay then? You'll do it?'

'I don't suppose I have much of a choice now, do I? But yes, of course. It's what we'd talked about anyhow.'

'Great stuff. I could really do with a girlie night. It's been ages since we had a proper get-together. So, when shall we set the date for?'

'Hah, I thought you'd have already planned that too.'

'Well, no, not quite. Though next Friday might just have been mooted.'

'I knew it. You are incorrigible.'

'Well, I had to get an idea of who might have which night free. We can all do that one.'

'And what about me? I might have a night of passion lined up or something.'

'Ah . . .'

'Just because I've been out of action for seven years. Remember that things have changed a little now.'

'Ooh yes, the delectable Max. How is he?'

'Good, thanks. But as usual, he won't be around until the Saturday, as far as I know. So yes, okay, my arms have been twisted so much they're nearly broken, but yes, let's go for it. Next Friday it is. Who's invited so far?'

'Holly's coming and is bringing a friend. Then there's Jo and Ali in our little gang, and I may have mentioned it to the practice nurse. She started a couple of months ago and is a hoot. Maybe you could ask your sister-in-law Chloe? And see if she wants to bring a friend?'

'Yeah, I'm sure she'd love a night out. Then I could ask Sheila from the grocer's – she is a bit of a gossip but her heart's in the right place – and her daughter, Laura, who's on Reception at the hotel. They are both good fun *and* if it goes well they are sure to spread the word about the prosecco parties once we get the licence sorted.'

'Hmm, good thinking.'

'So, that'd be about ten of us. A good number, bearing

in mind the size of the shop. We'll stick with that, give it a try and see how it goes. In fact, shall we go the whole hog and do a chocolate truffle-making session too?'

'Ooh yes, absolutely. Can you show me how to make those gorgeous Eton Mess ones, you know, with the meringue pieces? Though it'll probably just end up *a mess* with me involved.'

'Yes, no worries. You'll be fine, I'm sure, and then I'll think of a couple of others – the Baileys ones are always good, and maybe chocolate-dipped strawberries.'

'Scrummy bliss. I can't wait.'

8

Before Emma could catch a breath, it was the eve of the planned prosecco party. She was in the shop serving a lady who was choosing chocolates for a wedding anniversary gift box when the doorbell chimed and she glanced up. She felt her body go cold. There were prickles in the back of her neck. She couldn't believe her eyes . . . *Luke?*

But it could never be. This guy, though, he looked so like Luke it was unnerving. He was grinning at her and gave a small wave, realising that she was in the middle of serving a customer. Which was more than Emma realised at that moment in time. OMG – was it Nathan?

'Did you say there were some fruit flavours? Excuse me . . . ?'

'Oh, I'm so sorry.' Emma had stopped still and was just staring at the newcomer. 'Yes, of course,' she rallied, 'there's a lemon and blueberry, raspberry ripple, Eton Mess with strawberries and meringue pieces. All equally scrumptious.'

'Ooh, I'm sure they will be, they sound delightful. One of each, then.'

Emma placed them in dainty paper cases before adding them to the gift box. 'Just two more would make up your twelve.'

'Any other suggestions?' The woman smiled.

'Well, the sea-salted caramels are always popular, and the Irish Cream truffles are a personal favourite.'

'They sound ideal. Thank you.'

Emma looked up to acknowledge the man who was still standing there waiting. Oh my, his eyes were so very like Luke's – that same blue-grey. She found her hands were trembling as she wrapped the box with ribbon.

'That'll be eight pounds and twenty pence, please.'

The lady paid, saying, 'Thank you, I'm sure my husband will love them,' as she took the paper bag with the gift in.

As the space between her and the man who had just walked in cleared, Emma felt her heart banging in her chest. Luke's brother – it just had to be. It hit her suddenly, it was the only explanation. The last time she had seen him was at the funeral.

'Nathan? Is that really you?'

'Yeah – well I prefer to be called Nate, nowadays, but yeah, it's me. And, how cool is this?' he said looking around The Chocolate Shop and then settling his gaze on her. 'Hi, Em. Good to see ya.'

Emma noted a slight Australian drawl to his accent. Well, he had been away a long while.

'*So*, how are you?' She was coming out from behind the counter towards him. 'You look . . . wow, you look different . . . you look good. All grown-up somehow.' She stopped herself, realising she was beginning to sound like some maiden aunt.

'Well, I *am* twenty-six!' he laughed.

'Of course.' The same age Luke had been when he died . . . But wow, his little brother was here and all grown-up. Emma clapped her hands together. This was just wonderful. But God, he did look so like Luke. Her heart didn't know quite what to make of that yet.

He opened his arms wide to greet her and they shared a big hug.

'Wow, long time no see.' Emma could scarcely hide the emotion in her voice. Yes, the last time she had seen him was at Luke's funeral, eight years ago now, when he was just eighteen.

'I know . . . and hey, you don't look so bad yourself, Em. You've not changed a bit, honest.' He took a step back to take a proper look at her. 'And this place, it's brilliant. Your own business and everything. Mum and Dad told me all about it, of course.'

'Yep. Welcome to The Chocolate Shop by the Sea. It's been a long haul, to be honest, but yeah, it's good here . . . And you, how's life for you? Is this a passing trip? What are your plans?'

'Well, that's the million-dollar question.' He gave a cheeky smile, as though planning wasn't really his thing.

'Hang on, shall I make us a coffee while it's quiet here?

Have you got time? It'd be great to catch up.' There was only one customer in just now, who seemed to be happy reading their newspaper with a pot of tea and a chocolate brownie to hand.

'Yeah, why not. That'd be great.'

'Right, well take a seat and I'll be back with some coffee in a minute.'

'Do you do a flat white?'

'Ah, I'm afraid not, no machine for that as yet, though it's on my wish list. We're still on cafetières for the moment.'

'That's fine, no worries.' And he sat down, gazing out of the window. 'Sweet spot here.'

'Yes, it's a great village. I'll just be two ticks.'

Emma dashed off to make their drinks, realising she had a huge smile on her face. Mind you, once in the kitchen she felt a bit giddy and had to pause and hold on to the work surface for a second or two. Just seeing him walk into the shop like that, Luke's brother, being near him . . . it brought back so many memories. Nathan's hair was a bit longer, and the clothes far more casual than Luke would have chosen, but whoa, a quick glance and he could easily pass for Luke. And that made the hole in her heart she'd been trying so hard to heal, tear open a little more.

She told herself to get a grip and got on with making the coffee.

A few minutes later they were settled in the window seat together chatting about old times, about Luke, and the years kind of melted away. Yet they were both so aware that they were in such a different place than they would ever have imagined back then.

'God, I think I must always have been the annoying kid brother when you two got together. Hey Em, remember that time when our parents were away overnight and you and Luke were at our house? I was being a stroppy teenager and didn't want to go off to my room and I was on the PlayStation in the lounge for hours – no doubt getting in the way of your cosy night in. Then Luke got mad and got me in a headlock and something cricked badly. We ended up in A&E and he was terrified he'd really done something wrong.'

'Hah, yes. And I was left there at your house to keep an eye on the dog, and your parents rang to check everything was okay. It was past ten o'clock and I had to pretend you'd both gone off to sleep for an early night . . . *as if.*'

'Yeah, they did an X-ray to check, then let us home. No real damage, it was just a bit cricked. Mum and Dad still don't know about that one.'

'Brothers, hey?' said Emma.

'Still miss him.' He took a slow breath.

'Yeah, me too.' Emma didn't want to get maudlin, so switched the conversation. 'So, tell me all about your travels and adventures then. I've seen the odd photo online. Looks like you've been to some amazing places.'

'Yeah, it's been pretty cool. I liked the Far East the best. Some incredible places in Vietnam and Cambodia.

Temples, palaces, gorgeous tropical beaches, crazy tuk-tuk drivers in cities with seven carriageways, millions of motorbikes and a few cows crossing too. You have to see it to believe it.'

'Yeah, I bet.'

'And the people over there are just so friendly.'

A young couple walked in, so Emma had to pop behind the counter to serve, then she headed back to sit with Nathan – no, *Nate* – once more.

'So, what do you make of Warkton-by-the-Sea then?' she asked. 'Have you had chance to look around?'

'It's a cute place.'

'So, are you just on a day trip? What's brought you here?'

'Well, I heard you were up this way. Thought I'd check in, say hi and take a look at the place. It's an area I've always fancied visiting. Who knows, it might be a day trip or I might just stay a few days. I have no ties as such. I liked it down by the harbour and the pub seems pretty chilled. They do a nice pint of real ale.'

'Oh, so you've already been into The Fisherman's Arms . . .' Emma started. The other day made sense now. 'Were you here a week or so ago?'

'Yeah. I did try and call at the shop then too, but it was after closing. I hadn't thought about that, so I headed on up the coast for a few days.'

'Hah, I saw you. Thought I might have been going a bit crazy. For a moment, I thought it was Luke . . .' She felt a lump form in her throat.

'Oh, Em.' His hand went gently over hers. They didn't need to say any more. Sat quietly for a while. Lost in their own memories.

'It's been tough, hasn't it?'

'Yeah.' She had found someone who really understood. A shared love, a shared grief.

An elderly lady came in then and settled down in the other window seat. Em needed to get back to serving her customers and looking after her Chocolate Shop. It was no good dwelling on the past. It didn't change anything.

'Well, Em, I'd better get off.' Nate stood up, and the two of them shared a warm hug.

'I hope you can stay around for a couple of days at least. If you need a sofa for a night let me know. But if not, take care. All the best, whatever your plans for the future, Nate.'

'Thanks. Good to see you, Em.'

'You too.'

She watched Nate head out of the shop door, leaving a trail of strange emotions in his wake.

9

Emma found herself rather floored by the surprise arrival of Nathan yesterday – or Nate, she reminded herself. Her mind was still in flux. It was such a blast from the past, and yet he had changed so much from the teenager she remembered . . . was *so* like Luke.

Well, enough of the nostalgia trip; she had to shake herself up. Today was the day of Bev's trial prosecco party and now that she had closed the shop for the day, there was a party to organise! She'd decided to welcome all the guests with a flute of prosecco and a chocolate-dipped strawberry on the side. Then they could have a go at making the dipped strawberries themselves – they were really easy to do but looked delightful and tasted delicious. Just perfect with a glass of bubbly too.

Then they would move on to the truffle-making session. She'd lined up a selection of alcohol flavourings – Irish Cream, whisky and rum worked really well – so they could choose their own favourite. She'd also have some vanilla extract for a non-alcohol version, just in case. Hmm, that set her thinking – at the professional party nights there might well be a non-drinker, or perhaps someone pregnant. Yes, she'd put out a bottle of sparkling elderflower and some non-alcohol drink options too – the elderflower was still gorgeous and bubbly. It was good that she was doing this trial run – a useful business experiment. And, even better, it was a damn good excuse for a get-together with friends.

She set out the big round table in the window with a dozen champagne flutes – she'd had to borrow eight of them from Bev, as she rarely required that many. Next, she needed to go and turn on the tempering machine, so as to keep the melted chocolate just right. That way, the beginners could work with the chocolate easily. She then went upstairs to find her festive decorations that had been packed away after Christmas, pulling out a strand of white fairy lights to give the shop a pretty glow.

After setting everything out, she looked around The Chocolate Shop – it really was lovely. She felt proud of how much she had achieved in these seven years, both for herself and her shop. The new soft furnishings in their pretty shades of blue, grey and white gave it a cosy coastal feel for the summer months and a soft toy seal that one of her nieces had given her sat on the hull-shaped shelf rack along with the rows of goody bags of fudge and truffles. On the walls, there were some black-and-white photos of Warkton in the old days, showing the fishing boats down in the harbour. Old Mrs Clark, whose husband Jim had been a fisherman, had given them to her. One image was of his old coble boat, *Silver Spray*. He'd died over twenty years ago, so Mrs C had told her sadly.

It was after Emma shared a little of her own loss that the old lady came up with the photos, saying she wanted Em to have them, so they could be displayed in the shop for all to enjoy, far better than being tucked away gathering dust in her cupboard.

The shop was very much a part of this community, of its history. It had seen its share of love, laughter and loss too. But tonight, Emma had a good feeling, was going to be a particularly fun one.

Next some music. She took out her small portable speaker and chose some easy-listening tracks on her iPhone to give the shop a more relaxed ambience. Great.

It was soon time to dash upstairs for a quick shower and change. The girls were due around seven-thirty. She chose to wear her black work trousers, trying to keep her outfit true to how she might dress for the formal party nights, and teamed it with a soft-pink floral top. She popped her long red hair into a ponytail, to keep it neat and out of the way.

She was just about to head back down when she heard a knock at the back door and then Bev's voice calling up the stairs, 'Only me! I take it I'm the first. I'm a bit early. I'll come on up, shall I?'

'I'm nearly ready, so I'm on my way down, actually. Hang on.'

Emma was soon heading down the stairs.

They greeted each other with a hug in the hallway. Bev had brought a lovely square glass vase filled with pink and cream roses. 'For you.'

'Aw, thanks Bev. They're beautiful.'

'Well, I can't exactly bring you chocolates, can I?' She smiled. 'Oh, and these, to help with supplies.' Bev winked, and presented her with three bottles of prosecco, which Em placed on the kitchen side.

'Ooh, I'll put these flowers straight through into the shop. They will complete the look perfectly.' Em placed them carefully on the second window table. The first table being ready with the glass flutes, the bottles of alcohol to add to the truffles that she'd set out earlier, and a set of black aprons she had sourced online especially for the truffle-making session and had printed with The Chocolate Shop by the Sea logo and gold writing that read: 'Love, laughter, chocolate and prosecco!'

'Hah, these are brilliant.' Bev was opening one out.

'Thought it'd be worth the investment. Make it feel more professional, yet fun.'

'Love them. This is *so* going to work, you know, Emma. It's such a bloody good idea, dare I say so myself.' Bev was virtually preening. 'Prosecco parties are so *my* thing . . . Let's pour out a glass and toast their future success.'

'Oh, yes. Why not.'

There's nothing quite like the sound of the popping of a cork; the sight of straw-coloured bubbles rushing into foam down the side of a glass; that first blissfully refreshing mouthful.

'Cheers, Bev.'

'Cheers, hun. To the most fabulous chocolate and prosecco parties ever! And to The Chocolate Shop by the Sea making lots of money.'

'Yay! Now that would be brilliant.' A secure financial base would be just wonderful, for who knew what might happen next to the rent or the property after the bloody landlord's last visit. *But*, those negative thoughts needed to be pushed back for another day. Tonight was for enjoying themselves. 'Well, the good news is, it might not be too long before I can do the proper licensed parties. I've done my research and I've already booked a licensing course. Once I've passed the exam, I have to make an application to the council.'

'Ooh, landlady Em. You'll need to invest in some leopard-print gear, big dangly earrings and a push-up bra!'

'Hah, you're thinking Bet Lynch or Barbara Windsor's character at the Queen Vic!'

'Ooh ah, I bet Max'll love it.'

'Behave woman, but hah, he probably would. Though may I say, it'll be a much classier affair here.'

With that, two eager faces appeared at the shop door. Holly and her best friend, Jess.

'Come in. Come in. It's open,' Emma called out.

'Hi Em. Wow, it looks a-mazing in here. Love the new evening ambience.' Holly grinned.

'It's really pretty,' Jess agreed.

Within a half hour all nine guests were there, including Chloe and her friend Hannah, and were hands-on, dipping strawberries into bowls of white and dark chocolate that Emma had set out in the centre of the table.

'I want to eat them all already. How long do they take to set?' Jess asked.

'Um, about twenty minutes for these. I'll pop them in the cooler kitchen area for a while.'

That gave them time to have another glass of bubbly and have a chat. It all seemed to be going well, Emma mused.

'Top-ups anyone?' Bev was wielding the next prosecco bottle promisingly.

'I'll skip this time.' Em intended taking it steady for now whilst she was teaching and observing how the session was going.

The others were keen for refills.

'Okay, so next we are going to make the chocolate truffles. There's a little more technique to this.' Emma was trying to keep it sounding professional.

'Oh my, so I need to concentrate,' Sheila, from the grocer's, piped up.

'It's like being back at school,' added Jo, with a smile.

'Hah, school was never this fun!' Ali grinned.

'And since when did you ever get served prosecco at school?' Holly added.

'Good idea if they did, mind,' said Jess. 'Might ease the pain of exams.'

'You'd never get any work done, girls,' Sheila retorted sensibly.

Emma went off to fetch more bowls of tempered chocolate for the truffle-making session, to which they would add cream and their chosen liqueur. The mixture would then need to be chilled in the fridge for at least an hour before being moulded into small balls and dipped into even more chocolate to coat. Chloe offered to give her a hand.

'Seems to be going well. It's a really lovely idea, Em,' she said, once the pair of them were in the kitchen.

'Yeah, fingers crossed. Even if I could only do one or two a month to start, that'd be good.'

'Well, I'll help spread the word. There are lots of mums at the school gates, desperate for a night out. And this would be right up their street.'

'Thanks.'

They were soon back out carrying bowls of melted dark chocolate.

'Right, I'm going in with the Baileys liqueur.' Laura took the bottle of Irish Cream in readiness.

'I fancy the whisky,' piped up Ali.

'Ho ho ho, and a bottle of rum for me, then.' Holly took up the last bottle. 'We can share, Jess.'

'You only need a tablespoon for your mixture. So it'll go a long way.' Em was passing out the small dishes of melted chocolate – one for each person. 'Don't add the alcohol just yet, by the way. There's another step to do first.'

'Em, do you have any of that raspberry gin left?' Bev asked as the hostess-with-the-mostest reached her. 'You remember, we opened it at New Year.'

'I do remember, and yes, there's still half a bottle upstairs. Mmm, raspberry gin truffles, you might be on to something there, Bev.'

'I know. I have a taste for this stuff. My taste buds are the equivalent of Jo Malone's nose!'

The whole group creased with laughter at that point.

'Just saying.' Bev sounded slightly put out.

'I'll just nip up and fetch it.' With that, Em dashed up the stairs. She couldn't be long, or all the chocolate would start cooling. Kitchen cupboard, there it was. Result. She was back down in two ticks.

'Okay ladies, watch and learn. We all have a bowl of melted dark chocolate each and next I'll bring through the hot cream to mix. So, wooden spoons at the ready.' She poured a little into each bowl, judging the right amount instinctively. 'Don't worry, you can all have the recipe sheet to take home, so you don't need to remember all this. Okay, so now to add your chosen liqueur – just a tablespoon is enough – and stir through again.'

'This is fun.'

'Smells divine.'

'When can we lick the bowls?' Laura, from the hotel, asked cheekily.

'Hold fire on that. The mix needs to set in the bowls so we can handle it later to mould into truffles.'

'Darn.'

'Spoilsport.'

'Going to have to test a little on my fingertip then, if that's the case,' said Laura.

'Don't panic, folks, you can have the chocolate strawberries you made earlier while you wait,' added Em.

'And I suppose another glass of prosecco might help,' Bev said, grinning. There were still plenty of supplies, after all, as everyone who had come along had brought a bottle.

'Come on, then, let's have a brainstorm while you're all here. I'm always looking for new ideas for flavours for the shop; any suggestions for some new chocolates?' Emma was keen to hear their thoughts. 'And I promise I'll make the best suggestions a reality.'

'Ooh, now then . . .'

'Gin and Tonic.' Jo started the ball rolling.

'Toffee vodka.'

'Whisky and orange,' added Chloe's friend, Hannah.

'Hah, they don't have to all be alcoholic, mind. But what else can I expect with you lot!'

'Ginger beer,' came from Holly.

They all pulled a face.

'What? I love ginger beer.'

'Porn star martini,' called out Bev.

'Sex on the beach.' Ali.

'Now we're talking,' Jo rallied. 'What's that other one? Long slow screw up against the—'

'Okay, enough, enough. I think we'll stop the brainstorming now. You lot have one-track minds. I'd have to have an adult section in the shop with a black curtain over it at this rate.'

'Ha ha, yes, an obscured section in the refrigerated counter for X-rated chocolates. Hilarious! How can I help you, madam?' Bev winked.

'We could have chocolate willies,' Holly joined in. 'We had them at Ellen's hen do. They were brilliant.'

'Oh, just imagine handling those.' Jess pulled a face. 'Were they life-sized?'

'Nooo!'

'We are *not* that kind of an establishment.' Emma tried to keep a snooty voice going but ended up in a fit of the giggles. She should have realised a brainstorming session with her girlfriends after several bottles of prosecco may not have been the best idea.

The group chatted on about love, life and the latest village gossip, and it was soon time to do the next stage of the truffle-making. There was white and milk chocolate to coat, once the truffle centres had been rolled into little balls. This was the messy bit, and the girls had a hoot at this stage. There was much licking of fingers by the end.

'Mine look like little turds.' Jess wrinkled her nose at the end results laid out on her plate.

'How come all my decorating chocolate has slid off the outside?' frowned Sheila.

'The chocolate was probably a little too warm. Were you handling the bowl a lot?'

'Hmm, maybe.'

'Ah.'

'Well, look at these little beauties.' Bev was beaming.

'These are brilliant, Bev. Ooh, you can help me crafting in the shop, now I know you're a natural.'

'It's been so much fun,' added Laura. '*Now* do I get to lick the bowl?'

'Sure do. And when they are finally set, I'll give you all goody bags of them to take home.'

'That sounds great,' said Chloe. 'Better keep James away from them or I'll not get a look-in.'

'Brill, but can I take Bev's ones instead? They look so much more appealing than mine!' said Jess.

'Keep your hands off, you!' Bev threatened. 'Oh, okay, I'll donate one or two then.'

The evening carried on with the sounds of chatter and laughter, ending with an impromptu medley of chocolate and confectionery inspired songs. 'You're Sweet Like Chocolate' being Holly's contribution (they all knew she was singing about Adam), 'Sweet Caroline' a tentative link from Ali, 'Sugar, Sugar' from Jo, 'The Candy Man Can' from Sheila, and a fabulous twist on 'I Love Rock 'n' Roll' by Bev which turned into 'I Love Rocky Road' which they all chanted happily along with as a grand finale, with much table drumming and arm swaying.

All too soon, it was time for the group of ladies to go; the time had flown and it was nearing midnight.

'Past the Cinderella hour,' Sheila sighed. 'Sorry, folks, it's been great fun, but I have a shop to open in the morning.'

'Hotel Reception to run,' echoed Laura.

'Yes, "Doctors' surgery, how can I help you?"' Ali put on her best receptionist voice.

'Sixth Form . . .' Holly began. 'Ooh no, bliss, it's Saturday.' Holly was gleeful.

'But you *are* working for me,' Emma reminded her.

'Oops, yes. I'll be here, never fear.'

'Well, it's been amazing, Em.' Jo was sporting an extra-wide prosecco-fuelled smile.

'Just brilliant. Thank you,' said Jess.

'These prosecco nights will be fabulous.' Chloe gave her a big thumbs-up. 'As soon as you get your licence we'll all spread the word for you.'

'I'm sure the hotel guests will love it, too. Especially for birthdays, special occasions and the like. It'll be perfect,' Laura added. 'I'd be happy to put some fliers out for you. They already love the turndown chocolates as it is.'

'We'll be behind you all the way.' Sheila grinned.

'And if you ever need any more practice runs . . .' offered Ali with a cheeky smile.

'Aw, thank you. Love the support from you lot.' Emma gave them all hugs on their way out.

She closed the shop door with a happy sigh. There was just her and Bev, who'd offered to stay and help tidy up. It had been such a good night, and just what Emma had needed after the shock of Nate's appearance and that blast from the past.

10

Soon afterwards, that same evening, Bev was wiping down the tables so the shop would be shipshape for opening in the morning.

'Well, that seemed to go down well,' her friend confirmed with a grin.

'Yes, I'm so pleased. I really think it will work. Thanks so much for the idea.'

'You're welcome. Yep, it's been great tonight.'

Emma didn't answer. Tiredness, as well as all her tumbled thoughts over the past couple of days, were now creeping up on her.

'Em, you okay, hun?'

'Yeah, why?'

'Just, you seem thoughtful. And you were a bit quiet when I first got here? That rent man's not been hassling you again, has he?'

'No, it's not that.'

'So?'

There was no hiding from Bev. How did best friends manage to suss you out in that way?

'Okay, you've got me. I-I saw Luke's brother yesterday.'

'Oh, right. Whoa. That must have been a bit strange.'

'Yeah. The last time I saw him was at Luke's funeral. He was still a teenager, the kid brother.' Emma sighed. 'They got on so well those two, despite the age gap. Nathan adored him.'

The two ladies sat back down at the window-seat table. Bev placed a hand gently over Em's where it rested on the tabletop. Emma hadn't realised but she had started to cry.

'Hey, it's all right,' her friend soothed.

'Oh Bev, it was just weird yesterday. When I first saw him, just for that split second, I thought it was Luke. It was like an electric jolt right through my heart.'

'Aw, bless.'

'Of course, then I knew it couldn't be. He just looked at me with those eyes . . . I didn't think I ever would, but I had started to forget those eyes, how they really looked, and then the way he flicked his fringe out of them. Luke used to do just that when his hair got a bit longer. It took me right back . . .' Em snuffled a bit.

Bev fumbled in her pocket, then passed her a tissue.

'Ah, I'm sorry. This sounds silly.'

'No, it doesn't.'

'It was just such a surprise . . . Hah, who'd have thought. The end to a perfect party night and me blubbing like a loon. I should be pleased that he'd thought to come and see me.'

74

'Yeah, true. And I bet it's been hard for him too.'

'Yes, it must be. I suppose we have a lot in common, really. I think that's why he disappeared off abroad for all those years. Just to get away from all the memories . . . That's why it was easier for me to come here. To be somewhere else. I didn't have to look at where Luke worked, where he ate, the bed where he'd slept with me, every day. It was hard enough without that.'

'Yes, I can only imagine how awful that must be . . .'

'I'm okay. Really. It was just a bit of a shock, that's all. Come on . . .' Emma stood up, needing to get on with a task, stop dwelling on seeing Nathan. Get back to her life here and now in The Chocolate Shop, and the fact the kitchen area was still a mess and needed a good tidy before opening tomorrow morning.

Blimey, Max would be here with her tomorrow, too. She wondered what he'd make of all this with Nate. But then, a part of her thought, she should just let it lie. She didn't need to mention it. What if she got all upset in front of Max, like she just had with Bev? What might he think? They were just getting settled together. Yes, he knew about her fiancé Luke, but there was no point digging up the past. In fact, Nate might already be off on his way somewhere else and that'd be the last she'd see of him for years.

Bev stood up next to her, with her cleaning cloth in hand.

'Thanks, Bev.'

Her friend realised she was saying thank you for more

than the clearing up. 'You're welcome, hun. Hey, it was a *great* night. The prosecco party idea is going to be such a success, I tell you.'

'I think you may be right, there, my lovely friend!'

They headed for the kitchen where they hand-washed the flutes and stacked the dishwasher with all the chocolatey pots and spoons. Then it was time for Bev to go. Em felt a little lonely pit in her stomach.

'You okay? Shall I walk back with you?' Em offered.

'Don't be daft. If you walk me, then I should have to walk you safely back too. Then we'd be to-ing and fro-ing all bloody night.' She laughed. 'I'll be fine. This is *Warkton* we are talking about. The last major crime wave was when Mrs C left her walking stick at the post office section in the grocer's and was convinced someone – in fact "a right bugger" – had stolen it. And it was only that Sheila had put it behind the counter for safekeeping.'

The friends giggled.

'Night, Em.'

'Night. Love you, Bev. Thank you . . . for everything.' She found herself still feeling a bit emotional.

'You are so welcome, my gorgeous chocolate-shop friend.'

'Hah, you only love me for my chocolate.' Em was smiling.

'*Foiled* again,' was Bev's slick response.

The pair of them burst into laughter.

11

Emma's head felt rather delicate when she turned the pretty wooden sign to 'open' on the shop door the next morning, despite her efforts to take it easy on the prosecco.

She served the early customers with their teas, coffees and brownies on autopilot, looking forward to ten-thirty when Holly would come in and she could then retire to the kitchen to do some crafting – something straightforward like making a batch of fudge might be good today.

Stan and Hilda, a sweet old couple, regulars from the village, appeared for a pot of tea and some cake.

'So, how are you both keeping?' Emma asked cheerily, after taking their order.

'Grand we are, Emma. Just grand at the moment, thanks pet. Enjoying the better weather now that summer's just around the corner. And you, pet?'

'Yes, all fine here thanks, Stan. Keeping myself busy and out of mischief.'

He gave her a wink.

'It's lovely to be able to stop here a while now, Emma,' Hilda took up, 'what with the new café. It's made a real difference. Very cosy.'

'We make a morning of it now, don't we, Hilda. Fetch the papers at Sheila's on the way up, so we've got something to read. Then call back in for our weekend groceries on the way back down. Mind, when we saw Sheila earlier, she was looking a bit peaky. Reckon she's going down with a cold or something,' Stan added.

'Ah, maybe.' Emma smiled knowingly. There'd be a few sore heads in the village this morning for sure. She headed to the kitchen to prepare their tea and cakes. 'Won't be a minute,' she called back over her shoulder. 'Take a seat and make yourselves comfy.'

'Oh, we will, lass,' Hilda answered.

Holly arrived just as she was bringing a tray of drinks back out. Her assistant was carrying a brown paper bag that smelt suspiciously delicious.

'Morning, Em.' Holly sounded far too chirpy!

Oh, to have the recovery levels of a nearly eighteen-year-old, after a night out.

Emma served Stan and Hilda, then followed the aroma back to the kitchen. 'What's in the bag, Holly? And please, for goodness' sake, say it's for me or at least to share.' She suddenly found herself with the appetite of a horse.

'Hmm, thought you might like one. Mum made me a bacon sarnie just as I was coming out. There was one going spare, so I nabbed it for you before my brother could pig that down as well as his own.'

'Ah, you are an angel – and thank your mum from me. This is *so* what I need right now.' From feeling a little queasy when she'd got up, a little later than normal at seven-thirty, she had now turned ravenous.

She made a quick cup of tea for them both and dived into the soft malty bread and bacon. 'Mmm. Just bliss.'

'Right,' Holly said, 'I'll head out to the counter and make sure Stan and Hilda are fine and have everything they want. Last night was brilliant by the way, such fun. Jess and I have been telling our mates all about it already.'

'Great. Mind you, I'll not be able to serve you as a paying guest until you're officially eighteen, you know.'

'Ah, yes. Well, Jess is already eighteen, and several of my friends. It's only a month until my eighteenth birthday so I'm sure we can wait 'til then.'

'So, have you got anything special planned for your birthday?'

'I'm having a fancy meal out with the family. And then, I'm also planning a night out "on the Toon" in Newcastle with my mates. Yay – I can go out clubbing officially at last.'

'Sounds great fun. Right, let's get to work then.' Emma finished off the sandwich, had another slurp of tea, then washed her hands ready for her fudge making.

The morning and lunch shift passed quickly. There was a lull by mid-afternoon, and the pair of them found themselves yawning once the shop emptied. Em offered to make them both a coffee to perk them up.

Sitting with a steaming mug in hand, Em started, 'So,

how's the studying going? And are things still going well with Adam? All fine?'

'Yes, pretty good. Just keeping my head down with the studies – needs must. And Adam, oh, he's just so lovely. I don't know how I got so lucky.' Holly paused, looking thoughtful, then, 'It's going to be hard though, Em. I really want to go off to uni this September. I've got my nursing place for midwifery all sorted at Northumbria, as long as I get the grades in this summer's exams, but then Adam's going to be all the way back here because he's got his job at the hotel.'

With her long-distance relationship with Max going on, Emma knew exactly how that felt. 'Yes, it might be a bit tricky – but you know what, Hols? If it's meant to be with Adam, you'll make it work somehow. You need to think about your ambitions and goals in life too. You're still so young and there's a big world out there, Holly. Go grab it.'

'Yeah, I know. I've always wanted to nurse and to look after people.'

'Well, good for you. Hold on to your dreams, Holly, and your heart will work out the other stuff. If Adam's serious about you too, you'll both find a way.'

'Yes, I suppose. I just feel a bit anxious about it all. But thanks, Em.'

It was like her and Max: despite all her concerns and fears, they had found a way. So far so good, anyhow. She was looking forward to seeing him tonight.

They heard the shop door chime and were soon back

serving coffee and cake, filling gift boxes with truffles, and bagging up the new tray of fudge, then tying the bags with navy-blue curls of string. Delicious aromas of chocolate and fudge surrounded them, and Emma looked proudly out across the café where a host of happy customers were chatting and eating. The Chocolate Shop by the Sea was so charming with its cottage-style stone walls and cosy window seats – a place to truly warm your heart.

It was half an hour after closing time when Emma's mobile rang.

'Hi, Em. You okay?' It was Max. The sound was a bit echoey, tinny. He must be driving and on the hands-free.

'Yeah, where are you? Are you in the Jeep?' She was hoping he'd be here with her within the hour.

'Yes, but I've only just set off.'

Her heart sank. 'From *Leeds*?' That was about three hours away. 'What's happened?'

'I'm sorry. Having a 'mare of a day here. Been waiting on steel girders being delivered and they were on the back of a wagon that's been stuck in a jam on the motorway all afternoon. We needed to have them in place before we left today, to prop the structure securely.'

'Oh, right. Well, couldn't the others have stayed?' She couldn't hide the disappointment in her tone.

'It's *my* business, Em. Those girders cost a hell of a lot of money and they are such an important part of the structure; I needed to know it had been done right. You can't get it wrong at his stage.'

'Okay,' she conceded. It was just so frustrating – she would be waiting for nearly three hours until he was here. What with all that had happened this week – with the landlord, seeing Nate out of the blue like that, still nursing a mild hangover – all she really wanted was to curl up in Max's arms. She tried to buck up her mood. Max wouldn't want to be coming back to some grumpy woman. 'So, you'll be here in what, just over two and a half hours?'

'Probably, traffic permitting. It's still slow getting out of Leeds. I'm sorry, babe.'

'Ah, it's all right.' She tried to be a bit more understanding. 'I'll fix us some supper for when you get here.' The earlier plan of a fish-and-chip takeaway from the pub might not work out now, as they finished serving food by nine. Well, she was bound to have something in the freezer; maybe a pizza would do. 'Drive safely.' That's what really mattered, that he got to her safe and sound.

'Yep, will do. Oh, and yeah, how did the prosecco party thing go last night?'

'Really good. Well, a bit too good if my head's anything to go by.'

'Hah, don't expect any sympathy from me – all self-inflicted,' he jibed.

'Cheers. Thanks for the support. But yeah, I really think the idea's got potential and the girls seemed to love it.'

'That's great. And it should help keep the coffers full and Mr Miserable off your back for a bit.'

'Hopefully.'

'Right, well, I'll crack on. See you soon.' He sounded tired.

'Yep, I'll let you concentrate on the road. See ya.' She switched off her mobile and sighed.

It was work getting in the way again and the new job for Max down in Leeds was making things even more difficult for them. It was frustrating more than anything, but hey ho, such was life. She knew all about long working hours and short breaks. You just had to get your head down and get on with it sometimes.

She couldn't settle until he was there with her, so despite feeling tired, she used the time to make some raspberry-swirl chocolate bars – they looked so pretty with white and dark chocolate swirled together and freeze-dried raspberry pieces sprinkled over the top. She also made a batch of hazelnut pralines.

Alfie's excited bark was the indicator that Max's Jeep had finally pulled up outside. Em dashed through from the shop's kitchen and opened the front door to save him having to do the usual after-hours walk around the back yard. He came to the door looking pale-faced and shattered.

'Wow, what a day that was! Come here, you.' He managed to smile, his arms opening.

They shared a hug and a slow, sweet kiss, right at the shop door.

A couple of teenage lads happened to be wandering by, who gave a wolf-whistle.

Emma and Max pulled away gently with a smile.

* * *

After a casual supper of pizza and garlic bread – the freezer having come up trumps – they sat in the upstairs lounge of the cottage flat above the shop. Em, comfortable with her legs curled up on the sofa, rested her head back against Max's chest.

'So, tell me all about this prosecco party, then.'

'Yeah, it went off great. I thought the parties would need a bit of focus, so we made homemade truffles whilst enjoying the prosecco. And then there was time for chat and a bit of fun. The girls all loved it. I really think the party idea will work, once I get my licence completed. And, at least it'll be another chocolate string to my bow.'

'Exactly. It sounds good. What are you thinking of charging?' Ever the business mind at work with Max.

'Well, I've priced it out, and I was thinking, with say two glasses of prosecco included and all the chocolate-making ingredients, of charging £19.95 a head. That's similar to a top-end afternoon tea, and quite fair as a glass of prosecco out is usually about six or seven pounds. If the group want to buy any extra bottles, I can charge that on top. It'll keep the initial cost down per person but if a party are having fun, they can carry on with the bubbly that way.'

'Yes, that seems sound. You'll just need to keep an eye on your actual costs when you do the first few parties. You've got to make it worthwhile for the business too. You'll be giving up a whole night of your time, remember.'

'Yeah, I know, but I have to keep thinking of ways to

improve the shop's finances, especially with that bloody latest visit from Mr Neil.'

Max was stroking her hair gently as he spoke. 'I hate to put a spanner in the works, but it may well be that your landlord has plans to sell the freehold on the shop, Em. There's definitely something behind his month-on-month lease agreement.'

'Yeah, so he can get out of it quickly, I know. But I'm just trying to pursue everything I can to make this business successful and to be the best chocolate shop along the Northumberland coast. That's all I can do. There's no way I'm going to give up now.'

'That's the spirit, Em. Good for you.'

'Oh Max, if I think too much about the alternatives, the implications of maybe losing this place, it'd send me crazy.'

'I know. But whatever your landlord is scheming is outside your control. Just keep focussing on what you can improve to make the business even better, and if The Chocolate Shop ever did have to move premises, at least your reputation and your business can move with you.'

'Yeah, you're right.' But, even though his words made sense, the thought of ever having to leave this place, and maybe the village too, just broke her heart.

Later, as they sat, cosied up, watching some television, Emma realised Max's breathing had slowed and looked up from his chest to see that he had fallen asleep. She got up carefully so as not to disturb him and went downstairs to let Alfie out the back yard, before locking up the back door for the night.

On her return, she gently shook Max's shoulder. 'Hey, sleepyhead. Time for bed.'

'Wha—?' He looked up, bleary-eyed and a bit startled.

'You fell asleep in the middle of *Poldark*.'

'Oh, right.'

They were soon settled in bed and within a minute he was off again, breathing heavily beside her. It was the first evening since he had started staying over of a weekend that they hadn't made love. Emma sighed. He must be totally shattered, she reasoned. But still, she couldn't help but feel disappointed. There was a time when he could hardly wait until he'd got inside the door to make love with her. And now this . . . Had things changed so much between them already?

The next morning, being a Sunday and a morning off, Emma and Max decided to take Alfie for a stroll along the coastal footpath to the ruins of Dunstanburgh Castle. As they walked, they could see the ancient landmark, rugged and dramatic, perched on a grassy rise up ahead.

The walking was easy and they meandered along the track on the bright April morning. They passed a family with a labrador, who Alfie did his usual doggy meet and greet with – a sniff and circle manoeuvre – and some other ramblers who they said hello to.

It was lovely having a few hours together, holding hands as they strolled. There was a fresh sea breeze, but it was pleasant, invigorating. It was nice to get outside. Max seemed to have perked up a lot since last night. The colours of sky and sea, with the countryside rolling down to meet the rocks of the shore, were a bold mix of blues and greys and greens.

'It's beautiful here, isn't it? I can see why you've fallen in love with this place Em,' Max commented.

'It has a wild, rugged beauty, doesn't it? Still feels a little untamed. Just as it must have been years ago.' They were nearing the castle ruins now. Em always found herself wondering what battles and adventures had gone on there in the past. It was quiet here now, bar the odd cry of a gull, the crash of waves on the rocks that fell steeply below.

'I'm going to have to leave at lunchtime, Em. I'll go when you open up the shop.'

'Oh . . .' On a Sunday he usually stayed – sometimes helping her out in the shop, clearing plates and loading the dishwasher, or taking Alfie out for a walk – at least until after supper, and sometimes overnight too. 'So soon?'

'Yeah, sorry. I need to be onsite in Leeds to start at 6.00 a.m. It's a crucial stage on the project, and timescales are short. I'm going to head back down to the B&B digs there this afternoon. And you're working, anyhow.'

'Yes, it makes sense.' It also made her heart dip a little. Silly, how she could begin to miss him when he was still by her side.

They paused. Their stretch of track was empty for now

and she moved in to give him a hug, just wanting to feel him close. His arms came around her, keeping her to him. As she tilted her head up, his hands shifted to the back of her head and they shared a warm, tender kiss.

'Missing you already,' she admitted as she reluctantly pulled away.

'Me too,' he replied.

They stood close for a minute or so, side by side, just looking out across the rolling sea, until Alfie got bored and stood barking at them.

12

The afternoon in the café didn't run quite as calmly as Emma had anticipated. It was full-on in the shop with serving and keeping up with the orders. A sunny Sunday was bringing everybody out, locals and tourists alike. Emma was making her way out to the café, carrying a tray of lattes and two chocolate and raspberry brownies, when a voice stopped her in her tracks.

'Hi, Em.'

Oh goodness, Nathan was there in the shop, waving across at her. So, he'd stayed on in the area after all.

'Hi-i,' she mouthed back. She quickly served the couple in the window seat, then nipped across to see him. 'Hey, how are you? Still here in Warkton, then?'

'Yeah, fancied staying on a few more days. Been doing a bit of surfing on the beach here, actually.'

'Blimey, you're brave. I hardly get in past my ankles. It's usually freezing in the North Sea.'

'Yeah, well it's a darned sight colder than the sea in Oz.

But hey, chuck a wetsuit on and it's all right. It's been fun, actually. Nothing quite like it, catching a few waves, and I caught up with a couple of the locals on the beach too.'

'Ah, right.'

Holly was trying to catch her attention with a café order.

'Hey, I can see you're busy. Look, I'll get away and let you crack on.'

'No, honestly, stay. Take a seat. Can I get you a coffee or anything?'

'Well, if you're sure. A white coffee would be great, but I'll keep out of your way.'

'Great, coming up. I'll be back soon.' She didn't want him to leave just yet. He was like family. A link with her beautiful yet sad past. *And*, she was just getting to know him again.

She was soon back with the order that Holly had taken and Nate's coffee.

'Good little place you have here, Em. Seems popular.'

'Yeah, it's often busy on the weekends, especially through the summer months.' There was a queue forming at the till now. 'Ah sorry, got to help out at the counter.'

'No worries,' Nate said, smiling.

There was a constant stream of customers which was great for the takings but meant Em didn't get a chance to chat with Nathan again. She saw him getting up to go after spending a while browsing the local paper over his coffee.

'Hey, I can see you're really busy, Em. I'll get away.'

'Oh . . .' She couldn't help but sound a little disappointed.

'Look, why don't we meet up for a drink tonight? The Fisherman's Arms seems a pretty cool place. Maybe once you've finished work?'

'Yeah, okay, that'd be good. What time?'

'About sevenish? We can have a couple of bevvies, and chat.'

'Great. See you later, then.'

'Cheers, Em. Thanks for the coffee.' He got up without offering to pay. To be fair, he probably wasn't earning anything at the moment. Ah, that was fine, mused Em.

She watched him head out to the street. The profile so similar and the same jaunty walk as Luke . . .

'Who was that? Not seen him around Warkton before.' Holly was inquisitive.

'My br—' Em realised she was just about to say brother-in-law. But he wasn't quite. 'It's Luke's brother,' she corrected herself.

'Oh, right. Well, how come he's never been here before? You never mentioned a brother.' Holly had heard about Luke; how fate had taken away Emma's fiancé nearly eight years ago now and pretty much destroyed her life. Though she was much younger than Emma, she couldn't help but feel protective of her employer.

'He's been away – abroad. It's been a bit of a surprise.'

'Ah, right.' Holly paused, evidently thinking about this turn of events. 'You okay?'

'Yeah, I think so.'

Before they could chat any further, another customer came, wanting a gift box made up. Emma let her assistant deal with the order and went to clear the tables.

It was gone half-past five before Emma knew it. They served a little longer than usual today, making the most of the influx of customers. Em let Alfie out briefly, had a quick bite of toast for supper, and then dashed upstairs to get changed out of her work clothes. Weirdly, she felt a little nervous at the thought of meeting up with Nathan in the pub.

He was already there when she arrived, sitting with a pint of lager on a stool at the bar. Emma didn't fancy being on view quite so prominently and, after she bought her own glass of white wine, suggested they move to a corner table.

'So, is your shop always that busy? Looks like a little goldmine.'

'Nah, wish it was. That's just a weekend in what's nearly high season. Come along midweek or in January/February time and it'll be a different story.'

'Ah, right.'

'So, you said you'd done a bit of surfing the other day?'

'Yeah gave it a go. Nothing like the waves down in Oz, but yeah it was all right. The locals down there on the beach seem a pretty cool bunch.'

Emma thought it was probably the younger set from the village, some of the ones who'd be a couple of years older than Holly. 'Right. Okay. I don't really know them that well.'

'They seemed friendly enough. Surfers normally are as a rule. It might be chilly, but at least there's no sharks to worry about round here,' Nate added.

Only *landlords*, mused Emma wryly before saying, 'Oh, wow. There's no way I'd even try surfing if I knew there were sharks around.'

'Well, they don't come in often. Must admit, had a scare one time though, just off Melbourne, saw the fin right next to my board. Frightened the shit out of me. Just knelt up on the board and let it pass. My heart was going like the clappers. Pretty unnerving.'

'I bet.'

'Yeah, I love the travelling. New Zealand was stunning. The scenery, waterfalls, glaciers . . . I did a bungee jump there, down a ravine. Met some cool people on my travels too. Backpacker places are just great for making friends.'

His life sounded so very different from hers. She'd thought it a huge adventure to come up to Warkton and start her new life. But it seemed a pretty sheltered exist-ence now, compared to his. There was a whole world out there that she hadn't even ventured into. The furthest she had ever gone was to Paris on a weekend trip with Luke. She'd always wanted to go and see the paintings in the Louvre; the Mona Lisa in particular. And that day had been just wonderful. Luke generally wasn't one for public displays of affection, but outside, in front of the glass pyramid, they had shared the most romantic kiss, with the spirit of Paris upon them and their wedding to look forward to. It had been so special, so full of hope. Paris in springtime . . . Luke dead by autumn.

Emma felt a familiar knot in her throat, a tear misting her eye. 'Yeah,' she managed to reply.

'Em? You thinking of Luke?'

'Yeah.'

'Gets you like that sometimes, doesn't it. You can be happy doing something and boom, it slam dunks you again.'

'It still feels like it just happened yesterday, sometimes.'

'Hey, don't I know it.' He reached across the wooden table to take her hand.

Em let his hand stay there for a few comforting seconds. Then she spotted Danny moving their way collecting glasses. She wondered how it might look, the two of them touching like that, so pulled her hand away gently, and gave Nate a small smile.

'Hey Danny,' she called her friend over, 'come and meet Nathan, ah, Nate I mean.'

'Hi, Nate.' Danny gave them both a bit of an odd look.

'Hi. Hey, didn't I see you down on the beach the other day? Do you surf?'

'Occasionally, yeah. My mate Tom's more into it than me. The surf here's a bit hit and miss. Better to go off down to Tynemouth, really.'

'Ah, okay. I'll bear that in mind.'

'Everything all right, Em?' Danny raised his eyebrows.

Of course, everyone knew everyone's business around here. He'd know all about Max and Emma being a couple and would be wondering what the hell was going on here.

'Nate is Luke's brother, Dan,' she explained. 'You know, my fiancé who died.'

'Ah . . . right. Got it.' He looked relieved. 'Nice to meet you, mate.' He dropped a couple of glasses to the table and reached to shake his hand in greeting, his tone changing totally, and his shoulders relaxing.

Emma had to smile. *What was this place like at times?!*

'Right, well I'd better get on or I'll be getting the evil eye from Dave next.' He picked up the pint glasses once more, fingertips pinching them together, three to each hand.

Emma and Nate chatted on. He asked about her life here, which Emma thought sounded extremely boring compared to his worldwide adventures.

'It's a cute place round here. I like it,' commented Nate.

'So, where are you staying? A B&B or something?'

'Nah, I have my own camper van. Parked it down by the beach. No one seems to be bothered about me leaving it there. Free accommodation with a great view.' He grinned.

She didn't dare ask how he showered or went to the loo from there. Maybe the free and easy life wasn't quite for her after all. The flip-side of freedom! 'Well, if you ever need a shower or anything, you can always come to the shop. My flat's above it.' The offer had come out before she had a chance to even think about it. But he was just a friend. He'd be glad of a shower, for sure, if he was going to stay in the area a bit longer.

'Cheers, Em. I might just take you up on that.'

They chatted a while longer and she got another round of drinks in. It was pleasant catching up on old times, remembering moments with Luke, asking how their parents were doing. It was nearly ten o'clock when Em said she ought to be getting back.

'It's been good to see you again, Em.' Nate's eyes locked on hers.

'Yeah, you too, Nate.'

They briefly grasped hands across the table. It was like holding hands with the past. And yet, it also felt like there was still so much to catch up on. Seeing Luke's brother again like this, it was just so lovely. She realised she wasn't quite ready for him to up and go off on his travels again quite yet.

'I'll see you about, Nate. Call in whenever.'

'Yeah, I'll catch you soon, Em. Thanks for the drink.'

By the time she had reached the pub door, Nate was chatting away to one of the local lads at the bar – no doubt someone he'd met earlier down at the beach. He looked up and gave her a nod and a smile as she was about to leave. She smiled back, feeling strangely unsettled, and just as she got into her flat, her mobile started to ring. She saw the caller ID.

'Hi, Max. You got back to Leeds okay then?'

'Yeah. Sorry I had to rush away earlier. You all right? Had a good afternoon? I tried just before . . .'

'Ah, sorry. I've been out at The Fisherman's.' The phone signal was never very good down there. Weirdly, talking to Max now, she felt a little guilty, though there was no reason to be. Well, maybe she should have told Max about Nathan turning up the other day, but then she hadn't even known if she'd get to see him again. *And*, he was more or less family after all. 'Yeah, I had a surprise visit . . .' She didn't add that it had been three days ago. 'From Luke's brother.'

'Oh, right. Isn't he the one who's been living abroad?'

'Yes, that's right. He's back for a while. Come home to visit his family. He seems to be doing okay.'

'I bet that was a bit strange for you. Meeting up after all that time . . . after everything.' Max knew the guy had been away several years.

Em could hardly admit quite *how* strange, or how much Nathan reminded her of his brother.

'Yeah, it is a little.' She quickly changed the subject and they chatted for a while about work, both anticipating a busy week to come. Max mentioned he'd forgotten to tell her that he'd pitched for a job to follow the Leeds one, thankfully nearer to home this time. A barn conversion in a village outside Hexham.

'So give it a few months and things should settle down a bit, Em.'

A few months – that sounded such a long time. 'Well, that'll be good. Something to look forward to.' But would there ever be a period when work didn't eat up all their time, Emma wondered?

Ten minutes after they finished the call, each of them reluctant to say goodbye, wary of letting that sense of separation creep in, Em was standing out on the back step, letting Alfie out before bedtime.

There was an arc of crescent moon above her, high in the night sky, and a multitude of stars were glinting. She didn't really believe Luke could look down on her, but at times like this she somehow felt closer to him just gazing up at the vastness of the universe, with a sense of the unknown, the unexplored around her. She sighed. When would this heart of hers ever settle down? Could things really ever work out with her and Max when it always came back to Luke? She had worked so hard to open her heart once more, and yes, she really liked Max, but already she was afraid she could feel it starting to protect itself again. How could this new relationship ever be as good as the one she'd had all those years ago?

13

It was a lovely Tuesday in early May when the minibus of 'Golden Oldies' – the coffee group for the elderly that Shirley, Adam's gran, organised – pulled up outside The Chocolate Shop.

'Here we go, Bev. They've arrived.'

'Hah, I love this lot. They are so chatty and friendly. And the stories they can tell! I used to think Warkton-by-the-Sea was a sleepy little place, until I heard all about the old days around here.'

First off the bus was Adam's gran, a spritely grey-haired lady in her sixties. She helped with the weekly coffee morning in the neighbouring coastal town of Seahouses, and occasionally they would take a trip out to Warkton-by-the-Sea and Emma's Chocolate Shop for a change of scene.

Emma had reserved one of the window tables for them, though it was a bit of a squeeze with there being ten in the group. They could split up across to the other table, but they seemed to prefer being together. Bev let them get settled, and then went across to take their order. Cakes, brownies and a selection of chocolates were requested, along with a tray of tea and a couple of lattes.

When Emma brought the order along soon after, one of the ladies piped up, 'Ooh, and how's your young man these days? What a fine lad he was. Coming to help me at home like that.'

'Worth every penny wasn't he, Thelma?' the lady beside her beamed.

'Oh yes, he helped stack all those logs for me for the winter, *and* he put up some pictures for me and a mirror. Very handy.'

They'd won his 'services' in a charity Christmas auction and Emma had wondered if he'd ever make it back out of their sheltered accommodation in one piece after all the raucous banter that day at the Christmas Fayre. But he'd really enjoyed it, and the two ladies had been totally sweet and polite apparently. All bark and no bite, as Emma's own nanna might have said, had she still been alive today.

'Lovely-looking lad he is too. You two still courting then?'

'Dorothy, now that's enough. Don't you go embarrassing Emma with all your talk and quizzing,' Shirley warned.

'There's no harm in looking, Shirl. It's the best we're going to get at our age, isn't it, Thelma?' Dorothy winked kindly at Emma, who couldn't help but smile.

'So, who's for cake then?' Emma asked, serving out the gorgeous rich chocolatey slices.

There was a raising of hands, followed shortly by much happy munching and slurping.

'Delicious as always,' said one of the gentlemen, raising his teacup in thanks.

'Good to hear it. Enjoy!' And with that Emma went off to serve a young couple who were sat up on the stools by the counter.

It wasn't long before a family with a toddler arrived and took the other window seat. The café was then full. With it becoming more popular, and being a small cottage building, space was an issue. It was a lovely day out there, so it was a shame they couldn't put some tables and chairs out on the pavement in front of the shop, but it was way too narrow, and the customers would be too near the traffic as well as blocking the pedestrian access. Emma went out to the kitchen, taking a tray of used mugs and plates with her. She stood for a second looking from the kitchen sink out to the courtyard. That was when she remembered her light-bulb moment from a few weeks ago.

The courtyard. It could easily fit three or four tables. The walls would provide shelter and the space was light and sunny on a nice day. Walkers often liked to come along with their dogs too and they could only have a takeaway at present, but they could sit out there with their pets quite easily. She'd pop a big dog bowl of water out for any thirsty pooches. The Chocolate Shop's

Courtyard Café – a perfect addition for the summer. She felt a flutter of excitement. It was time to put her ideas into action. What with this and the prosecco parties, the shop's income might drastically improve.

She might even get to save a bit, and have some money kept by for any unexpected rent hikes – or, dare she even think it, towards a deposit on a business loan, though it might well take years to raise enough for that. Still, Emma felt a buzz of excitement and made up the next order happily humming away to herself. She couldn't wait to tell Bev and Holly all about her brainwave.

As she stood washing up, her mind rattled away. If she got a move on and found some outdoor seating (it would have to be second-hand for her tight budget), she might even have the courtyard area up and running by the Whit-week school holidays at the end of the month. In fact, she could ask her brother James to go along to any car boot or house sales on over the next couple of weekends as there was no time like the present. And if there was no joy with that, then Ron the local carpenter might have some ideas for wooden benches.

After the 'Golden Oldies' had set off with smiles, 'thank yous' and 'see you again soons', Em couldn't wait to share her idea with Bev who had just turned up for work. Emma launched into her plan as the pair of them stood behind the counter.

'That is *such* a good idea. It often gets a bit crowded in here, especially now it's almost the full-on summer tourist season.'

'Do you know what,' Em continued, the ideas flowing like melted chocolate now, 'I think I'll make a brand-new menu for the summer, with more emphasis on milkshakes, chocolate ice creams with fudge sticks in, choc-dipped waffles, oh yes and old-fashioned ice-cream sundaes too.'

'I think I've died and gone to heaven!' Bev said, then did an *oh-shite-I've-put-my-foot-in-it-again* face. 'Soz.'

'It's all right. It's just a saying. Anyway, we could source the ice cream from the local dairy to start. Their stuff is totally delicious, and we'll be helping another local business. So, we all win.'

'And the customers too. Summer chocolate bliss. Let me help you design the new menu, yes?'

'Of course.'

'So, how else can I help?' Bev offered.

Em loved that her friend was so keen to get on board with her new plans. It showed how much she cared for The Chocolate Shop too.

'Well, it shouldn't be too difficult to get up and running. The main thing will be finding some good second-hand furniture for the courtyard. If you can put the word out locally, that'd be great.'

'I certainly will.'

With that, another customer came in, Bev took the order, and Emma was back out to the kitchen again, with a cheery 'No rest for the wicked, then,' launched over her shoulder.

14

May sunshine streamed through the upstairs lounge window. She'd take Alfie out for his walk on the beach shortly, and then head back to make some more chocolate supplies before Max arrived. But what Emma *really* needed to do first, after a hectic Saturday in the shop, was to collapse on the sofa with a very large mug of tea. The summer season was already ramping up and she'd hardly had chance to breathe today. She couldn't wait to get the courtyard area organised and open to make the most of the increasing visitor numbers. But first the kettle was calling . . .

She had just plumped herself down on the sofa when there was a knock at the back door. Max wasn't due for another couple of hours, what with the long journey back from Leeds. Curious, yet irked at having to move so soon, Emma headed off down the stairs.

'Only me.' Nate was stood there, with a small rucksack

in his hand, and what looked like a towel sticking out from it.

She hadn't seen him for a while and had wondered if he might have left the village and set off on some new travels.

'You know that offer of a shower? Can I take you up on it? There's only so much you can do with a basin of water in a confined space. And my hair's got all salty with the surfing.'

'Yes, of course. Do you want a coffee or anything while you're here?'

'Yep, why not. A strong coffee would be great, ta.'

'Come on up to the flat. I'll show you to the bathroom, and then I'll put the kettle on.'

'Can I shower first? Can't wait to get into some fresh clothes and feel properly clean again.'

'Course. No worries.' As they reached the landing, Alfie came bouncing out to greet the newcomer.

'Howdy, mate. Cute dog.' He gave Alfie a good old head rub. 'Hah, our labrador, Barney, nearly bowled me over when I got home from my travels. You remember him, don't ya?'

'Yes, I saw him just a few months ago when I met up with your mum and dad. He's still very affectionate, just got a bit slower.'

'Hah, and a bit fatter. But crikey, he turned back into a big excited puppy when he saw me.'

'Aw, he must have missed you.'

'Yeah.'

'Right, well here's the bathroom. Go ahead. The water should be nice and hot. Take as long as you like.'

'Great. Cheers, Em.'

She headed to the flat's kitchen to put the kettle back on, then spotted the empty milk carton on the side that she'd just used up. Ah, not even a little drop left. And she knew the shop kitchen was out too, as there had been a busy spell just before closing with an order of three milkshakes – she'd only just had enough. She had intended calling Max and getting him to pick up some on his way and had forgotten. She glanced at her watch – five to six. It was the summer months, so Sheila should still be open now. If she quickly nipped down the street, she'd be in time.

'Nate, I'm just fetching some milk,' she called out. 'I'll be about five minutes. Okay?'

No answer. He might not be able to hear for the sound of the shower running. Oh well, she'd soon be back. She dashed out.

Max parked the Jeep up on the side street. He'd finished work early for a change and it would be lovely to surprise Emma, especially having been a bit late the last few weekends, and he was looking forward to a nice chilled-out evening together.

The back door, his usual port of entry out of hours, was unlocked, so he wandered in, calling out a 'hello' to Em as he entered. No answer, so he looked in the shop's kitchen. She wasn't there. Then he heard the sound of the shower running upstairs. Hmm, he smiled to himself, that could be a very nice welcome indeed! He swiftly made his way up the stairs.

He heard the shower stop, gave it a second or two and was about to stroll on in and take her gorgeous wet body into his arms, when the bathroom door was flung open.

'What the fu—'

'Ah, hi.' The young man had very little on other than a short towel which was wrapped around his waist area, and he was grinning away as though he had every right to be there.

Max's heart sank so low he felt physically sick. And then he had the strongest urge to punch the guy's lights out. His fist was prickling as he heard the back door go, just as the lad whose face had paled was saying, 'Ah, okay, it's not like it looks, mate.'

'Don't you *mate*, me.' Max's voice was a low growl.

It was then that Emma came up the stairs where all she could see initially was Max. 'Wow, hi Max, you're early.' Her voice came out a little squeaky, twigging who was still in her bathroom. Except, as she took two more steps up, she could see he *wasn't* still in her bathroom at all and was standing opposite Max, sporting a very small towel over a crucial area.

'Yeah, thought I'd surprise you . . .' Max's tone was full of irony, 'thinking that it might be nice to get a bit more time together. But I see you have other plans.' His voice was low, angry.

'Ah, right. This really isn't how it might seem, Max.'

'And how's that? That some guy's been staying over?'

'It's not just some guy!' She was floundering now, digging herself into a deeper hole, she knew. Dammit, she'd better get her explanation out quick or Max'd just carry on assuming the worst, but the words seemed to be stuck in her throat. 'Max . . . this is Nathan, L-Luke's brother.' She'd managed to find the words at last. 'He-he's just staying in the village for a time.' She looked between the pair of them. Max's face still a scowl. 'Okay, I can see how this might look right now, but it's only because he doesn't have a shower in his camper van.'

Nate was nodding. 'Yep, no shower facilities in the VW.' He tried a small smile. Max's face was totally stony in return. 'Well then, I'll quickly get dressed, and get out of your hair, Em.' Nate scurried back into the bathroom where he shoved on his shorts and T-shirt.

'What the hell?' was all Max could say, as Emma stood looking embarrassed, realising just how bad that had looked. All she did was hold up the milk carton as evidence, but she wasn't quite sure what of.

Nate was out of the bathroom again in a matter of seconds. 'Nice to meet you, Matt.' He offered his hand to shake.

'It's Max,' Max replied bluntly, with no intention of lifting his hand in response.

'Right, I'll leave you guys to it. I can see myself out. No worries.'

And he vanished.

'I was fetching milk,' Emma managed to say. 'I was just doing him a bit of a favour.'

'Yeah, I bet.' Max was struggling to shake off the feelings of anger.

'Hey, hang on, that's not fair. There's nothing at all going on. He's virtually family, after all.'

Alfie came out to the landing to see what all the noise was about. Max patted his head absently.

'And you didn't have to be so damned rude,' Emma continued.

'What? How the hell would you have felt if you came down to my house and some woman was walking out of my shower half-naked?'

'I'm sure I'd have given you a chance to explain.'

Max just raised his eyebrows at that. 'Hah – really?'

'Ye-es.' Though Emma wasn't totally certain herself.

'Ah, well actually, that would never happen as you never have time to come down to my place. What with your precious Chocolate Shop taking up all your time.' Max was so riled up it was all pouring out now.

That made the hairs on the back of Emma's neck rise – her Chocolate Shop was very precious to her; surely he could understand that? 'Well, if you don't like it, you can bloody well get out of it!' The words were out before she could stop them.

Alfie slunk back to the relative safety of the kitchen at that point.

'I might just do that,' Max retorted. But still he stood there.

Emma was frozen to the spot too, her face paling, the anger subsiding. Both of them afraid that he might really walk out at that point.

Max's features softened, his words said more gently now, 'I might just go and get some air. I'll take Alfie . . .' That way, they both knew he'd have to come back.

'Okay. That sounds a good idea.' Her voice was still curt, but there was a sense of relief between them.

Maybe a cooling-off time was just what they both needed.

Emma watched Max leave from the back courtyard and felt her heart sink. *What the hell had just happened there?*

Seeing him walk out of her door had made her realise how much she'd hate it if it ever happened for good. Thank heavens Alfie was there, trotting along beside him. He'd be back . . . he'd have to, this time.

She ran upstairs to the lounge and stood looking out of the window down the street, hoping to catch sight of them once more. She felt a bit queasy. She hated arguments at the best of times. Then she spotted the back of Max's tall, broad figure next to her brown-and-white spaniel. They were heading down towards the harbour, to the beach, no doubt. They didn't turn to look back at the shop, or her.

Was it just jealousy on his part? Most likely. But, what if he really believed she'd been messing about? That something had already happened between her and Nate? She realised what it must have looked like for Max walking in to find Nate half-naked like that. But really, talk about jumping to bloody conclusions. She hadn't even been in the flat at the time!

Ah, *love* – it swirled up your emotions like a damned whirlpool at times. Her battered heart was still getting a bashing. Was it really worth all the effort?

Oh, Luke why did you have to go and get killed? It would have been so much simpler if they could have carried on, had their wedding dreams come true, the life they'd thought they'd have together. When she didn't know that love could be a double-edged sword.

But as she watched Max's figure getting smaller in the distance, she felt such a pang of hurt and longing. A stark reminder that she wasn't ready to lose her new love for the sake of a misunderstanding.

She slumped down on the sofa, suddenly feeling exhausted, the angry emotions of their argument receding, leaving her feeling raw, vulnerable. She sighed, closed her eyes, and sat quietly for a minute or two. But this was no good, moping about like this, there were chocolates to make, her shop to keep going. She'd be better keeping busy anyhow; switch her mind to something more productive.

As she started pouring chocolate callets into the tempering machine, her mind couldn't help but drift back to the row with Max. It was so early in their relationship that it felt like they were on Bambi legs still. Could they pull through a blip like this? She knew she wouldn't relax until he came back, but she pushed on, getting the Baileys and cream measured out ready for the white chocolate-dipped truffles she was about to make.

And here she was back in the Chocolate Shop, with Max's words that it 'took all her time' now ringing in her ears. Okay, so she did work six-and-a-half-day weeks, with early mornings and late nights. But she had to do that to make sure the business survived, didn't she? Or, was it more her own survival technique, she wondered, a way of cutting off from the world . . . the world that could hurt you.

Max knocked at the back door before coming in this time. Emma had heard the back gate go just before and felt her heart rate quicken.

She swiftly rinsed her hands and wiped them on a towel, then headed for the back hallway. Max opened the door tentatively, Alfie already barging his way in.

'Hey.' Max stood there looking unsure of himself.

'Hi,' Em replied cautiously.

There was a second or two of silence, when they both seemed hesitant.

'Look, I'm sorry . . .' Max started. He was standing there with Alfie, both with a hang-dog expression.

She looked into Max's lovely green eyes.

'It was just such a bloody shock,' he continued. 'Walking in, seeing another guy here like that. Coming out of your bathroom . . . it just killed me, you know and I jumped to conclusions. I'm sorry . . . Look, I know he's Luke's brother, but he just seems the sort who drifts about from what you've said. He won't be around for long, Em, and I don't want you to get hurt or used or anything.'

'You did overreact, but I kind of understand why you did. I'm just getting to know him again, Max, as a *friend*, that's it.' She emphasised the word. 'I feel like I owe it to Luke to look out for his kid brother.'

'Yeah, I get it. Like I say, I'm sorry.'

'If this is going to work, Max, we need to start trusting each other.' She held his gaze. At this moment, she *so* wanted this to work.

'Of course.'

'And while you were out walking, I've been thinking things over. Some of what you said rang true. I realise that we need to somehow, in our busy, hectic working lives, make more time for each other too.'

'Yeah, I know it's been harder recently. But once this Leeds job is completed, and I'm back working closer to home again, it'll be a lot easier.'

'And then maybe I can get Holly and Bev to cover a few more hours and try and take the odd Sunday off too, so we can get a full day together at least sometimes.'

'That sounds good.'

She felt herself relax. He wasn't going anywhere fast. 'Do you want to take Alfie on upstairs? He looks a bit sandy. His towel's hanging on the peg above his bed.'

'Yes, of course.'

'I'll be up in just a few minutes. I need to finish off

making these truffles.' But even as she said this, she really didn't want him to walk away, not yet, even if it was only up a flight of stairs. She walked over to Max, who dropped Alfie's lead. The dog would probably just head on upstairs by himself anyhow. What did a few sandy footprints matter? Max's arms opened and she moved in to lean against the soft cotton of his T-shirt, finding the warmth of his chest below. It felt like where she should be.

She looked up, not realising at first that tears had misted her eyes, making her vision all fuzzy.

'Hey,' Max gently stroked her forehead, then moved his hand gently to tilt her chin so her eyes met his. 'It's okay . . . we're okay.'

15

Used to getting up at six for work, they spent what was for them a long, lazy Sunday morning in bed. Emma never tired of exploring Max's gorgeous body, and he seemed just as happy exploring hers. No alarms, no major deadlines, just a shop to open at midday.

It was ten by the time they were sitting, propped up against pillows, with a cup of tea that Max had got up to make. He'd also let Alfie out for her too. Emma decided to share her idea for the courtyard area.

'That sounds great, Em.' Max was enthusiastic.

In fact, she had heard of a car boot sale on today near to Alnwick. If they got their skates on an outdoor table set might be there waiting for her. She'd never get it into her little Fiat. But Max had a big Jeep outside.

'Ma-ax, just thinking . . . You wouldn't mind taking a drive across to a car boot sale this morning, would you? What I really need, to get this courtyard café off the ground, is some outdoor furniture – tables and chairs or maybe picnic benches, whatever I can find that's in good condition. It would be great if I can get this idea up and running as soon as possible.'

'Yeah, why not. No worries. Let's get going before all the good stuff goes.'

'Right. Brilliant. We're on.' Emma leapt out of bed. 'I'll just give Holly a quick call and make sure she brings her spare set of keys to open up the shop at twelve, in case we're not back by then.'

They were soon in the Jeep and winding their way out of the village. It was only a twenty-minute drive, and the roads weren't too busy.

The car boot sale was in full swing when they got there. A lot of the stuff on display was smaller items; knick-knacks, toys, clothes and suchlike. They stopped at a van which had several items of furniture outside, but there didn't seem anything suitable for outdoor use.

'You don't happen to have any outdoor furniture, do you? I'm looking for a table and chairs set for a patio area.' Em was being cautious, thinking he might raise his price if he thought a business was involved.

'No, nothing like that, love. Sorry. But there is a chap further down who has a few house clearance items. You might be lucky there. Look for the grey van and ask for Rick; he's a regular here.'

'Okay, will do. Thanks.'

She suddenly felt like she was on one of those antique programmes like *Bargain Hunt* or something. Em needed to get there before someone else did. She set off at a marching pace, closely followed by Max, who was smiling to himself at her focus and determination.

She saw the grey van and scanned the area next to it. Bingo! One wooden patio table, looking slightly battered paint-wise but which should sand down okay, and four sturdy-looking wooden chairs. A lady and gentleman were browsing far too close to the set for Emma's liking. She broke into a jog and manoeuvred subtly past them to ask the seller how much he wanted for the set. She held her breath while he stroked his short beard thoughtfully and eyed her. She levelled her gaze back at him with a hopeful smile.

'Seventy-five pounds for the set.'

Emma stayed quiet. If each set cost that much, she'd have to pay out several hundreds, which she really didn't have. She held her nerve while he added, 'This sort of thing would retail at around two hundred and fifty.'

'Yes, when it was new. But it's been overpainted, and that paint's all peeling away now. It'll need some work on it.'

Max was grinning as he reached them, hearing the stand-off. Emma was a lady to be reckoned with for sure.

'Okay, sixty-five then,' the chap came back with.

'Fifty.' Emma stood tall.

The trader shook his head. The other couple were trying out a chair now.

'Fifty-five. I have cash . . .' She had some notes in her pocket from yesterday's takings.

'Deal.'

They shook hands on it, both parties happy.

Sitting in the Jeep with a boot full of chairs and a wooden table that would soon spruce up again – on close inspection all the wood was in good condition – Emma and Max did a high five.

'Well done you.' Max was smiling. 'I loved the bartering technique. Think I might need you to do my negotiating when I'm buying materials in for the next job.' He gave her a wink.

'Any time,' she said, laughing.

They wound their way back along summer country lanes, with purple-pink foxgloves jutting tall from the stone walls, and cattle and sheep languidly grazing the green fields each side of them. As they reached the top of the village, they could see the fishing boats rocking gently in the harbour, the sea glinting silver in the sunshine, and the vista of the bay was just beautiful. It made the heart soar.

Emma looked across at Max in the driving seat, and they shared a warm smile. It was lovely that they seemed to be back on track, and that her dreams for the courtyard café were starting to become a reality.

16

At mid-morning on Tuesday, Emma was on her way to the grocer's, needing some fresh cream for the ganache she was planning to make. Bev was in and covering the shop.

She was halfway down the hill when a movement from the churchyard, which was set just up on the rise, caught her eye. It looked as though someone was unsteady on their feet and perhaps about to fall over. They appeared to be elderly. Emma couldn't walk on without checking that whoever it was, was all right.

The quaint stone church of St Peter's stood proudly on the hill behind the cottages of the main village street, looking out to sea. Emma diverted up a narrow path that was a shortcut to the church's wooden gate. As she entered the churchyard, Emma could see that an elderly lady was leaning heavily against one of the gravestones. On approaching, it was apparent that it was one of her regulars, old Mrs Clark, bent almost double.

'Are you okay?' Emma called. 'Mrs Clark?' She didn't want to just appear beside her and frighten her.

The old lady looked up then. 'Oh . . . just catching my breath, Emma pet. It's my knees. They're such cranky old buggers. Give me a bit of gyp now and then.'

She was still well enough to curse, thank heavens. 'Can I help at all?'

'Oh, I'll be all right in a minute. My, they get that stiff these days. I've been kneeling, sorting out the flowers for my Jim. But how else am I meant to do it? I come here every week, have a chat, fill him in on the news, you know.'

Emma smiled. She did know, but she didn't go to a graveyard for that; she just often chatted to Luke's photograph that was still on her bedside table. Luke had been cremated and his ashes scattered at a beauty spot near his parents' home and Emma always felt that it didn't really matter where the flesh and bones went, as long as you didn't forget, that you still held your loved one in your heart. In fact, she didn't really want to think too much about the flesh and bones. Everyone has to find their own way to grieve, and to carry on.

'Yes, I do.'

Mrs C was able to stand a bit taller now, with just one hand resting on the gravestone. 'He passed away twenty years ago. It was quite sudden – a heart attack. But there's never a week when I don't visit.' The old lady smiled fondly.

Emma noted the fresh bunch of bright-yellow carnations that were set in a cut-glass vase at the base of the headstone that was engraved with 'James Arthur Clark, much loved husband of Marjorie Clark'.

'How long were you together?' Em asked.

'Well, it was over forty years since I first met him. We were just a year off our Ruby Wedding Anniversary when he was taken bad.'

'Oh, I'm sorry, Mrs C.'

'Well, pet, we had our time, would have liked more, but we had our time. It was a good forty years together.' She looked at Emma kindly. 'I know you mentioned about your fiancé. That must have been so hard, losing him so young.'

'It was . . .' Emma felt a lump forming in her throat. 'Thank you.'

Was it any easier losing someone after forty years, when you'd had more time together, Emma wondered, or was that just more to be taken away?

'Well then, shall we head over to your lovely Chocolate Shop? That's where I was going next. 'Cos if I stand here much longer, the old knees'll seize right up again and I'll be back to square one. And I could really do with a nice cup of your tea.' Mrs C was a regular at The Chocolate Shop every Tuesday and Thursday, ten-thirty on the dot, and she popped in many other days too.

'Yes, of course.' She'd walk back with her and check the old lady was all right. She could nip out again later to fetch the cream. 'Mrs C . . . did you have any family?' Emma hoped she wasn't prying too much, but she was curious – she had never heard mention of any grown-up children visiting, or grandchildren.

'No, pet. Not that we didn't want them. But it wasn't meant to be for us.'

'Oh, that's a shame.'

'Ah well, we had a good marriage though, some happy times. And there were always lots of children about in the village to keep us entertained. Anyways, less of the bygones; how's your new young man?'

'He's fine. Just seen him at the weekend.'

'That's good. I used to worry about you there in that shop on your own for all those years. A young girl like you.'

'Oh, I was okay. But yes, it's nice having some company now.'

'I hope it's a bit more than that.' The old lady gave a cheeky wink.

Emma couldn't help but smile, especially remembering Sunday morning.

They were ambling back down the pathway now, soon to turn into the main street.

'I see you there in the shop, working so hard. You need a little fun in life too sometimes,' Mrs C continued. 'Life can be so short, Emma . . . but of course, you know that, pet.' She gave Emma's shoulder a pat. 'Don't hold back on the special things in life, that's all I'm trying to say.'

'I know . . . thanks.'

They were climbing the small hill up to the shop. 'Just need a breather a mo, pet.' Mrs C paused, her breathing a little laboured.

Emma guessed that she must be about eighty years old.

'Always a bit of a bugger, this hill. Keeps me going, though. I'm not about to give up now.' The old lady gave a wry smile that crinkled around her brown eyes.

'Nearly there,' Emma encouraged her, as they set off again. As they reached the door of the shop, Em opened it wide for Mrs C to go on through. 'There now, get yourself a seat and I'll fetch your tea. Do you fancy anything with it today?'

'Hmm, I might. Have you got any of those delicious brownies left?'

'Just made a new batch. There's plain or chocolate-and-raspberry ones.'

'Oh, I'll try a raspberry – they sound scrumptious.'

'Morning, Mrs C,' Bev called from the counter.

'Morning, Beverley. You okay, pet?'

'Yes, great thanks.' And they started to chat whilst Emma headed out to the kitchen to plate up the brownie, with some fresh raspberries for garnish, and make a pot of breakfast tea for one.

The old lady enjoyed her tea and her chat and a bit of a rest. Hilda and Stan came in too, so they shared a table. It was lovely to see the village community getting on so well. Her Chocolate Shop by the Sea was such a cosy hub at times.

17

In a quiet moment later that afternoon, when all the customers were served and happy, Emma chatted with Bev in the kitchen about her developing plans for the courtyard café. 'I'll need to get a move on mind, we are already mid-May now.'

'You'll manage. You can do anything you put your mind to, Em. I've seen you in action, remember. And I haven't forgotten, I've started asking about for you for furniture already. It's such a fab idea, I'm sure it'll work out.'

Emma told her about the table she and Max had managed to get at a bargain price at the weekend. 'So,' she continued, 'I just need to find three more sets and I'm ready for action.'

'We could do a moonlight mission in the village and steal all the good ones from people's back gardens,' said Bev wryly.

'Be-ev, you're terrible!'

'Only joking.'

'Yes, and I'd end up being tracked down by PC Bob straight away.'

'Hmm,' was all her friend responded with.

'What I need is to get some good second-hand ones, cheap. Mission Picnic Bench is about to begin!'

'Hmm.'

'Bev, you okay? You don't seem quite yourself today.' It was unusual for her friend to be subdued. 'Sorry,' Em continued. 'I've probably been prattling on about the courtyard and all my ideas for that, and no doubt been boring you out of your mind.'

'No, it's not that. It's been quite nice hearing you prattling away, to be honest.'

'Hah, so I was prattling . . . Anyway, what is it then? Something bothering you, hun?'

'Ah, it's probably nothing. It's just my mum. She needs to go for some checkups at the hospital. She's had a cough that just won't go away. Now they've recommended she goes for a scan. She's waiting on an appointment to come through and I can't help but worry.'

'Oh Bev, I'm sorry to hear that. No wonder you're worried. At least she's getting checked out.'

'Yes. She used to be a smoker. Stopped a few years ago now, but that's what's on my mind. What if it's something serious, Em?'

'Hey, why not cross that bridge when you come to it?' Emma soothed. 'There could be all sorts of other reasons behind it.'

'I suppose.'

'Have you talked about it with Pete? Let him know you're feeling a bit down just now.'

'Hah – he's hardly ever home these days. Spends more time at the bloody golf club. I know he loves his golf but this year he's become captain and honestly, there's hardly an evening we spend together.'

'Sounds like Golf Widow Syndrome to me,' Em said, with an understanding smile on her face, trying to lift the conversation.

'Yeah . . . I just hope it's nothing more than that.' Her friend's face dropped.

'What do you mean?' Em's tone became serious.

Bev looked concerned. 'Oh Em, you don't think he's having an affair, do you?'

'*Really?* Your Pete?' Em found that hard to believe. Those two were her closest friends and always such a team.

'I might just be being daft. But they say the wife's always the last to know.'

'I really can't see him doing anything to hurt you, Bev.'

'Oh, I'm probably just overreacting – with our Angus all grown-up and away now, and Pete out all the time, it can get so bloody quiet in the house.'

'Oh Bev.' Em put a hand on her friend's shoulder. 'You and Pete need to talk this through properly. About your mum – and him being out so much. And you know I'm always here for you too.'

'I'll try and chat to him, I will. But he's out a-bloody-gain tonight. Some golf charity event.'

Her friend looked like her confidence had taken a bashing, but Emma really couldn't imagine that Pete was straying.

'Right then, well, we'll go out too. Let's take a drive down to Low Newton. How does a walk on the beach and a fish-and-chip supper sound?'

'Sounds good to me.' Bev raised a small smile.

'Great. I'll come and pick you up after work.'

'I just want to pop and see Mum on my way home, but say after six?'

'It's a deal.'

With that, the shop door chimed.

'Come on then, we'd better step back to it again.'

At just after six o'clock that evening, Em pulled up outside Bev's bungalow.

Her friend was soon making her way down the front path, looking lovely, Em thought, dressed in navy capri jeans and a stripy top.

'Your carriage awaits, Madam.' Em smiled as Bev opened the passenger door. She wanted to make sure Bev relaxed and had a nice time this evening. Troubles had a way of building, then all you could see was the downside. She hoped to God that Bev's mum would be okay, and that Pete wasn't up to anything sinister; in fact, she'd risk a bet on it, but she'd be there to support Bev whatever the case. That's what friends were for. And Bev had been her crutch on many occasions in the past.

They drove through winding hawthorn-hedged country

lanes, with the windows wound down and their hair flapping in the breeze, the radio on. Parking up at Low Newton-by-the-Sea, Em let Alfie out of the hatchback and they headed down the short hill to the beach. The view of the sands, dunes and sea stretched all the way to the ruins of Dunstanburgh Castle on the horizon. As they reached the base of the hill, there was a cluster of quaint, white cottages set around a green by The Ship Inn.

They were soon strolling leisurely on the sands, Alfie in his element.

'So, how are you feeling after our chat earlier?'

'Ah, not bad. It's nice to come out and do something different, to be honest.'

'And how was your mum?'

'So-so. Still no appointment come through. I think I'll have to get on to them at the hospital, see if I can chase something up. It's hard not knowing what we're dealing with. Your mind plays all sorts of tricks on you. I can tell Mum's worried too.'

'She's bound to be.'

They neared a rocky area and rounded the headland, then the golden sweep of Embleton bay was there before them.

'Wow, I love this place. What a view,' stated Bev.

The castle ruins stood rugged and moody on the far cliffs, the odd gull circling the sky above it.

'Isn't it just?'

They walked in amicable silence for a short while, Alfie at their heels.

Emma was still mulling over Bev's relationship concerns. 'About Pete? And I don't believe it for a second, by the way, but has there been anything to make you suspicious? Or is it more about the amount of time he's away?'

'Well, he's a bit distant lately, I suppose. I think we just take each other for granted after all these years. And with all the captaincy stuff going on . . . Oh, I don't know! It might be nothing.'

'No, it's a real concern. Even if it is down to the golf, he's got to know you're finding it hard being on your own so much. That it's affecting your relationship. Don't let this drift, Bev. Promise me you'll discuss it with him.'

'Yes, okay. Blimey, you sound like bloody Oprah Winfrey.'

'Hah – if only I could sort my own life out as well.'

Alfie found a big stick of sea kelp that Emma launched across the sands for him. He went bounding off after it like a shot.

'And what about you, Em? What's the latest with Nate? Is he staying on in the village now? I spotted him at the grocer's just this morning.'

Em had already told her friend of the shower incident, and Max's reaction.

'Yeah, looks like he might be.'

'Just be careful, Em.'

'What do you mean?' Em paused to look across at Bev.

'Well, from what you've told me, he's the kind of guy

that comes and goes. He's been travelling the world, moving on all the time. He'll be off again before you know it.'

'Well, yeah.'

'Just don't let yourself get too attached.'

'He's Luke's brother, Bev. We're just friends!' Em pulled a face. Bev seemed to be going a bit over the top.

'Yeah, I get that. But there will be a special link there too, with what you've both been through. Something only you two can understand . . . Just wouldn't want to see you get hurt, that's all. Don't want us both in a bloody mess.'

'O-kay,' Em conceded. Of course she'd not get too involved. No doubt Nate'd be off again in a matter of days anyhow.

They moved the conversation to easier topics as they walked on. It was beautiful down there, the seascape colours muted to silvers and pale golds with the fading evening light. People were milling about enjoying the balmy weather, families, dog walkers, but it wasn't in the least crowded.

Emma suddenly felt her tummy rumble. 'Shall we turn around? Think I'm ready for my fish and chips.'

'Yeah, that sounds good.'

Half an hour later they were sitting on a wooden bench in the garden of The Joiners Arms, a glass of cider and a lager to hand, fish and chips smelling delicious before them. Oh, that crispy batter, salt and vinegar, melt-in-the-mouth fish delight – it seemed like seaside summer on a plate.

'It's lovely out here, isn't it,' said Bev.

'Yeah.'

'You know, I've been thinking of your courtyard café area back at the shop and it'll be great.'

'Thanks. I'm quite excited about it.'

'Yeah, I can just picture it out there on a sunny day, in your lovely stone-walled garden. Chocolate milkshakes, ice-cream sundaes – oh yes, and flowing chocolate fountains to dip marshmallows and strawberries in. I wonder if we could rig something like that up?'

Emma raised her eyebrows, grinning, 'Wow! I'm not bloody Willy Wonka. How do you think I'm going to create that?!' But Emma was glad that Bev seemed to be back on her chirpy form.

'Just letting my imagination flow. Don't stop me while I'm on a roll. It would be cool though, wouldn't it? It'd look like a water fountain, but instead it spouts chocolate. Brilliant. Anyway, Emma Wonka – you already make *the* most amazing chocolate creations.'

'Thanks, but we've got to keep it realistic and within budget.'

Bev pretended to yawn. 'Hah – ever the voice of reason.'

Emma gave her friend a playful punch.

They finished the last of their fish and chips, giving a very grateful Alfie the last few scraps. He'd been patiently sitting beside them, gazing up with hopeful hang-dog eyes.

'Aw, thanks Em. This has been such a lovely evening. Just what I needed.'

'You're welcome. I think I was in need of a bit of time out too.'

'You know, I think I'll have that chat with Pete tonight, when he gets in. No point letting things fester.'

'Yeah, that sounds wise. Good luck.'

When she dropped Bev off at home half an hour later, they shared a hug in the car, then Em watched her friend walk up the path and turn around to wave by the front door. She gave her a big thumbs-up sign in support and hoped the chat with Pete would go well. She'd be ready at the end of the phone tonight, just in case.

18

There was a 'toot' from outside the shop the next morning, just before opening time, then a louder and longer one. Emma headed out to see what the fuss was about.

There was her brother, James, in a white van, with Chloe beside him.

James jumped out of the vehicle. 'Hey, sis. We've got something for you. Best to take it around the back, I think. We'll park up by your back gate. See you there in a sec.' He was grinning – but giving nothing away.

'O-kay.' Em was curious. She dashed back through the shop and courtyard, opening the gate. She heard the van reversing down the track. She could hardly wait to see what was in the back of the vehicle.

Chloe got out first. 'Hi, Em.' She gave her sister-in-law a brief hug. 'I'm so chuffed with this find.'

With that, James pulled open the rear doors of the van. Inside was a lovely old wrought-iron table set with two chairs. Admittedly, on closer inspection it needed a bit of TLC.

'Isn't it delightful? I heard about a house clearance near Alnmouth and couldn't resist popping along. I saw this and could just picture it in your courtyard. James had told me all about your plans the night before. And there it was. Fate.'

'It's perfect.' Emma could see it now, repainted white (it was a tarnished pale green at present), looking like something from an English country garden.

'And there's more,' James announced proudly. 'Look behind.'

Emma clambered up into the back of the van, and there was a wooden pub-style picnic bench, which would soon perk up with a lick of varnish.

'Best thing was, that one was free,' James added. 'There was a pub closing down near Mum and Dad's. I was driving by a couple of days ago and saw it out the front, thought I'd be a bit cheeky and knock and ask if I could get it for a tenner or something. The guy there said to just take it. They were having trouble selling the place and he'd thought it might end up sitting outside for months, rotting away.'

'This is just great, guys. Thank you. So, what do I owe you for the wrought-iron set? I know that wouldn't have come cheap.'

'Actually, we'd like you to accept it as a gift for the launch of the courtyard café,' Chloe said proudly.

'You sure? You've already been brilliant finding it for me, and the delivery service too, of course.'

'No arguments,' James stated. 'We want you to have it.'

'Aw, that's so lovely.' Emma was touched by their kindness.

'There's one condition, though,' James added, looking serious. 'We get to call in for free milkshakes and chocolate cookies one day with the girls!'

'Of course, you daft things,' Emma said. 'You can call in for a whole month of free milkshakes and cookies as far as I'm concerned! Thanks so much, guys. I don't know quite where I'd be without your wonderful support.' And she meant both now and over the past eight years.

She helped unload the outdoor furniture, setting it out in the courtyard. Yes, it had seen better days, but she couldn't wait to give it a new lease of life. All it needed was a little TLC.

'Right, well I'd better get myself off to work now, sis, and get this van back to the hire place.'

'And I've got the supermarket shop to look forward to,' added Chloe. 'Oh, the joys.'

'Thanks so much for this.' Em had a tear in her eye as she stood at the courtyard gate and watched James and Chloe set off, waving out of the windows. Despite the uncertain future of the lease on the shop, it suddenly felt like Emma was starting a new adventure, that life was on the up. She just hoped Bev was going to be all right too. She still hadn't heard from her but she'd hoped that no news was good news as far as Bev was concerned, not wanting to pester her last night in case a heart-to-heart was underway. But by this morning she wondered how the 'talk' had gone, or if, indeed, Bev and Pete had managed to have one. She sent a brief text, knowing Bev was at work at the surgery: *All okay? xx.*

Bev phoned her back mid-morning. 'I'm on my break so I've only got a few minutes.'

'Can you talk?'

'Yep, should be okay for five mins.'

'So, how did last night go? Did you manage to chat things over?'

'*Noo*, after all that and me all hyped up ready, he didn't get back until past eleven. I was shattered by then and had already been asleep in bed for nearly an hour. He'd also had a bit of wine, I could smell it on his breath, so it didn't seem a good time.'

'Ah, sorry Bev. I'd hoped you might have got to the bottom of it by now.'

'Me too. Oh, well, maybe tonight. I did manage to get on to the hospital, though, and got an appointment for a scan for Mum tomorrow – someone had just cancelled. Oh, and before I forget – I've got another table set sorted for The Chocolate Shop. Jan, the nurse here, was chatting away about her fancy new dining set for her patio, that she's picked up in the sale. I cheekily asked what she was doing with the old set. I knew it was half-decent as I'd been sitting at it a few weeks ago. She said she was getting rid of it, just waiting for her hubby to get around to going to the tip. Well, I stopped her in her tracks. I'll see if Pete can collect it and drop it off for you this evening – if he's around, that is. She doesn't want anything for it.'

'Amazing. You're a star, Bev. Thank you.' Bless, even with all her own worries her friend was still looking out for Emma.

Em could hear another phone ringing down the line. 'Gotta go, Em,' Bev said. 'Catch you later.'

'Okay. Love you and thanks. Keep me posted on everything too.'

'Will do. Bye.'

The week flew by and suddenly it was Friday. Emma was looking forward to Max coming back up to stay the next day. He should be there by early evening, and she figured that if she set to work repainting Chloe's wrought-iron table set straight after the shop closed today, *and* got up early tomorrow morning, with a little extra help from Max on Sunday, she might have the Courtyard Café area ready for opening on Monday morning. She'd even been to the local garden centre and bought five small metal buckets to act as quirky plant pots for each table – with a miniature rose, a lavender plant, a lemon verbena, a mint and a strawberry plant ready to pot up – echoing the scents and flavours of some of her summer chocolates. It would be busy (hopefully!) trying to cope with all the extra customers, but that also meant extra security for her and her shop. She wouldn't have time to arrange a formal launch or anything before Monday, but maybe she and Max could share a cheeky bottle of prosecco and have some supper out there tomorrow night on his arrival, to mark the occasion. Yes, a glass of prosecco would *definitely* be deserved.

19

Emma was down on the beach early with Alfie, the sea air fresh in her face, blowing the cobwebs away.

She spotted a couple walking together further along the bay. They were hand in hand and looked happy, the girl leaning in towards the man who was a fair bit taller than her. They were evidently easy in each other's company, chatting and laughing. It was lovely down there for a romantic stroll, especially at this time of day when it was nearly empty and the sun was rising in the sky, diffusing a pastel palette of pinks, yellows and greys.

It was then she spotted the dark-brown curls and realised the girl was Holly, her assistant. Wow, she was looking so grown-up nowadays, and yes of course, she was with Adam her boyfriend. They looked the perfect couple.

Alfie spotted them too and went bounding over.

'Hey, Alf.' Holly leaned over to stroke him affectionately. 'Hi Emma,' she called across the beach.

Emma walked across to them. 'Isn't it lovely down

here this morning. You're up sharp.' She glanced at her watch – it was still only 7.30 a.m.

'Yes, Adam's just about to go on shift so we arranged to meet early.'

'Hi, Emma.' Adam smiled.

'Morning, Adam.'

'So . . .' Holly continued, 'we've got half an hour before he has to go in to help with breakfasts, and then I'll be getting ready to come to The Chocolate Shop. Well, I might fit an hour's revision in first. Gotta be done.' She rolled her eyes.

'All go for you two, then. I'll leave you to it. See you later. Got to work some of this spaniel's energy off.'

'Hah, yes. Bye, Em.'

Emma strolled on with Alfie, smiling to herself. Yes, she remembered the days of first love, when you snatched every moment you could. When love was young and still so new, and every second together was precious. *You never knew how many more seconds there'd be*, her sore heart reminded her.

She shook herself from that maudlin thought. It was a shame Max wasn't with her right now, though, that he had to be away so often. It would have been great to have him here, holding her hand as she walked the beach. Heading back to her flat together . . . Oh well, maybe tomorrow morning. He'd be here with her soon.

Despite her upcoming exams, Holly still worked on Saturdays for Emma, insisting she needed the break from her A-level studies, and this Saturday, with all the court-yard developments, Em was extra glad of the help.

When Holly arrived for work slightly early at twenty to ten, she made her way straight to the back yard through the wooden gate, desperate to see the changes.

'Oh wow, Em. This is so cool. What a great idea. I love it!' Holly was looking around at the new seats and tables that were set out on the pretty flagstone paving. She started to reach a hand towards the wrought-iron set.

'Ah, don't touch!' Emma managed to stop her just in time. 'That one's sticky with paint. I was still finishing it off this morning, so we'll not be using this space for the café until Monday.'

'Ah, okay.'

'The wooden one here's okay, though.' This one hadn't been started as yet. It was the one that Emma was yet to sand and paint grey. She darted a quick glance at her watch. 'Hmm, I guess we've got ten minutes for a quick coffee before we open. I've been up since the crack of dawn and so have you with your beach walk. I think that's just what we need to perk ourselves up.'

'Perfect, and it's so lovely out here, seems a shame to waste it,' Holly replied.

The sunlight was just peeping over the far wall of the back yard, warming the space and giving the old stone walls a honeyed glow. The varnish was drying on the picnic bench that Ron the carpenter had come in and revamped for her last night. She'd made sure that as well as his payment in cash, he took home some whisky truffles and a box of summer-berry chocolate cups for his wife Maureen, who still provided the shop with the most gorgeous supply of heavenly chocolate cakes.

The new plants were lined up in a shady spot ready to pot up, and Bev had arrived yesterday with a climbing clematis plant ready to position by one of the walls so it would grow and fill the space with delicate leaves and pretty deep-purple blooms in summer. Em had also set out one of Alfie's dog bowls, ready to fill with water for their four-legged visitors on Monday.

Whilst Em was in making the coffee, Holly sat for a few minutes, just taking in the peace of the place. It was like a little haven – and soon to be a chocolate haven. Bliss!

Her boss was soon back out with a cafetière for two, and a couple of homemade choc-chip shortbread squares – which were still slightly warm from the oven.

'De-lish,' Holly said with a grin after her first bite. 'I can't believe how much this place has changed in the last year. First the new café, the brainchild of a certain super-duper assistant, moi, no less, and now this gorgeous summer courtyard area.'

Emma had to agree; it felt good out here in the court-yard, a happy, positive space.

'My friends already love your shop,' Holly continued, 'but now we can sit out and enjoy the sunshine too. Just think: big creamy, chocolatey milkshakes out here on sunny days.'

'Oh yes, and I'm one step ahead. I've thought ice cream too. I've phoned the local Doddington's dairy to start taking delivery of some of their fabulous flavours, keeping close to the chocolate theme, of course. They do a dark chocolate ice cream, there's a gorgeous fudge chunk, and a vanilla – that'd be great drizzled with my homemade chocolate sauce. I can even make banoffee or choco-late-fudge sundaes with it too – what do you reckon?'

'Hah, I'm sold already. Ice-cream sundaes, like my nanna used to make. You'll have to get some of those tall glasses. Oh, and can you get some of those cute little tubs they do to take away, too? Yummy. Hah, I'm going to be the size of a house soon. Adam'll wonder what the heck's happening to me.'

'Aw, I'm sure he'll love you just the way you are. How are you two getting on lately? You looked very cosy there on the beach.'

'We're pretty good, yeah.' There was a touch of anxiety in her assistant's voice though.

'How do you mean, *pretty* good?' Emma queried. Usually Holly was all gushing and giddy about her gorgeous Adam.

'Ah . . . I think it's just all the studying I've had to do lately for these exams coming up, so it's hard to get much time to spend together.'

'Hah – tell me about it!' Emma smiled wryly, thinking of her and Max working all hours and Bev and Pete's current issues.

'And then, he seems a bit quiet when I talk about uni

and my midwifery course. I've tried to get him to open up about how he feels and he just says it's fine, that he knows if I get the grades this summer I'll be off up to Newcastle in September. Yeah, I'm a bit nervous, and I know I'll miss him like crazy, but it's what I really want to do, Em. It's my dream. Just love that *One Born Every Minute* programme.'

'Oh, I'm sure he'll want you to do well and go, Hols. Maybe he's just feeling a bit anxious about how it will be for you both? It's probably just the thought of you being apart soon.'

'I hope it's just that.' Holly looked worried.

'You need to really talk to him about it, Holly. Be honest. It's all about communication in a relationship. Yes, sharing your hopes and dreams, but also your fears.'

'Yeah, I know. Thanks, Em.'

'Right, well the time's ticking on. We'd better get the shop up and running and the sign on the front door switched to *Open*. It might well be another busy day.'

'Yeah. Can I make a notice for you later, Em, about your courtyard café opening on Monday? We'll need to let people know.'

'Of course, that's a good idea. And add "Walking boots and four-legged friends will be welcome", something like that.'

'Okay. Will do.'

And so, another day in The Chocolate Shop by the Sea was about to begin.

* * *

It had been busy all day; there were plenty of new faces, mostly tourists, and there was a lot of positive buzz and chat about the new courtyard café too. Stan and Hilda had wanted to hear all about it from Holly, and followed Emma out the back for a sneak preview, saying it looked 'Very nice indeed.'

The hours flew by and before she knew it, it was almost time to close up.

'Everyone's really excited about the courtyard for next week,' Holly said as she was wiping over the tables.

'That's great. Me too. I think it'll be a lovely new addition to The Chocolate Shop – perfect for sunny days. Let's just hope it's a good summer, weather-wise.'

'Ooh, yes. Well, I'm going to get all my friends around to try it out and spread the word this week. Not that they'll need much encouraging. What's happening with the prosecco parties? Did you get your licensing through yet?'

'Just an exam still to do. It's been so busy I haven't had a chance to complete it. But yes, we'll have those party nights to offer as well, which should be good for business all year through.'

'I admire you, Em. All your drive and energy. You never give up. Makes me want to go for my midwifery dream even more.'

'Good for you. And thanks, Hols.'

'So, anything else you need me to do before I leave for the evening, boss? I've only got a bit more tidying to get through.'

'Nope, I'm just about sorted. Going to head to the kitchen now to make some Eton Mess truffles for tomorrow, they seem really popular at the moment. Either that or Bev's been eating them all. They're her favourites.'

'Hah – yes.'

They both smiled.

'Let's just finish off here then.'

Closing time swung around and Emma was dead on her feet.

'Well, have a fab evening with Max,' Holly said as she wiped the last of the tables over.

'Thanks. And what's on for you? Are you seeing Adam again?'

'Yeah, we're off to the cinema down in Newcastle, and a bite of supper out, I think.'

'Very nice.' Blimey, she hadn't been out to the cinema in ages. When Max turned up of a weekend they were usually both too shattered to go out anywhere much. 'Oh, and don't forget to speak with Adam about how you're feeling. When you get the right moment, of course.'

'Yeah, I will do. Thanks for the advice. Cheers, Em. See you soon. I'll call in after Sixth Form one day next week with my pals. Milkshakes and ice creams are calling!'

Right, she had about an hour to make these truffles and prepare a homemade lasagne ready for Max's arrival. She couldn't wait to see him, especially after the stupid row about Nate and the shower incident last time, though they'd seemed to be back on track by the time Max left. She *really* liked Max, so much so that as well as feeling excited about their relationship, it also left her feeling fragile. It was all so new, letting someone back in, feeling warm and whole again when you were with them, yearning for them when you were apart. Although she was finally willing to risk her heart, she had to admit it still frightened her.

She wanted to make this evening special for them both and have supper out in the courtyard, just the two of them, to celebrate another new step forward in The Chocolate Shop's progress, and hopefully another step forward for them as well.

20

Where the hell was he?

If he was going to be this late, why on earth hadn't he phoned? Emma's anxiety levels were rocketing. She'd had to turn the oven right down for the lasagne that she'd specially made over two hours ago now and it was starting to dry out.

She'd phoned her mum and dad to see how they were and to fill some time, telling them all about the new courtyard area and inviting them to call in whenever they wanted. They lived about thirty minutes away in the small rural town of Rothbury. She also promised to pop across and visit them at home one evening after work next week.

She and her mum had chatted away for a while about various family members, and she heard all about Mrs Brown, a friendly neighbour from just down their street having a cataract op, and the new traffic warden in the village being super-efficient to the extreme and annoying everyone, locals and tourists alike. Apparently young mum Jessica, who lived over the road from them, had parked for two minutes on the high street to get some money out of the cashpoint. Having her little one in the car, she'd left it on a single yellow line so she could keep an eye on her. With her back turned to the machine for less than a minute, that was it: yellow parking notice slapped on her windscreen and a forty-quid fine. What was the world coming to, her mum sighed, when the real criminals were out there causing havoc?

The call had taken up twenty minutes, but there was still no sign of Max and it had gone nine o'clock now. He'd told her just yesterday how he'd try and get there around six-thirty. So much for their romantic supper and a glass of bubbly in the courtyard! The rain clouds had gathered and it was getting chilly out there.

She felt a bit queasy. No Max, no apologetic phone call. She couldn't help but worry; her worst day ever had come from her fiancé being so very late, and then . . . never coming home. That cold feeling of dread was creeping up on her. Of course, she reasoned, things like that surely only happened once in a lifetime and there was probably some very logical explanation this evening. But could she just have that explanation now, *please*, or even better, have Max turn up safe and sound and hungry on her doorstep.

Funny how minutes could seem like hours . . .

By the time Max's Jeep finally turned up at half-past nine – three hours late – Emma was distraught. The relief – at seeing the Jeep from her upstairs lounge window and a rather tired but all-in-one-piece Max get out – struck first, soon to be replaced by frustration and anger.

She ran down the stairs and out to meet him as he came into the back yard. 'Where the *hell* have you been? Why didn't you call?'

'Sorry, sorry! Nice to see you too,' he answered with a hint of sarcasm, holding his hands up, ready for his verbal shooting down. 'The job's been a total nightmare today, and my phone got smashed – fell out of my pocket from up some scaffolding. I would have called you otherwise, of course I would.'

'You could at least have called from someone else's phone.' Em was still up a height emotionally, and she wasn't coming down yet.

'Maybe, but all your numbers were stored in mine.'

'Google? It isn't *that* difficult, Max – the shop number would have been there!' Her tone was sharp.

'I'm sorry, I should have thought, yes. But I was just trying to sort out these supplier issues and then, by the time I was on the road, I was busy driving. I just wanted to get up here. But there'd been an accident on the A1 just before Durham, and I got held up again.' He looked tired, deflated. 'Some welcome this is!'

'Well, you should have thought to let me know.' She was still fuming.

There were a few tense seconds of silence between them.

But news of an accident made her think, soon taking the angry wind out of her sails. Max was okay. He was

149

here. He wasn't the one in the accident. 'I-I was just so worried.' Her voice trembled.

'Oh Em, God, yes.' It suddenly dawned on Max. Yes, anyone would be worried, with their partner three hours late, but for Emma this would feel so much worse. He took a step forward. 'Come here.' His arms went out and they met in a hug.

No more words, just the comfort of each other's body, chests pressed together, that life-affirming warmth between them.

'Sorry, Em,' he uttered gently above her, into the waves of her soft, red hair.

Her heart rate was slowing, beating next to his. 'It's okay.'

They stayed like that for a few quiet moments.

When she finally pulled back, Emma said, 'The lasagne's ready. Well, a little too ready.' She pulled a face. 'Like, the top is black, but I could scrape that off and we can have the remnants beneath. There's plenty of salad and some garlic bread too.'

'Sounds a veritable feast.' Max grinned, looking more like his usual self. 'I'm starving – my last bite to eat was a bacon butty at elevenses.'

'I had planned on eating out here, but it's getting a bit chilly now, and it'll be dark soon.'

'Yeah . . . hang on.' He looked about him. 'Hey, you've got a whole load of outdoor furniture and it looks really great. But yeah, maybe another time to eat outside, if you're feeling cold. Mind, we did manage a December picnic, remember.'

'Hah, how could I forget.' She remembered it well, the two of them and Alfie on the beach on a cold winter's evening under a blanket and a canopy of stars. It had been such a special night and seemed a world away from how they were now – overtired, arguing.

She felt shattered, anxiety having dissolved into fatigue. 'We'll save the courtyard for another time.' *And the bottle of prosecco too*, she mused. It didn't seem the right time for bubbly any more. She just wanted to curl up with him on the sofa and have supper on their knees.

'I do have a bottle of red in my car. I'll go fetch it, shall I?'

'Okay, yes, lasagne with a glass of red sounds pretty good.' Though the way she was feeling so tired suddenly, she feared she might be asleep before they even finished it.

After the meal, they were sat chatting.

'Hey, I'm sorry that your plans for us to have supper in the courtyard didn't work out for tonight.' Max looked genuinely apologetic.

'Ah, it's okay. I know you couldn't help being so late.' Emma had calmed down by now. She could see how Max was trying to juggle life and work with travelling up to see her.

'We could always take a glass of wine outside?' he suggested. 'Have a few moments out there at least.'

'We'll need a fleece on. But yeah, why not.'

'Or my arms around you?' He gave a cheeky smile.

'Now *that* sounds a good idea.'

'Come on then.'

They wandered down to the quaint courtyard that held Emma's latest Chocolate Shop dreams within its walls. There was enough light coming from the kitchen to flood the space nearest the cottage, and a half moon shone above them too. Alfie followed them out eagerly, wagging his tail and sniffing around.

'You've worked really hard on this, haven't you?' Max said, taking in all the revamped furniture, the little touches with the plant pots.

'Yes, this place means so much to me, Max.'

'I can tell. It's got that warm friendly feel, with a little bit of magic that spells *Emma* to me. Your heart and soul really has gone into this.'

'Aw, that's so lovely.'

He placed his wine glass down on the table beside them. Emma did the same, anticipating what might come next. And he took her into his arms as he'd promised, tenderly placing his lips against hers, tasting of red wine and Max, with a generous sprinkle of passion and a hint of her future.

There was no Sunday morning lie-in. Emma woke feeling restless and had got up early to sand down the last of the table sets, ready to paint after work. However, on the radio, whilst making herself a coffee to keep her going, she heard that rain was forecast for later. Argh, how was she going to paint a table in the pouring rain? She'd have to get it into the shop somehow, but how was she meant to do that, with a kitchen full of chocolates, and a café full of customers?

Still, she sanded until the grit made her eyes itchy and her back was aching. She must have been at it for nearly an hour-and-a-half before Max appeared.

'Hey.'

'Hi.'

'You look busy.'

'Yeah. I have loads to do today.' She could feel her stress levels rising. The shop would be opening again at lunchtime, and there was a long list of things she needed to do first. So much to do, so little time!

'Coffee?'

'Yes please.'

When he came back a little later, carrying two mugs, he said, 'Can I help with anything? I've got a few hours this morning, then I'm gonna have to head off again. I have a pile of paperwork to sort out – bills, admin stuff. It's been mounting up and I'm going to get into trouble if I don't get on with it.'

'Oh . . .' Emma felt disappointed. *Here we go again.* 'But you haven't even been here twenty-four hours, yet.'

'I know, babe. But at least I made the effort to come all the way up here to see you.' He didn't sound that happy that he had. Emma could feel the magic of last night quickly melting away.

'Whatever.' Emma's response was curt; she had enough on her plate. She'd just crack on with what she needed to do to get this place ready to open tomorrow. If it wasn't raining, that was. Some grand opening that would be, with two people, probably Bev and Holly, sitting with umbrellas.

The two of them sipped their coffees, unsure of what to say next. Emma bit the inside of her lip. Maybe they weren't as okay as they had imagined. Their relationship was like a yo-yo at the moment.

21

On Monday morning, Emma was woken by the sound of singing and a guitar strumming. It sounded a bit like Ed Sheeran. Had she left the radio on loud in the flat's kitchen or something last night, whilst she was busy painting the table and chairs which she'd managed to drag in out of the rain? Was someone there with her in the flat?

Nope, there shouldn't be, it was definitely Monday and Max had left at midday yesterday.

She rubbed her eyes, beginning to come to, and glanced at her watch. It was only six-twenty. The singing continued somewhere nearby. Was she actually still dreaming? She opened and closed her eyelids again pointedly – they were definitely working. She hauled herself out of bed and walked across to the old-fashioned cottage window, pulling up the sash.

'Wha-at?' She looked down to see a figure sitting at the new wrought-iron table with a guitar in his hands. The rains had stopped and the sun was shining.

'Morning!' He stopped singing and looked up. Nate.

'What on earth are you doing?'

'What does it look like?' He grinned. 'Heard you were opening your courtyard café today and thought I'd give it a good start. Wish you luck and all that.'

'O-kay . . . But it's not even six-thirty yet.'

'Well, I've been up since four watching the dawn. It was amazing this morning, like the calm after the storm. That view you get from the dunes. The sun was like a golden ball rising out of the sea. So cool. You can't just go back to sleep after seeing something like that.'

'No, I suppose not.' It did sound stunning. But she also wondered if he'd been drinking late and might still be just a little bit tipsy. She'd heard he'd started to work behind the bar at The Fisherman's Arms as he'd decided to stay on over the summer and perhaps they'd had an after-work 'sesh'. Oh well, whatever; he was here now and he did have a nice singing voice.

'I didn't know you played guitar.' Em was hanging out of her bedroom window, in her slip of a nightie.

'Learnt a bit at school. Then I picked it up again out in Oz. Got this little beauty second hand.' He tapped his guitar fondly. 'It's a great way of chillin' with friends.'

'Go on then, sing something else. Even though it might wake up the neighbours.' She smiled. Crazy guy, that he was.

'Any special requests?'

'No, you choose. Maybe not ACDC at this time of the morning, though.'

'Hah, no worries – I'll keep it chilled.'

'Hang on then, I'll just get my dressing gown on and come down and join you. Do you fancy a quick coffee with me before I start work?'

'Absolutely, that was my ulterior motive. Coffee sounds great. Your stuff is delicious and I've run out of instant at the camper van.'

'Okay. Just give me two ticks.'

As she arrived in the courtyard five minutes later, in her flip-flops and dressing gown, with a tray of coffee and two warmed chocolate croissants, Nate was strumming away once more and singing Ed Sheeran's 'Thinking Out Loud', which was lovely but sent a little shiver through her too. She always thought of Luke when she heard this. They never had their chance to grow old together.

Alfie had followed her out too. He settled beside her as she sat down on the other chair next to Nate. 'Well, this is a nice way to start the day. I've never been serenaded before,' Em said with a poignant smile.

'There's a first time for everything. In fact, there are lots of firsts you still need to experience, I think. You need to live a little, Em. From what I see, you spend all your life working.'

'Well, yeah, but needs must. And today is definitely a day for working, I have this whole new area to open.'

It was warm already in the courtyard, with the sky above a summer blue with the odd puff of white cloud. Despite the rains of yesterday, it looked like it was going to be a lovely day for the opening. She looked proudly around her; the outdoor space looked charming. She just needed to bring out the final table and chairs set, which she had painted an antique grey late last night in the shelter of the kitchen.

'I need to keep you here to entertain the guests,' Emma said, half-joking, but that would in fact be rather special. She poured out some coffee into two white mugs.

'No way, it's just for you, Em. And actually, my second motive was to grab another shower. I don't think your customers would be too chuffed sat next to this stinky surfer dude, even if he was singing.'

'Hah, of course.' As she spoke she felt a little anxious. After the antics of last time, Max was suddenly very much in her mind. What would he make of all this, her being serenaded early this morning? Ah, but it was harmless, just Luke's brother doing his stuff.

They chatted briefly over coffee and croissants, Nate saying he was enjoying his few hours' work in The Fisherman's and that he was getting to know the locals more. Emma then said she'd better get to work.

'Big day ahead,' she said with a smile.

She asked if Nate would mind helping her out with the table and chairs that were taking up most of her kitchen, so she'd have space to work once more, and after they'd done that, she told Nate to go on up and shower while she got on with some baking downstairs – she'd go and get ready herself later. The implication being very much *after he'd gone*. Leaving no room for any confusion.

22

The ice cream delivery arrived at 8.30 a.m. much to Emma's relief. She already had a large fridge-freezer in the shop's kitchen, so she hoped there'd be enough space in it. With a bit of clever stacking and juggling around, she managed to shut the freezer door on it all. If it proved popular, she might well invest in a further countertop freezer for all the individual pots. The flavours were delicious – she'd already tasted most of them, with it being her favourite local ice cream. The Utter Chocolate and Alnwick Rum Truffle were just the bee's knees.

Her mobile rang just after nine. It was Max. 'Hey.'

'Hi, there.' Em sounded chirpy, looking forward to the day ahead.

'All going okay? Ready for the grand courtyard opening?'

'Yes, thanks.' She thought it wise to say nothing about her morning serenade. No point putting the cat out amongst the pigeons again. And she was certainly *not* going to say anything about her visitor showering there too.

She looked around her, the tables had their herb and fruit mini flowerpots on and she'd cleverly thought to paint a number on each so it would be easier to keep track of which table had ordered what. The tables themselves were totally revamped, all freshly painted and varnished, and the mix-and-match furniture worked well. Even her original put-you-up set for two sat quaintly in one corner. Her new clematis from Bev was planted next to a wooden trellis that Ron had helped secure against the stonework.

'It looks good. I wish you could be here to see it.'

'I know. About that, and the way things were this weekend . . . I'm sorry it's all been so crazy lately. It will get better, honestly. I'm not always going to be working so far away.'

'Yeah, and I need to make sure I get down to see you too,' Emma conceded. 'Even if it's after work and we snatch an evening together at your house. It'll save you always being the one to have to come up here.' A little give-and-take might be just what they needed to help them move on. She could see things clearer today, the frustration of Saturday night having subsided.

'Well, I hope it goes really well.'

'Cheers, Max. Thanks for the call.'

'Bye then. Chat later.' It sounded like he was busy on site. There was a noise of drilling in the background.

'Bye.'

*   *   *

It wasn't long before a cheery face appeared at the gate.

'Helloo! All ready to go, hun?' Bev said.

'As ready as I ever will be. I hope we can cope between us.'

'Well, there is a queue like the Harrods sale snaking down the high street.'

'Really?' Em fell for it for a second.

'Now come on, this is Warkton we are talking about. It's not even ten o'clock – even the seagulls are still a bit dozy. But Stan and Hilda are waiting outside. I said I'd come around the back first and then let them in. No point keeping them waiting.'

'No, absolutely not. It's all set and ready here, so I'll keep an eye out here as well as minding the kitchen and orders. If you can take the orders as usual out the front, that'd be great. I should be able to manage, but I'll shout if I need you.'

'No worries.'

'Hey, how's your mum, hun? Any better?'

'Much the same. We went for the scan, and she's just waiting on the results. There'll be a follow-up appointment soon with the consultant.'

'Send her my love and best of luck.'

'Thanks.'

'And Pete? Did you finally talk?'

'Yeah, it's all good.' Bev smiled.

'Phew.'

'He's a bit stressed with it all too. The captaincy has a lot more to it than he'd imagined. Says he'd never have time or the energy to fit in an affair. But yes, he's going to try and not take on so much from now on. We're actually going out to the pub for supper tonight.'

'Thank heavens. I don't think I could have coped if you two weren't right.'

'Well, hun, let's get this show on the road. The courtyard café is about to open. We're keeping poor Stan and Hilda waiting!'

The kitchen was full of fresh baking. This morning, after her serenade, as well as setting out the final touches in the courtyard, Emma had made a batch of fresh brownies, croissants and some choc-chip shortbread. Maureen had delivered two fresh chocolate fudge cakes too. She and Bev would manage fine, she reassured herself.

She gave Bev the keys to open up, gathered her nerve in the kitchen with a deep breath, and then headed out to see Stan and Hilda. They were standing by the counter with a gorgeous bouquet.

'Oh!'

'These are for you and to wish The Chocolate Shop every success with its new venture.'

'Thank you so much. They are just beautiful. I don't know quite what to say, it's such a surprise.'

'Well, pet, you've always made us so welcome. It's our favourite spot in the village, isn't it, Hilda? Come rain or shine you're always here ready with a smile and a kind word.'

Emma had tears in her eyes. 'Oh, that's so sweet, but don't say any more or my mascara will be running.'

'Hold on. Stay just like that the three of you. With the bouquet in the middle. Perfect.' Bev took a snap on her mobile phone. 'I'll put this on the shop's Facebook page if you all don't mind.' She liked keeping that up to date for Emma, who had enough to do as it was. 'It'll be a great picture to celebrate the courtyard opening and help spread the word.'

'So, would you like to sit outside or in this morning?' Em asked.

'Well, I think we'll have to try outside.'

'It's nice and sheltered there.'

'Sounds lovely.'

'And as you are the courtyard café's very first customers, it'll be on the house.'

'Oh, no need for that, pet,' Hilda said.

'It'd be my pleasure, honestly. I won't take no for an answer.'

'Well, thank you, Emma.'

The bouquet of flowers took pride of place on the countertop as soon as Emma had put them in a vase. Her first customers were very happily ensconced outside at the wrought-iron table that was still in the shade, not wanting too much direct sun, Hilda had said. The pair of them sat with their newspapers spread out, and a pot of tea, along with a large slice of chocolate cake to share and two shortbreads.

'This is the life.' Stan grinned at Emma and gave a big thumbs-up as she stood on the back step of the cottage taking in the scenic image, just as a chap and his dog appeared through the back gate.

Several people came in through the morning, sitting both in and out. The orders flowed and Emma and Bev coped really well. It was only at around two, when a flurry of café clients appeared at once (with it being half-term week there were several families about) just as a gentleman came in who wanted a large bespoke box of chocolates made up, that a queue formed for orders. Em asked them to take a seat, mentioning the courtyard space too, and said she and Bev would be around to see them all shortly. A deep breath, a calm head and her usual kitchen routine served her well. They were all catered for within the half hour and, much to Emma's relief, seemed pretty content.

Wow, the day had passed in a whirl. Emma knew she was certainly going to have her hands full during the high summer season, but it would be so worthwhile to see the shop flourishing and her rent being paid, with perhaps even a little left to save. It had been lovely seeing locals and holidaymakers alike sitting inside and outside today, enjoying The Chocolate Shop café as a welcoming cosy space, just as it was meant to be. Just as she'd dreamed.

Bev had left just a few minutes before with a big hug and a massive thank you from Emma. They worked so well as a team, even during that manic mid-afternoon phase. Em was so grateful. She now felt like wallowing in a deep, hot bubbly bath, but there was a spaniel waiting patiently upstairs, ready for his evening exercise. She went up, gave him an affectionate pat, and reached for his lead.

'Come on then, Alfie. You know what this means.'

He wasted no time, leaping out of his basket and straight down the stairs after her. There were still several people milling about in the village. She said a few 'hellos' as they walked down the hill and gave Sheila a wave as they passed the grocer's shop which was still open, making the most of the summer trade.

At the beach, Emma let Alfie off the lead and he ran about contentedly. She'd thought to bring a ball as she wasn't sure how far her tired feet would want to take her and Alfie never seemed get worn out. Even better if she launched it into the foaming waves and he could swim after it. A couple were strolling the sands and it made her think of her and Max meeting here that very first time and the many times they had walked here since. She hoped they could work this present glitch out. It was probably just life getting in the way. And she thought of Luke and Nathan, and how life could change in an instant. She felt Luke would have been proud of her achievements today and everything so far with her Chocolate Shop.

It was time to head back, Alfie had had his fresh air and runabout, and it had helped her zone out from her working environment. The bath tub was calling, followed by an easy supper and, remembering her new supply in the shop's kitchen, a wonderful tub of local ice cream. Hmm, now would it be Utter Chocolate or the Rum Truffle? Decisions, decisions.

23

For every step forward, there always seemed to be one back again.

Two days after the courtyard's opening, there was an unwelcome visitor.

Holly was taking a brief respite from her studies and was helping out in the shop while Emma was up to her ears in the kitchen, getting the truffle order of mini boxes ready for The Seaview Hotel, as well as keeping up with all the café orders.

'I hate to break the news, but The Eel's here!' Holly marched in, pulling a grimace, as she handed over the next order slip. They both knew full well who she was referring to. Em then spotted her landlord snooping around the new courtyard café area, where he pulled out a camera from his pocket and began taking photos. The girls stood and watched him through the kitchen window for a few moments.

'Don't trust him one bit.' Holly was shaking her head.

'Nor me.' Emma let out a sigh as she tried to keep her mind off what this might mean.

He was soon in with his slick-backed black hair and slimy smile, loitering at the counter where Emma had positioned herself ready to catch and politely quiz him on his way past.

'Can I help you with anything?' She tried to sound calm, but her heart was already pounding in her chest. This man was like the harbinger of doom as far as The Chocolate Shop was concerned, and he held her future in his grubby little hands.

He said he didn't want to order anything, though Emma did offer him a cup of tea or coffee on the house, trying to keep him sweet. He didn't have much time apparently.

'No thank you, Emma. I'm just here to take a look at the new developments I've heard about. *Interesting.*' He dragged out the word. 'You've made a nice job of them. The property is looking good, I must say.'

Why did something that should be a compliment sound so ominous coming from his lips?

'Well, thank you.' Emma thought she'd best be polite.

A customer appeared at the counter behind Mr Neil, looking to place an order; she gave them a nod of acknowledgement, hoping The Eel would get the idea and move on. She had a shop to run after all. He appeared slow to move, saying, 'You don't mind if I take a few photographs, do you? Just for my portfolio, it's looking very nice now it's all been done up.'

'No, of course, that's fine.' She could hardly argue; he owned the place after all, and she needed to get on with serving her customers.

Off he slimed. She heard a click, then saw him take a picture of the interior of the shop. Suddenly Holly appeared, popping up at the shelf area where he next had his camera angled. She began shifting with her cloth and spray around the room, photobombing him at every opportunity, intent on 'her cleaning' and ultimately spoiling the shots.

Emma couldn't help but smile to herself, but equally she knew it was a risky business upsetting the man. He tutted loudly, then started to frown.

'Holly,' she said tersely under her breath from behind the counter. 'What are you doing?'

'Well, he's obviously up to mischief. Scheming something. We can't make it easy for him.'

'Well, that may be. But he does also own this place. And the last thing we want to do as tenants is upset him.'

Holly stopped her cleaning with a hmph.

Mr Neil wandered past them, back outside to the courtyard for a while.

He was soon on his way, with just a nod in farewell. Emma was busy serving a customer with a fudge and truffle order, so she nodded back, forcing a smile.

There was something about him that always made her skin prickle. She didn't trust that man one bit.

As soon as the door closed behind him, Holly caught Emma's eye and pretended to gag. Emma pursed her lips into a tight smile, trying her best to remain professional at the counter.

The next day, Thursday, trouble seemed to come in twos.

'Have you seen what's going on down by the harbour?' Bev was striding in to The Chocolate Shop for her morning shift.

Emma, who was occupied filling up the refrigerated counter with some fresh cream pralines she'd just made, raised her head. 'No.'

'Well, it looks like someone's doing up that old wooden fish shack. Not sure what into, mind. I haven't heard anything about it on the village grapevine – surprisingly.'

'Hmm. Oh well, it'll tidy that area up a bit,' Emma commented. The old shack had been empty ever since Emma had moved into the village eight years ago, and probably had been for many years before that too. It looked rather ramshackle and its wooden panels were starting to rot.

'Yes, there's new sheets of timber and all sorts there, laid out ready to use.'

'Well, that sounds good. It'll give the village a facelift.'

Emma didn't think any more of it as they set to work, getting ready for their early opening.

'My, there was a lot of banging and hammering going on down at the harbourside there this morning. What a racket. I called in to see Sheila in the grocer's on my way up the hill and she's heard there's going to be some sort of new shop down there. She's keeping her ear to the ground on it, trying to find out a bit more. Hmm, I wonder if that shack's going to be another fish shop, like in the old days?' This from dear old Mrs C, who'd called in for her Thursday morning coffee and cake.

'Maybe,' Emma responded.

'Ah, yes, Ford's fish shack. I remember it well. All sorts of fresh fish, smoked fish and crabs they had in there. I remember my mum going there for her kippers. My dad loved them with melted butter on – it was his treat on a Saturday morning. Not me, mind you, I hated the smelly buggers: they stank the whole house out. I was glad to get out to play on a Saturday.'

'That's probably why they did it.' Bev was grinning knowingly.

'Oh! I hadn't thought of that.' The old lady looked taken aback, then chuckled.

Emma smiled too. 'Right, I'll go and fetch your coffee. A slice of chocolate cake today, Mrs C?'

'That'd be grand, Emma pet.'

She left Bev and Mrs C chatting over possibilities for the future of the old fish shack. It was far too small to be a house, Bev was saying, more like a kiosk of some kind. Gifts, arts and crafts maybe?

It seemed to be the talk of Thursday, with several customers coming up with their own theories throughout the day. That was until Sheila, nose-to-the-ground and ear-to-the-wall woman that she was – in fact, the equivalent of a gossip bloodhound – came into the shop at four o'clock. And it wasn't going to be a fish shop, oh no.

'Hello, Emma.' She almost bounced in the door with the news. 'All that commotion down by the harbour? Well, I've had Councillor Fraser in. It's been approved for a sweet shop, a *candy kiosk*, apparently, very American sounding if you ask me. Sticks of rock, boiled sweets, fudge, that kind of thing. I hope it's not going to be all Kiss-Me-Quick hats and the like. Well, why on earth do we need that, I said to him, we've already got a chocolate shop in the village. They're looking to encourage new business, apparently, and the new owners have agreed to do up the kiosk in keeping with the original building and preserve a bit of the local heritage.'

Oh crikey, just as things were looking up for her and her Chocolate Shop – now there was to be direct confectionery competition in the village. This wasn't good news. 'Oh,' was all Em could manage to say.

'Well, us villagers could always boycott it, I suppose,' Sheila suggested. 'We wouldn't want to see you losing business, Emma. And it'll affect *my* sweet sales too. Humph, these incomers with their new-fangled ideas.'

'I was an incomer once too, you know.'

'Ah no, I didn't mean you, pet. You're part of the village now, one of us.'

But Emma knew how it felt to be the new kid in town, trying to make a new start and a living somewhere. 'Well, Sheila, although it's not the best news I've had all day, I think we need to give them a chance at least.' She didn't want anyone to feel an outsider or not welcome here, even if they *were* selling sweets and taking some of her trade.

'Well, yes. I didn't mean to sound unwelcoming,' Sheila conceded. 'It's just hard enough to make a decent living as it is these days and it's bound to hit my trade.'

'Tell me about it . . . But let's just wait and see, hey? Maybe we can all work together to make Warkton-by-the-Sea *the* place to come to on the coast, and we can all gain.'

'As you say, let's just wait and see.' But Sheila didn't sound as if she was hopeful of a positive outcome and despite putting a brave face on it with Sheila, that night thoughts of another sweet-selling business in the village were spinning in Emma's head. Why was it when you took a step forward in this business, there always one back? It was like snakes and bloody ladders. She sighed in the dark, listening to Alfie snoring from his bed in the kitchen next door. Emma knew that she could only do her best, and that was what she intended to keep doing, but it didn't always help to ward off the nightly worries that often spiralled and kept her wide awake.

24

A week later the fish shack by the harbour had been turned into a cute little sweet shop. Emma had observed its gradual transformation on her evening dog walks. The wooden kiosk gleamed with new varnish and looked so quaint down there by the harbour. The hatch was open one day and she saw that the interior was being painted in alternate blue and white thick stripes and looked rather jolly. There was a newly-painted sign along the top of the shop's frontage saying *The Rock Shop*, and a sign announcing it was due to open the next day.

That Friday, Em needed to call down to Sheila's for some extra milk before opening herself, so thought she'd do the right thing by calling to say 'hello' and introduce herself, even if the business was in competition with hers. It was half-past nine, and Emma could hear someone inside the shop. The side door was ajar and when Emma peered in she saw sticks of rock, jars of lemon sherbets, cola cubes, mint humbugs, and those old-fashioned seaside sweets that looked just like beach pebbles, lined up in rows. There were strawberry laces, large swirly-striped lollipops, fudge and more. The new owners had evidently gone all-out with the old-fashioned sweet shop idea. Emma had to admit that it did look good. She spotted a middle-aged lady with grey-tinged shoulder-length brown hair, sorting out some stock.

'Morning,' Emma called brightly.

The woman looked up with a smile.

'Hi, welcome to Warkton-by-the-Sea. I'm Emma, from The Chocolate Shop just up the road.'

'Oh hello. I'm Anne.' The woman paused for a second or two and then came across. 'Yes, I've seen that shop up the hill,' Anne continued, sounding a little cool.

'So, are you opening here today?'

'Yes, I'm just about ready. We used to run market stalls down Durham way, selling sweets and the like, but we thought it might be a nice idea to get somewhere more permanent. This place turned up for sale, slightly quirky, but it felt right, you know? And this looks such a lovely village.'

'Yes, it is, and the locals are a friendly bunch when you get to know them.' Em hoped to goodness they wouldn't let her down and start the boycott they'd initially threatened. She could only offer this olive branch of friendship herself, and hope others might follow suit.

People were always curious around here (well okay, yes, *nosey*) so they were bound to turn up and chat to this new lady, if only to find out where she was from and what her intentions were. It was like being a suitor to the village. There were unspoken tests you had to pass as a newcomer. No one quite knew what they were, but they were there nonetheless, to see whether you fitted in or were branded an 'incomer' forever.

'Oh, I've already met . . . ah, Sheila, is it? The lady from the little supermarket?'

Well, that was no surprise. She'd have been loitering down there for the past week, no doubt, trying to catch the incomer with a list of questions about her intentions. 'She seemed . . .' Anne paused as if trying to find the right words. 'Well . . . nice and chatty.'

'Oh, she is that,' Emma replied, with her eyebrows slightly raised.

Anne gave a small, hesitant smile, saying no more.

'Well, I wish you all the best with the new venture,' Emma offered kindly, and she genuinely meant it. She wouldn't wish ill on someone new to the area trying their best with a business. As Emma rescanned the goods for sale – it was always wise to check out the competition – the only thing they both would be selling by the looks of it was fudge, so it wouldn't mean too much direct competition, hopefully. And hey, who knew what might happen; people might come especially for the old-fashioned sweets at the harbour *and* the chocolates up the hill. Warkton might become the confectionery coastal hub of Northumberland. She could dream, right?

'Thank you, that's kind of you. I'm feeling a bit nervous about it all, to be honest. A lot of our savings have gone into this from our retirement fund so there's a lot at stake,' she confided. 'My husband's still working part-time as a heating engineer at the moment, but that will finish soon, and he'll be helping me on the weekends. We've just moved up to the area, got ourselves a little bungalow in Seahouses.'

'Oh yes, it's nice over there.' Emma was aware that the time was ticking on and she had her own shop to open. 'Well, nice meeting you, Anne. I'm sure we'll catch up with each other again soon. All the best.'

'Thank you.'

Emma set off to Sheila's with a small wave. It didn't hurt to be welcoming. And the new lady seemed friendly enough.

This village could be big enough for the both of us, Emma thought in a John Wayne kind of voice. If she was going to cling on to her own Chocolate Shop dreams, it would just have to be.

25

On Saturday, Adam popped into The Chocolate Shop just before closing.

'Hi Hols, you know tonight, what do you think about calling in at the pub later? There's meant to be a band on. Should be a fun night. What do you think?'

'Yeah, I'd be up for that. There's usually a good crowd in on a Saturday night too. Hey,' she turned to Em, 'what about you and Max? He's coming up tonight, isn't he? Be something different for you to do.'

Yeah, that might be good, she and Max hadn't been out in ages, and a few drinks, some chat with the locals, spending time with Holly and Adam and some live music, sounded good. Max and Adam always got on well too, despite the almost twenty-year age gap.

'Yeah, okay. Thanks. What time are you heading down there?'

'About eightish,' Adam answered. 'We'll see you there then, shall we?'

'Great. Yes.' That'd give them time for a bite of supper once he got here, and then to wander down. She was sure Max would be up for that.

It was twenty to nine by the time Emma and Max got to The Fisherman's. Yet again, he'd been held up. It was getting so tedious. What was it with this job down in Leeds? There always seemed to be something to delay him.

An hour earlier Emma had found herself sitting waiting in her lounge, worrying. At least this time he had managed to call her to explain as he left. But then all sorts of weird thoughts began whirling around her head. Maybe it wasn't just the job. Was it a cooling off in their relationship? It happened to couples all the time. Why not them?

But then, she countered her own argument, it didn't feel like that when they were together, most of the time it still felt precious. But spending all week apart, well, who knew how he was really feeling? And hey, she'd done it herself, with a couple of short-term relationships she'd tried since Luke, when she realised they were getting nowhere and eased off, drifted away.

Ah, these thoughts were getting her nowhere fast. She'd stopped herself and gone downstairs to make a start on some chocolate bars – yes, chocolate she could always count on to calm her nerves.

So, they finally made it for their night out. It was rammed in there – The Fisherman's Arms at full pelt on a Saturday night. There was a younger crowd in for the music as well as some of the regulars that Emma recognised. A buzz of excitement filled the warm air, along with sounds of animated chatter and laughter. Pints were being poured on repeat and drinks passed across the bar. The band were doing their final sound checks and looked as though they were about to start.

Holly was standing up, waving, in the far corner; she and Adam had managed to get a table in the main bar area. Max did the 'What do you want to drink?' universal glass-tipping hand signal, and they got a round in before heading across to join them.

'Hi, guys, sorry we're late,' Emma said, her voice raised above the din.

'Hey, no worries,' Holly replied.

Max delivered a pint of pale ale across to Adam and a gin and tonic for Holly, her drink of the moment. Em had chosen the same.

The first sip of the gin was dry and fragrant with a touch of lemon that was delicious.

They were soon chatting, but once the band started, it was hard to hear over the music, so they relaxed and listened to them. They were a male duo and Emma had to admit she was really impressed – they were much better than the usual fare down at The Fisherman's. They played guitar, and keyboard as well as singing, performing several covers of Coldplay, Kodaline and the like, then they did some of their own original tracks too, which were great.

Adam got another round in and the night was going well. The band took a break and Emma's group could talk more easily then.

'Hey, they're really good,' Em enthused.

'Yeah, I loved their version of "Paradise". Just brill,' said Holly.

'Pretty talented,' agreed Max.

'Good to get some live music too,' commented Adam. 'The pub should do it more often, seeing how busy it is. I've sent a few customers down from the hotel too.'

'How's it going so far this summer, mate?' Max asked.

'Good. Bookings are up on last year, so it's looking promising. We've just completed the renovation of our executive "bridal" suite too.' He showed the inverted commas with his fingertips. 'It looks great.'

'It's a-maz-ing,' Holly butted in, pulling a 'wow' kind of face. 'Honestly, I *sooo* want to stay in that room.'

'It's always booked out,' Adam continued. 'It's been all done out really well, all new soft furnishings, and has got a huge super-king bed—'

'That I just want to bounce on,' Holly interrupted cheekily. 'Oh, and they've had an interior designer in and everything. The colours are divine – all soft seascape style.'

'Sounds lovely,' Emma commented.

'Yeah, then you go outside and it's even better,' Adam added. 'There's a deck, and you're like at the top of the hotel there. The view across the bay is brilliant.'

'And,' Holly took up again, 'there's a Jacuzzi up there

with champagne in ice buckets all ready to go. Proper outdoor lounge chairs, and those huge lose-yourself-in-them comfy towels. It's so lush.'

'It's proving really popular already.'

'I bet. Sounds brilliant.' Max was smiling.

'It's such a lovely village here,' Emma said. 'It's so nice people can come and really enjoy it. The hotel upgrade has been such a good thing for Warkton.'

'And they're still enjoying their turndown chocolates, too,' Adam said, grinning.

'That's good to know.' Emma smiled.

'Right, anyone for more drinks?' Adam stood up and went off to the bar with Max, where Em noticed they were being served by Nate. She felt slightly uncomfortable about that; perhaps she should have warned Max that Luke's brother had started working there. But to be honest, after the whole shower debacle and row, she hadn't particularly wanted to bring up his name with Max.

With the lads at the bar, Em turned to Holly. 'All okay, Hols? Did you two get a chance to chat things over?'

'Yeah, a bit. He just seems a bit reluctant to talk about it in any depth, though. Says it'll sort itself out somehow. But we seem okay for now.'

'Well, that's good. Yeah, some men aren't that great at discussing their feelings, are they?'

'True.'

'Well, best of luck to you both.' Em saw the two men heading back towards the table and thought it wise to draw that particular conversation to a close.

The lads were chatting as they came back over with the drinks. Max had a frown on his face. 'Hey, Adam, how do you find that guy?'

'Uh, he's not too bad. A bit full of himself at times, but pretty harmless.'

'Ah, okay, fair enough.'

'He's your ex's bro, isn't he, Em?' Adam asked, as he popped the girls' drinks before them on the table.

'Yep.' Em's voice was slightly taut.

Holly shook her head. 'Becca said he was chatting her up the other night. She said it's bad enough with Danny on the case behind the bar and now there's two of them at it. Mind you, I think she quite enjoyed it.' She laughed.

Em could see Max's jaw tighten. 'Well, he's bound to be chatty behind the bar,' she said, trying to lighten the tone. 'It's all part of the job.'

Max just gave her a look.

'Right, well, cheers guys.' Em took a sip of gin and tonic. 'Ooh look, I think the band's about to come back on.' She swiftly moved the conversation on.

After the band's second set, which was easily as good as the first and got the whole bar singing along, the pub started to empty out a bit. Nate was clearing the tables and eventually reached theirs.

'Hey, Em, guys. Good night in here, wasn't it? Loving the act.'

'Yeah, they've been brilliant.'

'By the way,' Nate added, 'I'm thinking of having a beach BBQ next weekend. We used to do that a lot down in Oz. Saturday night, if you'd like to come along. Just turn up at the beach down on the sands near the car park and bring a few beers. It'll be pretty casual, but it should be a bit of fun. You're all more than welcome.'

'Oh, thanks Nate. Sounds great.' Em smiled.

Max didn't say anything.

Holly sounded enthusiastic. 'Aw, cheers Nate. Sounds brill.'

Adam nodded next to her.

'So, that's next weekend sorted.' Holly grinned. She loved a party, whatever or wherever it was.

'We'll go, won't we?' Em questioned Max.

'Yeah, probably.' He sounded rather lukewarm about it. 'I'll just have to check everything at work, mind. We absolutely have to meet our contract deadline on the Leeds flats.'

'Ah, okay. Well, thanks Nate.'

As the pub emptied out there were just a few locals left. It was warm and cosy by the log burner that was lit even though it was summer, and the four of them were chatting comfortably. The two singers were sitting with a couple of pints, and then one of them took up his guitar and began strumming away. Soon, Nate finished off behind the bar, and, bringing his own guitar, sat himself down with the duo and joined in for an impromptu jamming session. It was pretty cool, sitting there, listening in, watching, whilst the four of them finished their drinks.

There was a moment when Nate had held Emma's

gaze, just for a few intense seconds, as he sang the lyrics to Coldplay's 'Yellow' along with the lads – and as he sang about the stars shining just for the girl in the song, a lump formed in Emma's throat and all sorts of mixed emotions filled her. Then Max had spotted Nate's focus and given Emma a look of his own which was rather stormy and she'd had a feeling the green-eyed monster was upon him.

What was she meant to do, hey? Totally ignore the guy? He was a part of her past, a link with all that – and oh my God, at times he looked so like Luke . . .

26

Despite the numerous drinks and late night at The Fisherman's, both Emma and Max woke early. Having been used to early starts every day for work, it was often hard for them to sleep in, so by seven-thirty on Sunday morning, they were down on the deserted beach, walking Alfie. The sun had risen on a gorgeous summer day, the sea rippling with glints of silver light bouncing off the waves.

'So, it sounds like you've had a good week at the shop . . . and the courtyard café's going well? I was sorry I couldn't be there for the opening day,' Max said as they strolled on the golden sands.

'Hey, no worries. I do know you have a lot on just now. And yeah, it's going really well – and did I tell you I even had a guitar serenade from Nate on the opening morning?' The words just fell out of her mouth before she had time to think.

'Oh great. Good old Nate.' Max sounded huffy.

Em carried on in a bright tone, regardless. 'Yeah, it was quite nice actually.'

'So, you think I'm boring then because I don't sit around strumming Bob Dylan tracks on the guitar?'

'It was Ed Sheeran, actually. Max, what is up with you? And where did you get that idea from? Of course I don't think you're boring, maybe just a bit – a bit fixated right now.'

'Because I've got a real job and a business to run, and I happen to be rather busy?' Max's voice was taut.

'It's not that!' Blimey, he was sounding like a stroppy teenager. Emma started walking ahead with Alfie; she couldn't be doing with this. Surely she should be able to mention Nate's name? He was just a friend, more or less family. This jealous side of Max was getting a bit tedious, if she was honest.

'I can be carefree too, you know.'

Emma turned to glare at him.

And Max started stripping off his T-shirt.

What was he doing? Em just stood and stared, wondering what on earth had brought this on – though it wasn't a bad sight at all. Just a little out of character. Then he started undoing the belt of his jeans, the top button . . . She was amazed and a little taken aback. Was he intending to remove the lot? What the heck had set all this off? Jealousy? Was it to do with Nate?

Good lord. 'Max . . . what if someone . . . ?' Em started. But glancing up and down the beach, it was obvious they had the whole bay to themselves.

The jeans came off, the boxer shorts next. And there was her gorgeous, if rather grumpy boyfriend, standing stark bollock naked on the beach. Her mouth creased into a wry smile.

'Joining me?' he asked, smirking somewhat. 'Or are you too bloody scared? Or, in fact, *boring* yourself?'

Ah sod it. If you can't beat 'em join 'em. But this was the North Sea, and despite it being summer it was *always* chilly if not bloody freezing. She'd only ever braved it up to her ankles before and that was bad enough; it had set her off shivering for hours.

'Right then,' she snapped back, taking off her clothes in a rush before the cold air or the appearance of a dog walker made her change her mind. Spaniel Alfie stood staring at the pair of them, barking, then leapt into the water.

Max ran at the sea and took a dive into a foaming white wave, Emma dashing in after him. OMG! Just up to her knees and it was flippin' freezing! In to her waist now – oh crikey, this was torture. She plunged forward after Max in a now-or-never moment of madness, the chill of the water taking her breath away as a frothy wave washed over her.

'You silly bugger. You're mad!' she shouted across the boil of the surf. It had been windy last night, and the sea was still a bit whipped up. As another blast of icy wave slammed against her, she shouted, 'We're going to die of bloody hypothermia.'

Max was laughing now, the anger zapped out of him

by the chill of the sea and the craziness of the situation. He swam across to her and she kicked up an arc of cold water at him.

'Now *that* means trouble.' He was grinning as he splashed her back, soaking her hair, her face, the salt stinging her eyes now.

'Right, that's it!' With both hands she scooped up as much seawater as she could and launched it at him, then doused him again, over and over.

He ducked and was there next to her, pinning her arms beside her. She could feel his strength, but it was measured with playfulness. He was shaking his head exaggeratedly, as though wondering what to do with her next.

He took her into his arms and planted a wet, salty kiss firmly on her lips.

And they both felt a sudden huge relief; that this was still good, that they were still right.

'I can't believe you've got m-me into this, Max Hardy.' Emma tried to remain indignant as she finally pulled away, her teeth chattering now.

He wrapped his arms about her and lifted her feet up off the sand-bed. They rocked together, laughing and shivering for a while, getting bashed by the pulsing waves, then he carried her back to the shore. This was the moment they should lie back on the sands in the breaking waves of the shoreline and make love, but *that* was in the movies and probably on location in the Caribbean – it was too bloody cold here for that. Though, they might just continue this back upstairs in The Chocolate Shop – maybe after a thaw out in the shower first.

All too soon it was time for her to open up the shop, and for Max to leave. The afternoon had turned to rain, so the courtyard had to close, which meant the shop's café was rather crowded. But at least working single-handedly this afternoon, as Bev wanted to spend some time with her mum and Holly had to get back to her studies, meant she didn't have to be in three places at once, just the two – the shop and kitchen. Emma's own exam for the licensing was this coming week too, so she'd cram in a few hours of study herself later.

Emma sighed; it was exhausting, it seemed like she was on a hamster wheel at times. Working, chocolate crafting, baking, serving, paying bills, seeing Max, studying, working . . . It'd all be worth it in the end, though, it had to be. And, if she passed this exam then she could start her prosecco parties for real. Something which would take her through into the autumn and winter months too.

She just felt so very tired of late, but there was no chance of taking a rest just yet. With The Rock Shop on her heels – oh yes, she'd spotted the stripy pink-and-white bags making their way past her shop, clutched in the tourists' hands – she needed to keep The Chocolate Shop as appealing as it possibly could be to keep drawing the customers in. It took a hell of a lot of determination to get that chocolate crafted, and Emma knew she couldn't afford to take anything for granted. As long as people wanted their day brightening with a fix of cocoa and a friendly smile, Emma would be there, ready and waiting.

27

'Sorry, Em, but I'm not going to manage to get up to see you this weekend,' said Max down the phone line. It was already mid-week, the busy days having passed quickly.

'Oh Max, not work *again*.' Emma couldn't hide her disappointment.

'It'll be the last big push on this Leeds project, and we'll need both Saturday and Sunday to get it to finishing by Monday, handover day. I know it's a pain, but after this is done, life'll be much easier for us, and we'll have a bit more time.'

Time . . . it was so precious. Living an hour apart as they usually did, and both of them running businesses, was bad enough, but the Leeds job had meant they were nearer to three hours apart.

'Okay, there's not much I can say or do is there? But yes, I get it,' Em conceded.

'The contract has time penalties, as you know, so I absolutely can't afford for the job to run over. But after that I can't wait to come back up to Warkton and to chill out with just you and a bottle of lager.'

'Ah, and who said romance was dead?' Emma joked. 'Well, maybe I'll try to come down to your house after work and see you one night next week, then.' She was trying her best to sound upbeat. Max was working hard, after all, and she did admire that he was dedicated and ran his own business – she knew herself how much time, organisation and energy that took. She had, in fact, only been down to his place a couple of times in the whole of their eight-month relationship, being holed up working in The Chocolate Shop all hours too.

'Yeah, that'd be great, Em. I'd like that. But I'm likely to be wrapping up here in Leeds, at least for the first part of the week.'

'Okay, well, let me know which day might work best.'

'Will do.'

'Everything else okay with you there?' Emma asked.

'Yeah, not bad. I'm tired and fed up with staying over in B&Bs, but that's par for the course.'

'No, it'll not be like home, will it?'

'A bed, four walls, TV and a coffee machine. But I could be worse off, I suppose.'

'Yeah, look on the bright side, you're nearly done there.'

'Of course. And it will be so worth it in the end. It'll boost my business no end, both profits and reputation. That's why I want to do the best job I can this weekend and get it finished on schedule too. You know how powerful word of mouth is.'

'Yes, well, I'll see you in a week or so. It'll soon go by.'

They chatted for a while, but it was hard sounding upbeat when they were both so tired and so far apart.

'Love you, Em,' Max brought the call to an end.

'Love you, too.' It was becoming easier to say that now. To say those words to someone new. Emma turned off her mobile with a sigh. Was loving someone enough?

So, it looked like she'd be going to Saturday's beach BBQ on her own then.

The following morning a van pulled up alongside The Chocolate Shop, blocking the light. Emma was about to go outside and remind them that that was a yellow line area and no parking – after all, it wouldn't be nice for her café customers to sit and look at the side of a van – when she saw the sign on it. Something inside her went cold as she stood in the shop and watched the male driver get out and remove a set of ladders from the roof rack. He then climbed up beside the shop window and the next thing she heard was a hammering noise.

She felt a bit light-headed and had to steady herself by holding on to the counter's edge before her emotions swiftly turned from shock to anger. Out of the shop door she marched, past the van with 'Fawcett's Estate Agents – Your Home in our Hands' emblazoned on the side.

From the base of the ladder she shouted up, 'What the hell do you think you're doing?'

The ladder shook a little as the man was startled.

'Instructions from the owner, madam. It's up for sale,' he called down.

Of course, the owner wasn't her. He had the right, the slimy little eel, but he could at least have had the decency to inform her in advance. Oh, her precious Chocolate Shop up for sale. Yes, she'd feared this moment for over a year now. But this was it, it was now a reality. She felt her knees buckle.

'Whoa, hang on there,' came a voice beside her. With that she felt a pair of strong arms around her, supporting her. She felt herself sink into them. Her head was a bit woozy. 'Em, you okay?' It was Nate.

'Is the lady all right? I'm only doing my job.' The chap was down off his ladder, his task completed and the 'For Sale' sign mounted next to Emma's lounge window.

Suddenly Sheila appeared on the scene along with old Mrs Clark, who'd been taking her time ambling up the hill.

'What's happening here, then?' Sheila raised her voice. 'Ah, looks like she's feeling a little faint. Give her some space, people . . . And let's get her back into the shop, young man.'

Sheila and Nate helped Emma inside and to one of the window seats, where they sat her down. She seemed to come to a little then.

'Ooh, sorry, I'm not quite sure what happened then,' Emma said, her head starting to pound.

'I'll make a cup of a sweet tea, shall I?' said Holly. She was helping again today as revision was 'doing her head in', and had been serving in the back courtyard at the time of the drama.

'Yes, pet, that'd be a good idea. Thank you.' Sheila's voice was calm and kind.

Nate had sat himself down next to Emma. 'You feeling better now?'

'Yes, I think so. Uh, is that sign really up outside my shop?'

'The "For Sale" one? Yes. Sorry Em,' Nate replied.

'Surely they can't just do that without telling me?'

With that, in waltzed The Eel himself, her back-stabbing landlord – now she knew what all those photos were about.

He'd evidently overheard Emma's comment. 'My apologies, Emma. They were meant to be coming to put up the sign in an hour or so's time. I'm here to advise you now. So yes, the property is for sale, and the lease will continue on its month-by-month basis as agreed with yourself at Easter. I will, of course, inform you if there are any developments.'

'That's shocking,' Mrs C piped up.

'Disgusting, if you ask me,' Sheila added. Both ladies stood with arms folded stiffly across their chests in matronly battle pose.

'I am *well* within my rights to do this.' Mr Neil dabbed his forehead with his cotton handkerchief. He looked a little uncomfortable, unusually for him.

'You may well be, but it's not a polite or gentlemanly way to do business at all.' Mrs Clark was indignant. There was a chance she was about to bash the landlord over the head with her Queen-sized handbag, from the telltale twitch of her wrist.

'It's okay, Mrs C. Thanks for the support, but it's just one of those things,' Emma countered. The last thing she wanted was for Mrs C to be carted off by the local constabulary for causing grievous bodily harm. And despite her age, someone of Mr Neil's surly nature would surely take her to court or at least inform the police.

'It's a disgrace, that's what it is,' Sheila added.

'Well, I think my job here is done. This is the notice in writing for you.' With that, he placed a crisp white envelope on the tabletop in front of Emma, just as Holly appeared with the cup of tea.

'Time for you to go then, Mr Eel,' Holly said loudly, making no effort to hide the misnomer.

And the four of them watched as the landlord slid his way out of the door without so much as a backward glance.

'Oh pet, we'll find a way through this for you, won't we. He can't just chuck you out,' Mrs C said determinedly.

'Of course we will,' Sheila rallied.

'Thanks, but I'm not sure how.' Emma was being realistic. 'If he sells the shop from under me I can't do anything about that. And I can't afford to buy it.' Her shoulders sank.

No one knew quite what to say to that.

Nate put an arm around her and gave her a comforting squeeze, but she still felt so very cold inside. The future for The Chocolate Shop by the Sea suddenly looked pretty bleak.

Emma persevered through the day, keeping herself busy and putting a brave face on things. But, as soon as the shop sign was turned to *Closed*, she headed back to the kitchen and sank down on a stool with a huge sigh. She could still hardly believe it – her wonderful Chocolate Shop and her home up for sale. The tears flowed freely. She wasn't a crier generally, but her heart felt so sore. All those hopes and dreams, all those years setting this place up. She let it all out in big snotty tears, then went and fetched a tissue and gave her nose a good blow.

Emma gathered herself, then pulled out her mobile phone from her pocket. She really needed to speak to someone . . . and that someone was Max.

The dialling tone droned on and then switched to the annoying standard voice of the answerphone. 'Argh!' That was all she needed.

Okay, okay . . . She talked to herself as she felt the sting of tears building in her eyes again. Her brother James was always level-headed, he'd be good to chat with about this too. She redialled. This time it was answered within a couple of rings.

'Em, hi.' He sounded cheery.

'James . . .' She didn't even want to say what had happened out loud, for fear of the tears breaking free once more and her becoming a blubbering mess.

'Hey, what's up, sis?'

'Oh, James. The Chocolate Shop . . . it's been put up for sale.'

'Ah, no way. Bloody hell, Em. It's that prick of a landlord again, trying to sell it for a small fortune no doubt.'

'*Ja-mes.*' She heard Chloe call to him in the background. 'The girls are here.'

'Sorry, sorry.' One apology seemed to be for Chloe and one for Em. 'But that's what he is.'

'Yeah, you're probably right. I haven't had a chance to check the price or the details yet. It's up with Fawcett's.' She didn't want to see it there on some website, up for sale . . .

'I'll take a look for you in a mo.'

'I don't think it'll make much difference. Even at a bargain price I could never afford it. I'd never be able to raise enough cash for a deposit. I'm going to have to leave, aren't I? And that makes me feel so sad.'

'Hey, shall I come round? Do you want some company? I can be there in twenty minutes.'

'No, it's okay. I'll be all right, I just needed someone to talk to. Just stay on the line and chat a while. About anything. Tell me how the girls are or something.'

'Okay, well, they've been to school today. Been making books on what they did at half-term. Your Chocolate Shop features prominently.' They had in fact been in for their milkshakes, cookies and ice-creams in the courtyard – twice. 'Honestly, it's like having promo for you at the school. It's soon sports day, and there's lots of trips coming up for them. In only a few weeks it'll be the end of term, so we'll have the long summer holidays to fill. And they are already excited for that to say the least.'

'Is that Auntie Emma?' A high-pitched voice could now be heard in the background. 'Can I talk to Auntie Emma, Daddy?' 'And *meee*,' another voice piped up.

'Hang on. They want to talk.'

'That's great. Put them on.' And that was just the lift she needed, hearing all about their swimming lessons and the friend they each had coming for tea tomorrow when they were going to have pizza and ice cream as a special treat.

James came back on. 'You really okay? It's no bother to call around, you know.'

'I know, but I feel a bit better already, just chatting. It's not like it's going to happen overnight, is it? It's no good me moping about. I'll just have to keep my head down, keep the business running as well as it can, and be prepared to keep my options open.'

'That's the attitude, Em. You take care of yourself, sis. And if there's anything you need . . .'

'Yes, I know where to come. And, thank you.'

A few minutes later there was a knock on the back door, which opened more or less at the same time.

'Em?' It was Bev's voice. She'd had to take her mother to the specialist's appointment so hadn't been at work today, which was why Holly had filled in. 'I heard about the bloody "For Sale" sign.' News travelled fast in a small village. 'You all right, hun?'

'Been better.'

'Yeah, I expect so.'

'It's funny how two little words can just go and wrench your heart out.' Em sniffed. *For Sale.*

'Oh, Em. Come here.' With that, her best friend gave her a hug. 'Can I make you a cup of tea? A stiff gin and tonic?'

'That might be more like it, but I don't have any.'

'I could always pop back home and grab a bottle from the drinks cabinet.'

'I think the way I feel right now, I'd just down it in one, so thanks but that's maybe not such a good idea, Bev.'

'Right, well, tea it is then.' Bev headed over to the kettle. 'Why don't we go and sit outside. It's still bright out there in the courtyard.'

She made their tea and they wandered out to the little wrought-iron table and chairs set Emma had hand-painted, full of hope and plans for the future, just those few weeks ago.

'Well, it's an absolute bastard,' Bev uttered angrily. 'All the work you've put in here. And now he's selling it from beneath you. How are you feeling, hun? Or is that a silly question?'

'Pretty shite.'

'Yeah, I bet. I'm so sorry.'

'Hey, it's not your fault. And I can't do much about it, can I?'

'No, I suppose not. That horrid man owns the place

after all. But maybe something good will come of it, Em.' Bev was trying hard to find a bright side. 'Maybe you can start looking for a place somewhere else?'

'But where? There's nothing like this in Warkton. And then what? In the next village, the one after that? Away from here, away from you lot?'

'No! We couldn't let that happen.'

'I've spent so much time and effort getting this place just right, how I wanted it to be . . . the courtyard, the café. I just can't imagine being anywhere else. And this village, this community, is my home.'

'I know.' Bev rested a hand on Em's shoulder. 'Come on, let's have a slice of Margaret's scrummy chocolate cake to go with this tea. It's the least we can do in the circumstances. Needs must.'

Emma felt slightly sick, to be quite honest, but she didn't have the heart to protest.

Bev soon came back out with two generous slices of cake, on pretty tea plates with forks.

'A slice of cake can't really change things, I know, but it might just make us feel a teensy bit better.' Bev gave an encouraging smile.

Tea and cake – a sliver, or slab in this case, of light in the gloom.

'Oh Bev, how's your mum? Sorry, I've been so wrapped up in my own problems, I didn't ask how you got on at the hospital.'

'Well, the good news is the scan has shown it's not cancer, which was my biggest fear.'

'Oh, that's such a relief.'

'But the not-so-good news is that she's got bronchitis, which she's had before and they think it's left some scarring on the lungs this time. She's on medication now, which should help her pick up generally, but unfortunately there could be some long-term damage. She's just going to have to take it really easy for a while and let herself heal.' Bev looked concerned.

'Bless her. Well let's hope she gets much better soon. Send her my best wishes.'

'I will do.'

'It's just a gesture, but might a few coffee creams help cheer her up, do you think?' Em remembered they were one of Bev's mum's favourites.

'I think they might.' Bev smiled.

'I'll box some up before you head off, along with a bag of Eton Mess truffles for you. Hey, gotta look after the carers too. And I know you'll be doing a good job of looking after her.'

'Thanks.'

They sat in the courtyard that sadly might soon no longer be Emma's, and chatted about other things for a while. Em remembered the BBQ on the beach that she was meant to be going to on Saturday and Bev said she hadn't been invited, not really knowing Nate, but she'd heard Holly talking about it.

'I may as well still go,' Em mused aloud. No point moping about here on her own, dwelling on things. 'Holly and Adam'll be there and I'm sure to know some others.'

'Yeah, sounds as though it might be fun. You get your-self out there, let your hair down a little, Em.'

As Bev was getting up to go, chocolates in hand, Emma's mobile went off. She looked at the screen. Max. Finally.

'Hi.'

'Hey, Em. Sorry I couldn't answer earlier. I was just in the middle of a team meeting, putting the last plans in place.'

'Right.'

Bev was mouthing 'Max?' and as Em nodded, she whispered, 'I'll get away, then. Call me if you need anything, hun.'

'Will do,' she spoke to Bev. 'Thanks.'

'Everything okay there?' Max sounded concerned.

'Not really.' Emma sighed heavily, then gave him the whole story. By now, she was all cried out, and sounded fairly calm.

'Oh Em, that's so shit. I'm so sorry. I know how much that place means to you.'

'Yeah . . .' Her head was throbbing now.

'I'm sorry I can't be with you right now, Em.'

'Me too. I could really do with one of your bear hugs, Max.'

'Sending one right down the phone for you, madam.' He tried to sound upbeat.

'Thanks.' But it really wasn't the same as the real thing.

They talked about options for the future of the shop, which were limited, and whichever way they looked at it, involved having to leave the place she loved.

'We'll work this out somehow. I'll be there soon with you, Em.'

'Yeah,' she uttered. But the word felt empty.

'You take care.'

'I'll try.'

'I love you.' His words were heartfelt.

'Love you too.'

And she sat quietly for a while, still in the courtyard, with a sparrow hopping at her feet looking for cake crumbs. The sun was on her back, and she was sheltered from the breeze by the stone walls. Bev's gorgeous vivid purple clematis was now climbing proudly and about to bloom and her herb pots stood on each table, smelling of summer while a drift of cocoa aromas came from the kitchen. It was such a special place here.

She wondered who would be sitting here this time next year, or even in a few months. Would it still be run as a business or be someone's house or a holiday let? Whatever happened, she wasn't going to give it up that easily. Knowing Mr Neil, he'd be asking a high price, and it might not sell that quickly. She'd just have to keep going, make a success of The Chocolate Shop this summer season, save as much as she could – which she realised would only be a small dent in the kind of deposit needed for a business loan on this place – and come up with some alternative ideas. But there was no denying it, The Chocolate Shop was up for sale, and the thought of having to leave this place made her feel so terribly sad.

28

On Saturday morning Emma lay in bed in a bleary fog. She'd already pressed twice on the snooze button on her alarm. She'd heard the 'For Sale' sign creaking in the wind in the night, taunting her. She'd tossed and turned, trying to come up with some way out of this nightmare situation, until her head and heart were sore. Now she felt totally wrung out. This really needed to be the biggest duvet day ever.

Alfie had managed to sneak in at some point and was there on the covers beside her.

'Oh, Alfie boy.' His fur was soft and warm under Em's palm as she gently stroked him and he snuggled closer. Thank heavens for our four-legged friends.

She let a few stray tears hit the pillow.

'Come on, Emma,' a small voice inside began to kick in. 'You've fought bigger things than this.' And she had, she really had. But this morning it felt like the final straw, the kick in the balls that brought you tumbling down. She lay there a little longer, with her arm around Alfie.

On the third snooze alarm, she forced herself up. The shop had to open, after all.

She blasted herself under a warm shower, letting it stream down over her. Walking into the kitchen to make some tea and toast, she turned on the radio which was playing 'Life is a Rollercoaster'. Hah, she'd had enough of that particular rollercoaster for now.

Despite it all, she forged her way through the day on autopilot, bravely fielding queries from her customers about the estate agent's 'For Sale' sign that was hoisted up on the front of her shop like a stake through her heart. Her hopes and dreams for the future up in smoke once again. Why was her life such a bloody car crash?

She so needed some time out – which was why, soon after closing time, she was heading off down the hill with a bottle of rosé and a picnic basket of goodies to Nate's beach BBQ. She'd found some pork sausages she'd bought from the local butcher in the freezer, and had some brownies left over in the shop that she'd cut down into smaller squares and put in a Tupperware box. That'd do.

It looked as though the weather was going to hold, and though clouds were starting to gather there was no sign of rain as yet. It was a warm evening too, a bonus. Past the harbour she went and into the dune car park, where she passed what must be Nate's camper van, making her way down the sandy track to the beach. She could hear sounds of chatter and laughter, as though the group had already gathered. And as she came out on to the sands there they were, about twenty people so far.

'Hi, Nate. Hi, all,' she called, smiling as she approached. It was always slightly daunting when you didn't know many of the gathering that well, Nate having made friends with more of the younger group in the village. She so wished Max had been able to come.

'Hey, Em, hi. Come and meet Des. He's a mate of mine from Oz, now over here travelling in the UK.' Nate introduced them and handed her a bottle of lager from a plastic crate doubling as a makeshift ice-bucket. She was soon chatting away with the guy, who had tousled blond hair, a deep tan and looked in his mid-twenties. He seemed friendly enough, though he made her life seem rather narrow with his tales of diving with sharks at the Barrier Reef and getting stranded for several hours in the desert after trying to climb, illegally by the sounds of it, Mount Uluru.

As more people joined them, Em recognised a few local faces, including Danny from the pub. She waved across at him. He came over, saying he only had an hour to go before his shift in The Fisherman's started, so was desperate for the BBQ food to get going.

Nate took the hint and investigated the contents of Emma's picnic basket. Her food offerings seemed to go down well with the group, resulting in a whoop from Nate and several smiling faces as the chocolate brownies made their appearance. The sausages were added to the stockpile of baps and burgers set out on the table beside the BBQ, a big metal half-drum that was loaded with charcoal, ready to light. Nate took out a box of matches and set it alight, much to Danny's relief.

Em finished off her lager and Danny fetched her another bottle. It all seemed pretty laid-back and relaxed, which was just what she needed.

Some of the surfer lads started a game of rounders down on the beach in front of them. They had set out posts made from driftwood and were using an old tennis ball and baseball bat someone had brought along. Holly and Adam turned up at that point, along with Laura, Sheila's daughter, and her boyfriend Angus.

They all ended up joining in, fielding firstly, and Emma stunned herself with a lucky catch that impressed the gang and raised a 'Whoop! Go Em!' from Holly.

Nate started cooking the food, alongside the guy from Oz, both of them looking very at home in shorts and T-shirts, with a large BBQ in front of them and cans of beer in hand. Scanning the group, Emma suddenly realised she must be the oldest there, being well into her thirties, but she didn't feel left out in any way. They were a friendly crowd and easy company.

After a delicious supper, and her chocolate brownies going down extremely well with lots of 'Oohs', 'Aahs' and 'Scrummys' from the partygoers, Emma found herself feeling pretty chilled-out, sitting on a rug in the lower dunes with a bottle of lager in hand. She was watching the embers flickering in a firepit Nate had made earlier as the sun started to go down, the odd spark still flaring.

It was dark now, she suddenly realised, so it must be fairly late as the sun didn't set until after ten this time of year. It was a shame Max couldn't have come. He'd have enjoyed this. Always work, bloody work.

As she looked up from the fire, she realised that most of the others had gone and she had said several goodbyes as couples and friends had drifted off. Holly and Adam now got up to leave.

'Bye, Hols, Adam.' Emma smiled, feeling very comfortable where she was.

'You okay, Em? Want to walk back with us?' Holly asked.

'Nah, I'll be fine. It's been such a nice evening that I'm not quite ready for home.' Emma felt pleasantly buzzed from the lager, and she'd also had a glass or two of rosé. It was one of those evenings that you didn't want to end. She could just sit and listen all night to the rush of the sea to shore in the cosy shelter of the dark. The beach had always been her special place.

'Bye, then. Take care.' Holly looked slightly concerned.

'It's okay. I'll walk her back. See she's all right,' Nate offered.

'Thanks,' Adam said. 'Night then.'

'Bye-e.' Emma was smiling, happy and mellow in her little beach BBQ world.

Holly and Adam left, arm in arm.

Just Emma and Nate there now . . .

Nate was sitting watching Emma, strumming away on his guitar. She recognised the lyrics of Ed Sheeran's

'Photograph' – about keeping a photo in your jeans pocket. Memories of someone you love. She was sure they were both thinking of Luke then. She smiled across at Nate. God, he looked *sooo* like Luke, it was uncanny. She wondered how it must feel for him looking in the mirror every day: it must be as though Luke's shadow was there with him.

She felt a shiver run through her.

'You okay?' Nate stopped singing, his tone was gentle, concerned.

'Yeah.'

'Here . . .' He put his guitar down and moved across to sit beside her on the rug, wrapping his hoodie around her shoulders. She could feel the warmth from his body.

They were quiet for a few moments.

'It's been a pretty shitty week for you with the shop and everything.'

'Yep.' She didn't want to talk about that just now.

'I'm sure something will work out Em, with The Chocolate Shop.'

She shrugged her shoulders, couldn't see how at all. But still, she said, 'Maybe.' She didn't seem capable of forming full sentences just now. Like her fragility might just break free if she voiced it.

She felt Nate's arm wrap around her, his hand resting on her far shoulder. It felt natural, comforting. She let it stay there, feeling tired, a little woozy, in fact. They sat like that for a while, neither saying much. Looking at a sky full of stars, suspended over a black, inky sea, she felt her eyelids relax, the slow whirr of alcohol through her veins . . .

'Come on, I'll walk you back. It's getting late – and cold.' Nate's words made her eyes ping back open. She wasn't sure if she had dozed, or for how long. Had her head been resting on his shoulder?

'Oh . . . yeah, that'd be good. Thanks, it's been a nice night.'

He looked at her intently for a few seconds with those eyes just like Luke's. 'It has, hasn't it.'

They made their way back up from the beach, along the track in the dunes to the car park, where Nate's camper van was parked up for the night. There was no way he was driving anywhere after the many bottles of lager he'd had.

Em realised she wasn't walking that well, kept veering to the right. Nate steadied her. She felt a bit light-headed now. She giggled.

'You all right?' Nate asked.

'Oooh, just give me a second.' She paused, taking a gulp of air. She looked up and the sky suddenly took a little spin. *Oh no, don't look up too long . . . made the legs wobblier. Be nice if she didn't have legs to get in the way right now. Then she could fly and soar and be free.*

Nate had his arm firmly around her, steadying her along as they walked. *That was better. No wobbles at all.*

'It's bee-en such a lovely night.'

'Good. I'm glad you've enjoyed yourself. Time you got a bit of a chill-out for yourself.'

'Y-y-ee-ss.'

'And you're sure you're all right?'

'Abso-blooody-lutely!' Then she felt a bit of a spin going on. 'Ooh, do you have some water, Nate?'

'Yep, no worries. There's some bottled water in the van.' They had nearly reached the camper van, anyhow.

'Right.' Nate unlocked the side door of the unit. 'You may as well sit in a minute, while I find you a bottle. I bought some at the supermarket earlier.' He rummaged in a cupboard under the sink, whilst Em perched herself on the sleeper bench. 'Here.' He'd found a large plastic water bottle and poured some out into a glass for her.

She took a long sip, still feeling a little woozy. Nate sat down beside her, his hip touching hers, leg to leg. It was a pretty small space. The door of the van had been left open.

'I still miss him.' The words came out before Emma knew she had been thinking them.

'Yeah, me too. Every day.'

They didn't need to say who.

Nate's arm drifted around her again. There were a few seconds of silence. Then Emma turned to look at Nathan. Their eyes met, held each other's. She could see the glisten of a tear in his.

She didn't know who moved first, but suddenly there were lips pressed against hers. She didn't stop it, responding gently. Oh God . . . That smell of his after-shave. The touch of his lips. She'd missed him so much . . . *so much*.

She opened her eyes and it was Nathan there. *Nathan.* The past tangling with the present. She was surprised, yes, and she tried to fathom how she felt . . . It was okay, nice, her emotions over seeing Luke's brother again, the confusion and heartache of the past few weeks, the disappointment about the shop, finding an outlet at last.

It was a good kiss, tender, with a hint of passion.

But it didn't feel like Luke's kiss . . . This wasn't Luke. Luke was never coming back. *And* it didn't feel like Max's kiss. God yes, she and Max had shared their first kiss here in this car park, that day when they'd first met. She felt a prickle of guilt.

And then a realisation. Kissing Nate didn't make her toes curl.

What on earth was she doing?

Holly and Adam made their way up the track from the beach. They'd taken a stroll along the sands in the dark after leaving the others, wanting to make the most of some extra time just to be together. They were both aware that the summer would pass all too soon, and the time would come when Holly would take up her university place and have to leave Warkton-by-the-Sea.

They were walking hand in hand as they reached the car park.

They saw the camper van with its side door open, the light on inside. They spotted Nate in there and then, Emma – her wavy red locks apparent even though she was facing the other way.

In fact . . . Holly stopped walking and took a closer look. Yes, it was definitely Emma and she was facing Nate. Kissing him.

29

What the hell had she done?

The next morning Emma woke with a head that felt like it had been used as a rugby ball and the most horrid hangover, and yet she remembered last night's incident all too well. There had definitely been Nate . . . and a kiss involved. *Bugger.* That was before she'd asked him to walk her home and left him politely on her back doorstep. She felt terribly sick, probably the dregs of alcohol kicking around in her system, but also the awful realisation of what had happened. She thought about Luke. Oh God, she'd gone and kissed his brother! What was she thinking of? And then Max, gorgeous Max. Yes, it had been a bit tricky with work lately, but he was a great guy, and now she'd gone and kissed someone else, in a moment of bloody madness.

It was a mistake. Just a mistake. We all make mistakes. She tried to put it into perspective. But it had happened – and she couldn't change that.

It hurt to open her eyes, but she needed to check what time it was. She squinted at her wristwatch: ten past ten. Oh my, she ought to get up soon. The thought stayed a thought, however; there was no subsequent action. Her whole body felt like she'd been kicked by a donkey.

Alfie must have heard her stirring and came through to her room. He stood patiently beside the bed and nuzzled his nose to her hand that lay on top of the covers. Emma gave him a gentle pat.

'Oh Alfie, what have I done?' she groaned. She'd need to let the dog out. Face the day. Get ready to open The Chocolate Shop at noon. But she'd just take five more minutes . . . just five, yes.

She woke up over half an hour later; Alfie had snuck up on top of the covers, which he was rarely allowed to do, and had curled up beside her.

There was also a missed call on her mobile, which was on the bedside table. Max. She groaned loudly. That was one call back she wasn't ready to make just now.

With a thumping head and a heavy heart, Emma took Alfie out for a short walk down to the harbour and back, then she forced herself into the kitchen and set about making some chocolate bars to replenish the shop's supplies. They were fairly straightforward to make, she just needed to melt the chocolate and add a touch of flavouring – Grand Marnier orange and then mint options this time. She found her rectangular moulds and set them out on the countertop. Yes, she thought she could manage to make these even with a headache. She could work on autopilot.

However, standing in the shop's kitchen, looking out over her newly spruced-up courtyard, she couldn't help but think. Okay, so the shop and café might be up for sale, but that was just the building, the bricks and mortar, she told herself. Her Chocolate Shop was so much more than that. It was all the things *she* had put in there: the furniture, the displays, the chocolate creations, including her heart and soul.

Argh, as if she didn't have enough on her plate . . . and now her crazy late-night kiss with Nate. Oh my, she'd be mortified when she saw him next time. She'd have to apologise, say it was all a mistake.

She had a fleeting flashback to the end of the night before. Nate had walked her home and they stood there on her back step, an awkwardness already forming between them. There was no chance of a repeat-performance goodnight kiss. She didn't need another lover – all she'd needed was a friend, a brotherly figure, no more. She hoped she hadn't gone and messed that up too.

And then there was Max. Should she come clean and tell him? It was just a blip, after all. But would he understand? She poured milk chocolate callets into the tempering machine absent-mindedly, spilling a few. Stupid, stupid woman. If she did tell Max, would it ever be the same between them? After that silly shower incident with Nate, he might just think his instincts were right all along.

Her head was thumping even more now. Time for a couple of paracetamols, a drink of water and a large cup of tea. Then, she'd make some choc-chip shortbread: kneading and rolling the dough might prove therapeutic.

So, life threw you curveballs every now and then. She'd have to ring Max back soon, or her silence would be telling in itself. But she didn't know quite what she was going to say . . . some things were bigger than words could express.

30

Emma left it until that evening before calling Max, after the shop had closed and when her headache had subsided to a low throb.

She stood with the phone in her hand, thinking back over the disaster of last night. She hadn't seen anything of Nate all day, thank heavens. Maybe he had decided to lie low too, which was definitely for the best.

She just had to dial. It would be fine. All she had to do was act normally, speak normally . . . ask Max about his day. So why did she feel so sick all of a sudden? Emma paced the room, paused, took a slow breath, then punched in his contact. She heard the dialling tone, and felt a lump form in her throat.

'Hi Max,' she managed to say.

'Hey, Em, been busy there?'

'Yeah, sorry, one of those days.' *One of those days where you go around remembering kissing someone else,* her mind heckled.

'Yeah, me too. Never got a chance to call back after this morning.'

'Did you get finished on time, then? Is the contract completed?' This felt safer ground. This she could cope with.

'Yep, by the skin of our teeth. But yeah, the owners seem really happy with the work. I'll need to be available over the next few weeks just in case there are any teething problems at all. On such a big job there's always something. But the flats are basically finished and ready for the owners to go ahead and sell now.'

'Great – well done you.'

'Ah, I'm so relieved, Em. I cannot tell you how much. This was such a big project for me and the business and boy, was it a long haul. I'm shattered, if truth be told, but the lads want to go out for a beer tonight, to celebrate.'

'Oh yes, you must.'

'And you? How's the shop been? How are you feeling after the bloody "For Sale" sign going up and all that? I'm sorry, I've been so tied up here. Such bad timing. I really wish I could be there with you, Em.'

'It's all right. I'm coping.' Em felt distinctly uncomfortable. Oh yes, what *had* she been up to these past two days? She certainly did not feel ready to share that with Max just now, not now he was so happy about finishing his contract.

It was *way* too risky telling him over the phone too. She couldn't see his reaction or gauge the truth from his eyes. He was already riled up about Nate being about as it was. The knowledge of that one kiss might just fester within him and then she'd never be able to explain properly. Who said honesty was the best policy, anyhow? What would it achieve telling him the truth? It would stir up a hornet's nest. And for what? She knew she'd *never* do it again.

Only she and Nate knew of it, after all. It could stay that way . . .

Why ruin Max's night and possibly their whole relationship for a silly moment of madness?

'Max . . . I love you,' was all she said.

'Love you too, Em.'

His words bruised. Guilt was a gnawing horrid thing.

'I'll come down and see you mid-week if you want, like we talked about,' Em offered. She needed somehow to make it up to Max, even if he never came to know why.

'Thursday would be good. I'm working back at Hexham that day so I'll be home by five.'

'Great. I'll come down straight after work.'

Maybe she ought to come clean on Thursday, face to face, when she could explain everything properly. But oh, if she did, would everything they had just fall down?

What a bloody mess – and this time it was a mess all of her own making.

31

Emma was nervous about opening the formal-looking white envelope. With all the havoc going on in her life, she had put the recent application to the back of her mind. It was Monday and the postman had just called. She slid open the seal and scanned the typewritten letter. It was from the local council.

'We would like to inform you . . .' Wow, she'd been approved! Yippee!! She was now an official licensee. Which meant she could go ahead with her prosecco parties. Well, she could certainly do with some bubbles in her life right now.

Word had already spread since the success of the girls' trial party night a couple of months ago. Laura at the hotel had already mentioned that one of her friends was getting married just before Christmas – she had already booked the wedding reception there at the hotel and wanted a summer hen do with a difference. With the new courtyard available and having experienced the chocolate-prosecco party first hand, Laura had recommended Emma's Chocolate Shop venue. Maddi, the 'hen', and her group of girls were desperate to be the first to try out the party nights.

No time like the present, Emma thought, she'd give the bride-to-be a call. Laura had already left her all her details.

'Maddi, hi. It's Emma from "The Chocolate Shop by the Sea".'

'Oh, hi Emma.'

'Hope all the wedding arrangements are going well?'

'Great, thanks.'

'Well, Laura asked me to give you a call about your hen do. The good news is, I am now licensed so I can go ahead and take bookings for the Chocolate and Prosecco Party nights.'

'Ooh, fab. Me and the girls can't wait. It sounded such a lovely night when Laura came along. And The Chocolate Shop is already special to our engagement.'

'Is it?' Emma was curious.

'Yes, your amazing Easter egg – that was my fiancé, Mark.'

'Aw, how lovely. So you evidently said yes.'

'How could I not after all that effort? It was just stunning. I don't know how you crafted it, all that detail. I didn't want to spoil it by eating it in the end. Mind you, I did scoff all those delicious truffles inside. The chocolate shell opened out perfectly, though, so I've kept it. And then it was such a surprise when I found the ring.

Mark was down on one knee when I looked up.' She sounded a little happy-teary down the line.

'That's so lovely to hear. I'm glad it all worked out well for you both. So, have a think about the hen do and just let me know if you have any dates in mind.'

'Actually, I already have a day in mind. We've set the date for a winter wedding, so no point hanging around and I'm thinking that two weeks this Friday would be perfect . . . if we can. I know it's one of the few nights when all of the girls are free.'

'So . . .' Emma checked her calendar. 'That's July 13. Oh, are you okay with that? Friday the Thirteenth?' Emma wasn't usually the superstitious sort, but it made her think for a second. After her trial of a weekend she didn't want to tempt fate any more than she had to.

'Ah, yes, doesn't bother me. It's the date we can all do, so we'll stick with it.' Maddi sounded very relaxed.

It was Maddi's night after all, so Em answered cheerily, 'Okay, I'll pop that in the diary right away, and I'll give you a call in the next couple of days to chat about details. Do you have an idea of numbers?'

'About twelve of us, I think.'

'Yes, that's fine. I'm looking forward to making it a special night for you all.'

'Thank you. This is brilliant.'

'Bye. Chat again soon,' Em replied.

How fabulous that it was the very same girl who the chocolate-engagement-egg creation had been for. Being a chocolatier was just the best job, especially at times like this. It was so wonderful to have a part in making other people's dreams come true. Even if her own life struggled a bit in that department at times.

Three days later, Emma popped in at the grocer's. At the till, Sheila started going on about rumours she'd heard – apparently, The Rock Shop lady had been making disparaging remarks about The Chocolate Shop. Em had enough on her plate, and just poo-pooed the comments as gossip, making it quite clear to Sheila that she wasn't interested in getting involved in any tittle-tattle.

That was when Nate walked in. It was the first time they had bumped into each other since that fateful Saturday night and Emma found herself frozen, only just managing to squeak a 'hi'. This really wasn't the place for a heart-to-heart. The walls had ears in that shop, and Sheila could spot signs of embarrassment, awkwardness or a cover-up a mile away. So, after buying her bag of potatoes, bacon and orange juice, Emma swiftly left.

But she felt there was so much unsaid, so much to say, and she'd hung around along the street, following Nate down the hill to have a quiet word.

'Nate?' She caught up with him down by the harbour wall.

They instinctively walked away from the road that led to The Fisherman's and diverted along by the harbour where it was quieter.

'About Saturday night . . .' Em paused. She really didn't want to have to say the word 'kiss'.

Nate stopped and looked up at her. Oh my, there were still so many shades of Luke there in his eyes, across his face. 'I know,' he started.

Emma realised she was holding her breath.

'Look,' Nate continued, 'I'm sorry, it shouldn't have happened.'

Phew, at least they were on the same wavelength.

'I know, I feel so awful, like I've let everybody down,' Em tried to explain. 'Luke, Max, your parents, even you. I shouldn't have let you believe there was more to it than there was. I think I was feeling a bit emotional, you know.'

'No worries, honestly Em. I've been feeling rotten about this too. What the hell was I thinking? Don't take that the wrong way – you're lovely, really lovely. But you were always, *will always*, be Luke's. I had no right. Dammit, I have *so* messed up.'

'It is pretty messed up, isn't it?'

Nate just nodded, Em wasn't sure what was going on in his head, but he looked like he was really blaming himself.

'Nate, can we just keep this between ourselves?'

'Of course. My lips are sealed.'

Both of them had got caught up in a crazy, stupid moment. That was all.

'Thank you. Well, I'd better get back,' Emma had plenty to do in the shop, and she didn't want to drag this out any further. The last thing she needed was someone overhearing or seeing them together like this. Sheila might well be peering out of the grocer's window as it was.

'Yeah, me too. I'm on shift soon. Don't worry, Em. No one will hear anything from me. We're all good.'

'Thanks.'

That they'd had this conversation was a relief – but it still didn't change what had happened. And Emma knew she had done wrong by Max, and that felt horrid. But no one could change the past; all she could do was be the best person she could be in the future.

Normally Emma would be really excited about seeing Max, but guilt and worry were doing terrible things to her insides and so, the drive down to Hexham that evening was a little stomach-churning. How would she be when she saw him? Could she act the same as normal? She'd never been any good at lying. James would come up with all sorts as a kid, *and* get away with stuff, yet her mum would just see right through Emma. Normally that wouldn't be such a bad trait; honesty. But this evening she could really do with a good poker face.

She parked outside Max's end cottage in Whitstone village just outside of Hexham. Alfie was with her too, nestled happily in the back of the car. He was always pleased to go wherever Emma went. He barked as they came to a halt. Max's Jeep was parked outside, *so* he was home.

She didn't need to knock on the door. As she walked up the front path, Max was already there with it wide open and a smile on his face.

'Hey, beautiful.'

'Hi, gorgeous.' Their usual waking-up together phrases flowed easily, but it also made Emma feel so very sad. How could she have ever thought of risking this? Her first real chance of love in the eight years since Luke's death . . . argh.

She let herself melt into his arms and breathed in the comforting, sensual aftershave smell of him.

'God, I missed you.' He sounded so honest.

'Missed you too.'

'Hey, Alf.' The spaniel had followed Emma in and was now receiving a warm pat from Max.

Max closed the door on the outside world and took Emma back into his arms, his kiss tender at first, then firmer, passionate, stirring sensual thoughts and sensations all the way through her. This felt so very right . . . and yet had she trashed everything in that one crazy moment?

As the kiss eased off, Em realised tears were forming in her eyes. Oh my, she couldn't be seen to cry now, or there'd be some explaining to do. She moved in for a big hug, her head bowed. She took some deep breaths as she leant against Max's broad chest, composing herself.

'Well then . . .' After a short while, Max shifted back and started chatting. 'I've been home for an hour, so I thought the least I could do was prepare us some supper. There might be a little something for Alfie too. I had thought of a takeaway, but reckoned you'd prefer something home-cooked. Mind you, I warn you now, the takeaway option may have been the safer bet.' He grinned.

'Ooh, what's on the menu?' Emma resurfaced now she had blinked away her tears.

'My go-to gourmet dish. Steak and chips.'

'Sounds wonderful.' She could never afford steak herself.

'But first, seeing as I haven't seen you for a whole ten days, I think we have some serious catching up to do . . .' He didn't need to say any more, as he took her back into his arms and kissed her again, their tongues entwined, her hands in his hair. She could feel the firmness of his erection against her hip.

She wanted this too.

They started for the stairs, laughing, dashing up them, then pausing at the top landing for another kiss. Emma undid several of his shirt buttons, traced his gorgeous torso with her fingertips. He pulled her summer dress up and over her hips, her chest, her shoulders and then discarded it, the pair of them bolting to his bedroom. Underwear was tossed aside, the bed then beneath them, a tangle of legs, skin on skin, lips on lips, making sweet and very sexy love. A sigh, a groan, and that beautiful, blissful moment where they became one.

'Emma, my love . . .' he breathed, his words tender by her ear.

She was lost to him, with him.

They dozed after making love, Max tucked behind her in tumbled sheets, the tiredness from working so hard these past weeks catching up on them both. Alfie had crept up into the room too and had made himself cosy on the floor, curled up in Max's discarded clothes.

When they woke, they didn't rush to get up, just stayed in bed, chatting about their lives, work, how Emma felt about the shop being up for sale. Max trying to reassure her about the future, that her business might carry on in a different, new way. How life had a way of working itself out.

He stroked her hair where it lay splayed out on the pillow. 'Did I ever tell you how much I love your hair?' He smiled at her.

'Maybe once or twice,' she answered softly.

'It makes you look like a flame-haired goddess.' And he couldn't resist kissing her again.

They finally got up. Max cooked their steak supper and they chatted over red wine, chilling out with some music on, until it was time once again for bed.

It was dark; Max had fallen asleep, and was breathing deeply, their hands were still entwined. It had been such a lovely evening, and Emma relished having him beside her. She never wanted to lose that.

And she knew, then, that she could never tell him.

32

Max made a breakfast of bacon sandwiches with some fresh white bread he'd fetched from the village shop whilst Emma was still snoozing. They sat eating at the small wooden table in his kitchen, drinking orange juice and good coffee. Delicious.

Morning had come around all too soon. Emma felt sad having to leave already, but they both had work to get to this morning, and Emma needed to be back to open up the shop by ten. They took Alfie for a quick stroll around the village green, and then it was time to pop her overnight bag in the car and head back to Warkton.

'I'll catch up with you at the weekend, yeah?' Max smiled, his green eyes full of love.

'That'll be great.' The thought of leaving him felt like a weight on her this morning.

'Miss you already.' He took her into his arms.

With Max it was that physicality she so loved. His

warmth. His body next to her, that feeling of closeness. It was addictive. 'Miss you too.' It seemed so hard to be leaving him, even for a few days.

Emma told herself to get a grip, not to be so daft. They'd be fine. They were used to living like this, spending time apart. She wondered why she felt so fragile. Was the secret of her misdemeanour scratching away inside? She needed to stop overthinking.

She put Alfie in the hatchback, popped her bag in, then got into the driver's seat. She waved out of the window as Max stood on his doorstep, waving back.

'See you soon,' he shouted.

'Yes. Love you.' She called from the window of her car, not at all bothered if the neighbours heard.

And once she turned the corner, her smile faded and her heart felt as heavy as a lead balloon. What on earth was up with her?

That day and the next rolled on with Emma's focus back on her Chocolate Shop. Business was fine but seemed slightly quieter than usual. Sheila came into the shop that Saturday afternoon to buy a box of chocolates for her mother-in-law's birthday.

The chat soon turned to Anne, the owner of The Rock Shop down in the harbour.

'You know, she's not as friendly as she seems, that lady from the kiosk. I'm still hearing talk that she's bad-mouthing your business, Emma. Have you noticed if it's been quieter in here of late?'

In fact, there had been a turndown in takings, and spare seats in the café lately, just when the summer season was gearing up. She'd hoped to fill both the café and courtyard, but that didn't seem to be happening as yet.

'Well, my grocery store is definitely down on confectionery sales since she got here.' Sheila shook her head with a sigh, whilst Em got on with selecting chocolates to fill the bespoke gift box.

'Oh Sheila, there's always gossip flying about whenever we get newcomers to the village. We just have to give people a chance. Take them as you find them, is what I say.'

'And I agree. But, in this instance, I think you're being far too kind. I'm just looking out for you, Emma. There's more than one I've heard it from, that have found her to be meddling and spreading rumours. She's certainly not been very complimentary about your Chocolate Shop.'

'Well Sheila, time will tell.' Emma really didn't want to get caught up in the gossip-mongering. 'She's never been anything but polite to me.' She'd not seen the lady often, to be fair. Just that initial conversation and the odd wave as Emma had passed by the kiosk.

'Well, she wouldn't, would she? It's always behind other people's backs with her sort. That's the whole point.' Sheila gave a loud tut.

Emma sent Sheila off with her box of handcrafted chocolates for her mother-in-law, initially dismissing her gossip. But a while after she'd gone, Emma began to think. Customer numbers and her takings *had* seriously dipped since the arrival of The Rock Shop. Maybe some of that was natural, with people trying out the new confectionery rivals, but she'd thought things should have picked up again by now. There were certainly lots of tourists about in the village. She'd seen plenty of people wandering by with their telltale stripy pink-and-white bags of fudge and goodies from The Rock Shop, but most of them weren't stopping or even looking in at The Chocolate Shop. Maybe she'd been naïve and she should be worried, after all.

Max had called her earlier in the day. There were some small but pressing issues with the Leeds project and there was no way around it but to go and sort them out in person. He had anticipated some teething problems and had warned her that there was always something to follow up with projects on this scale. It was best to deal with them swiftly and keep the client happy, he'd explained. Max had then apologised and said he'd definitely make it up to her the following weekend when he'd be there to see her in Warkton, come hell or high water.

Emma said she understood, even though her heart sank. She'd so wanted to see him – to put things right after her stupid moment with Nate, not that Max even knew. And then she did what she usually did: concentrated on her own business, making more chocolate supplies and dashing about keeping her customers happy.

The 'For Sale' notice hanging outside the shop was still lingering in her mind, immovable. And she knew that there might be viewings on the property soon, even if she hadn't heard anything so far. All she could do in the meanwhile was forge on and keep her eyes open for any suitable property up for rent. There was so much out of her control. All she could do was put one foot in front of the other, even if she felt like everything might soon come tumbling down.

33

Two uneasy weeks later, with the Wimbledon tennis tournament due to start on Monday, Emma decided she'd spend a couple of hours after the shop closed on Sunday evening re-jigging her window display with an 'Anyone for Tennis' theme using a few brightly coloured balls, her tennis racquet (it didn't get used often!), and the most divine champagne truffles, together with a dish of her chocolate-dipped fresh strawberries and some home-made meringues.

It looked great, but she wasn't altogether happy; customer numbers had dropped off this past weekend more than ever and any drop in turnover was a massive concern. She couldn't afford to get behind with the rent like she had last year.

On the Monday morning, Emma needed to nip down to the grocer's to fetch some extra cream and eggs and after a quick stroll over, Sheila was smiling at her from behind the till. 'How are you, pet?'

'Oh, pretty good.'

'And how's business?' A frown creased Sheila's brow.

'All right.' Emma was noncommittal, not wanting to give anything away. The next thing would be the whole village hearing all about her misfortunes.

'So, you're not down on customer numbers, then?' Sheila fished.

Emma stayed quiet.

'I'm still hearing rumours, you know. Look, Emma pet, I know you think I'm a meddling thing at times but I don't like to see anyone unfairly treated. I've a mind to go down there and have it out with that Rock Shop woman myself. It's not the way we work in this village. And I'll not see your Chocolate Shop harmed by this tittle-tattle she's spreading. She's telling people your shop is about to go out of business, that's why it's up for sale.'

'Really?!' Emma was taken aback. But was it just rumours? Just the village grapevine doing Chinese whispers and getting its knickers in a twist? She'd hate to accuse someone of wrongdoing if it wasn't true. But maybe there *was* something in it . . . 'Well, I'll take note of what you're saying, but I'll fight my own battles, thank you, Sheila.'

'Okay, pet. I wouldn't take too long about it, though. Things'll only go from bad to worse otherwise. It needs to be nipped in the bud, so it does.'

Wow, yet more troubles lining up for her. As she paid for the cream and eggs, Emma tried to keep a sensible head on. She'd need to somehow verify if there was any truth in this. The only thing was, she wasn't quite sure how . . .

Emma really needed something to look forward to, and she was both excited and relieved when Maddi's hen do rolled around the following week – the first formal 'Chocolate and Prosecco Party' for Emma and The Chocolate Shop. She really needed it to go off well because her reputation was at stake and her nerves were jangling somewhat.

'Holly, can you just give me a hand over here, please?' Emma was balanced precariously up a stepladder, trying to swoop a string of outdoor fairy lights along the side wall of the courtyard. 'Just keep me steady while I reach across. Don't want to end up in A&E before the party even starts.'

'No worries. I've got your back,' Holly said, grinning up at her from the base of the ladder.

'Thanks.'

With fairy lights now strung up on both side walls, tealights and an old-fashioned teacup filled with sweet pea flowers (a gift from Hilda and Stan's garden) set out on each outside table, it was going to look so pretty there in the courtyard when the girls arrived and dusk began to fall. It was a calm clear night, thank heavens, so her plans for using the outdoor space had come together perfectly. Em was going to start the party outside, serving her bubbly and the chocolate-dipped strawberries to begin. She'd give the ladies time to chat and relax, and then they were to have a go at making the choc-dipped strawberries themselves out in the courtyard.

Then, as it would cool down into the evening, they'd head back into The Chocolate Shop after dusk, where Bev was now setting out all the ingredients and bowls ready for the truffle-making session later – raspberry gin truffles being Maddi's choice.

Bev was thrilled that her recipe idea from the first prosecco trial night had been selected. Emma was even making them for the shop now – they were summery and delicious, and equally scrumptious dipped in white, dark or milk chocolate to coat. One of each was a nice way to start, to be honest!

With the deposit money on the booking, Emma had bought a set of glass flutes for the shop, which were already set out on a tray in the kitchen awaiting the cork-popping moment once the girls arrived.

There were ten minutes to go – the group being due to arrive at eight o'clock. Holly and Bev were inside the shop making some last-minute touches to the arrangements, and Em paused for a moment to stand on the back step, gazing out at the courtyard. Her mind drifting off to her own engagement with Luke. They had been so damned happy and excited. They'd held a party for their friends, family and schoolteacher colleagues at a small hotel just outside Durham. It was great fun with a disco and dancing until the early hours, with all the people that were special to them there.

The proposal itself had been at their home and was

quiet but just right. Luke was not a showy character, but he'd made it special all the same. She smiled as she remembered. It was the night she took an after-school baking class, so she never normally got back until around seven. When she opened the front door, she could smell that something delicious was cooking. She walked through to the living room, on the coffee table was a hand-tied bouquet of soft pink, white and cream flowers. And, even better – Luke knew how much she *loved* chocolate – was a beautiful heart-shaped box of artisan chocolates.

She'd thought it was just a romantic meal he had planned, and how lovely was that? But as she walked through to the kitchen where she expected to find him cooking, he was down on one knee, with a huge grin on his face. It tugged at her heart all over again.

She and Luke had never had their special day. Her wedding dress still hung in the wardrobe in her mother's spare room – she couldn't bear to give it away. She still felt so very sad even after all these years, but not bitter. She wished Maddi and Mark the best for their big day ahead and for their future because she wanted to cling on to the fact that love could work out, and that most of the time the world was a good place. If she wasn't meant to get her happy-ever-after, then at least other people could have theirs.

That's why she'd worked extra hard to make tonight special for Maddi and her friends. A night for them to remember. A night of chocolates and prosecco, but so much more than that too: of fun, friendship and love.

Right then, Emma, let's do this thing.

She wiped away a tear that had crowded her eye and headed through to the shop to be with her assistants, who had both been keen to help out tonight. 'Ready?'

'Yep.'

'Looks great in here. Thank you, ladies.'

'You're welcome.'

Emma then opened the shop door, just as a white minibus pulled up outside.

There was fun, there was laughter, there was popping of corks, and tasting of chocolates. The courtyard worked wonderfully for the first couple of hours, and as the dusk began to fall and the pinky-peach glow of the sky gradually darkened, the walled garden began to change into something truly special, with white lights twinkling magically.

Glasses chinked, and Emma raised toasts to the bride-to-be, Maddi, and then her hens. There was such a lovely atmosphere within the group.

They moved inside for the Raspberry Gin truffle-making session, which proved messy, somewhat chaotic, but heaps of fun. There was much hilarity, especially when one of the girls, Rachel, no doubt aided by a glass or two too many proseccos, managed to get her long brunette hair dipped into the melted white chocolate. (Maybe she ought to provide optional hair caps, or at least hair ties at the next function, Emma mused.)

'Hmm, chocolate-dipped hair.' Maddi started laughing

and joked that it looked like a new style of balayage and that it might just catch on.

'At least you could eat it when you got bored with it,' one of the others added.

'OMG, I am in such a mess,' Rachel admitted.

The girls all ended up in a fit of the giggles.

Once the hands-on session had ended, the girls ordered a couple more bottles of the prosecco and sat and chatted excitedly about all the wedding arrangements and their plans for the weeks ahead. There were make-up sessions, hair trials, dress fittings and much more to come.

Maddi had already chosen her dress, and couldn't resist showing Emma, Holly and Bev a picture of it. It was just beautiful, floor-length ivory lace with a prettily embroidered bodice.

Em could picture her looking stunning in it. 'Wow. That will be just perfect on you,' she said.

Holly was swooning at this point and Bev said, 'It's wonderful.'

'Thank you. Ooh, there was something else, yes. The favours.' Maddi became animated. 'Emma, would you be able to make me up some cute mini boxes of your truffles for my wedding favours? I've seen the ones in the hotel in the village and they are *so* pretty. I'd just love that, and I'm sure they'll be popular.'

'Definitely.' 'Absolutely!' the girls called out around her.

'Of course. It would be my pleasure, and we can style all the colours of the box and ribbon ties with your wedding theme.'

'Perfect. I think we have over a hundred guests coming now, so there will be lots to make.'

'That's no problem at all.'

Typical that her new business idea was starting to flourish, just when she might not have a place for it to be any more. But Emma knew she had to stay positive. No one had come to view as yet so she'd carry on as normal for as long as she could.

It was soon nearing the midnight hour.

'We've had such fun. It's just been the best night.' Maddi was giving Emma a big hug.

The others were all putting coats on and gathering their goodie bags. Clutching them like they were the best-ever kid's party bag, full of truffles and dipped straw-berries. Emma had thought to place a couple of business cards in each too – not one to miss a promotional oppor-tunity. She'd also included a mini bag of fudge each as a thank you for their custom.

'Thank you for making it all so wonderful tonight,' Maddi said. 'And thanks for starting all of this off with the most beautifully crafted Easter egg. I'm going to keep it for my wedding day you know, and give it pride of place next to the cake. It was the start of this magical journey. It's been such a special year so far already.'

'Aw, and I'm sure your wedding day will be just as magical too. Laura and Adam and everyone at the hotel will see to that.'

'I can't wait. It's not just about the party you know . . . though all this is such fun. I *so* want to be Mrs Johnson, and what that means for us as a couple, for me and Mark. That's what it's really all about, isn't it? Loving, sharing, caring. Being there for each other.'

'It certainly is.' Emma found she had a lump in her throat.

The white minibus drew up outside once again, ready for the hens' journey back home.

'All the best, Maddi. All the best, girls,' Emma said.

'Thank you. Cheers. To you too.' 'To Chocolate and Prosecco Parties.' 'Woo-hoo!' 'Long live The Chocolate Shop by the Sea!'

And they gave a resounding 'Hip, hip, hooray!' as they made their way out of the door.

The Chocolate Shop team of three cleared up and Em shared out a half-empty bottle of leftover prosecco into three flutes.

'Come on over here, Bev, Holly.' She passed them a glass each. 'Cheers, ladies. Thank you so much for your help tonight – and always. I couldn't do all this without you two beside me.'

'Aw, it went off really well, didn't it,' said Bev.

'Brilliant,' added Holly. 'Chocolate and prosecco is the way to go! And I just love working here.'

And then all was quiet. Holly and Bev left to walk home together, and Emma stood for a few moments on the back step looking out at her twinkly courtyard, and then up at the stars in the sky. It looked perfect out there.

This was her happy place – her Chocolate Shop by the

Sea. The place where her heart was, her home. Would she really have to leave it soon? She crossed both sets of fingers and sent a little wish to the stars.

All she needed was a miracle.

34

Despite the success of the hen party the night before, Emma was still wondering why her daytime trade had dipped so much since the opening of The Rock Shop, or if there was any link at all. Was there any truth in the rumours?

She now had a plan. She was going to send James and his family down to the harbourside undercover today. Anne, the kiosk owner, wouldn't know they were related to Emma or that they had connections with The Chocolate Shop. Mission Rock Shop Rumour was underway.

It was a nice day, the tourists out in force – Wimbledon Ladies' final or not – and Emma's shop and café were *still* only half full. She spotted James, Chloe, Olivia and Lucy walking past mid-afternoon on their mission. The girls gave her huge smiley waves, and Lucy added a thumbs-up. The plan was that they were going to hang around the harbour, listen in on any conversations going on at The Rock Shop Kiosk and then move in themselves to buy some sweets and monitor if any adverse comments were made. Em felt slightly anxious.

Twenty minutes later, down on the harbourside, James and Chloe hadn't yet managed to hear anything untoward from the kiosk, though it wasn't always easy to listen in without risking looking a bit odd or suspicious. Chloe moved right in to browse the shelves at one point, whilst a middle-aged couple were being served, but hadn't heard any mention of The Chocolate Shop. She went back to her family, as though to consult the girls on what sweet options were there.

'Right then, I think we need to make our move,' said James.

'Yes, can we have some sticks of rock?' Lucy said, grinning.

'Or one of those big lollipops?' Olivia said, eyes wide, taking in the huge lurid whirls of pink, blue and yellow – pure sugar and food colourings on sticks.

'Blimey, I'll have to risk their teeth for the sake of the bigger cause,' Chloe sighed.

'Nothing a good toothbrushing session won't sort out later.' James winked. 'Come on then, guys.'

They strolled across, in apparent holidaymaker mode.

'Now then, girls, what would you like?' James asked.

'Hello.' Anne greeted them with a smile, but was it one of those Big Bad Wolf smiles?

'Can I have a rock stick, please?' said Lucy.

'And I'd like a big lollipop . . . please.'

'Okay, which colour rock, darling?' the lady asked.

'The stripy pink one.' Lucy pointed.

James needed to open the conversation a little. 'Lovely place here, cute little harbour.' He smiled. 'Have you been here long?'

'Just a few weeks and yes, it is lovely.'

'Is there anywhere you'd recommend for, say, some coffee and cake?' James angled.

'Oh, I love *chocolate* cake,' added Chloe exaggeratedly.

'Hmm, didn't we spot that chocolate shop up the road?' James looked thoughtful.

'Oh no, I wouldn't go there,' Anne started up animatedly. 'It's up for sale, you know. Heard it's gone downhill lately, standards have fallen, so they are having to sell up.'

James paled, but stayed calm, just nodding. There was an angry twitch in his cheek though.

Lucy bristled, crossed her six-year-old arms, and then she couldn't help herself, despite the warnings not to mention they knew anyone at The Chocolate Shop. '*Well*, that's my Aun—'

'Right then, I'll bear that in mind. Thank you,' James butted in quickly over Lucy, so as not to give the game away. 'That's been . . . most helpful.'

Chloe quickly paid for the sweets, handing a bag each to the girls, trying to keep up the play-acting. Unusually for two little girls who had just been given sweets, they weren't smiling at all.

'*Anyway*, her fudge is way better than yours,' added Lucy dramatically, having been cut short before.

'And we love it there!' piped up Olivia as a grand finale.

The four of them turned and walked away. James and Chloe couldn't help but smile at the girls' protective comments about their aunt. But this wasn't good news for Emma's Chocolate Shop.

Back at The Chocolate Shop, James nervously began to tell Em the whole story. It was when he got to the part about 'standards having fallen' and the shop being 'about to close' that Emma blew.

Right, that was it. *Enough was enough!* Emma felt red rage burn right through her. So, there *was* truth in this talk. NOBODY bad-mouthed her Chocolate Shop without good reason.

'James, can you mind the shop for ten minutes?' Emma's voice was clipped.

'Of course.'

'We'll help too, Auntie Emma.' The girls grinned sweetly. 'Yes, go and tell that naughty lady off,' added Olivia.

Emma set off at a marching pace.

Trouble had brewed and revenge, or at least justice, was about to be poured . . .

She found Anne busy with a customer and bided her time until the gentleman had been served before moving in. She hadn't planned what she wanted to say, but approached with her head held high.

'Hello, Anne, we met a few weeks ago.'

'Yes . . .'

Emma's gaze became stern. 'Well, since then I heard

talk that you'd been saying things about my Chocolate Shop, disparaging things, but I dismissed it as gossip at first. Now I find out that my brother has just been down and you tried to put him off visiting my shop by spreading talk that it's about to close due to falling standards and lack of customers.'

'Well . . .' Anne looked distinctly uncomfortable. 'I saw the "For Sale" sign up.'

'And? Where did you get the falling standards idea from? Make it up, did you?'

'Ah . . . I umm . . .'

'If you must know, the sale is to do with my prick of a landlord, not anything to do with the quality of my chocolate or the way I look after my customers.'

'I'm sorry. I just assumed . . .'

'Well, don't. My old nanna used to say "To Assume makes an ASS OUT OF YOU AND ME" and I'll not have it.' Em darted a warning finger at the kiosk owner. 'I have a business to run, the same as you. All I ask is a bit of support and fair play. And so do my friends here in Warkton, so I'd tread very carefully from now on if I were you.'

A small group of tourists had gathered to listen in. Emma turned around, having said her bit, and spotted them. Also, though Emma couldn't see from here, Sheila was hanging out of her shop door halfway up the street, trying to make out what was going on.

'Okay folks, show's over,' Emma called across to the harbourside gathering. 'Anyone fancying coffee and cake, or some lovely chocolate truffles, feel free to pop up to The Chocolate Shop up the road.'

She left Anne in shock, standing behind her kiosk counter and rather red-faced, but thoroughly deserving to be.

'Hey, you okay? How did that go?' Chloe asked kindly as Emma got back.

'Oh, fine. I don't think we'll get any more talk. Blimey, I feel shattered though.' Em didn't enjoy confrontation – but needs must at times. The emotional impact was exhausting, though. James came over to give her a brotherly hug and Lucy rushed up to say, 'I hope you gave the nasty lady a good telling off.'

'I did.'

Four of the people from the harbour had followed her back and came into the shop.

'We couldn't help but overhear. We haven't been in before, but we thought we'd give you a try.'

'Thank you. I appreciate that.' Emma found herself feeling a little teary.

Chloe spotted it. 'Look, I'll serve these people and you take five minutes out the back if you like.'

'Thank you, Chloe.'

'No worries. Come on girls, you can help me,' added Chloe with a smile.

'Yay. Yippee!' Olivia even took Emma's little notepad with her across to the window table where the group had settled in, ready to write the order down. The girls often played 'chocolate shops' back at home. This time they were getting to do it for *real*.

Emma gathered herself in the back kitchen and popped the kettle on, ready for the likely drinks order as well as her own cup of tea.

'All right, sis?' James came through.

'Yes, thanks for your help with this. Well, I think that's nipped it well and truly in the bud! Blimey, Sheila was right all along. She grabbed me on the way back up the hill, by the way, wanted to know all that had happened. And I'd thought it was just her gossiping again.'

'Don't blame yourself for thinking the best of people, Em. That's no bad trait.'

'No, I suppose not. But it was really starting to damage my business. There's so much on at the moment with it being for sale and everything, it's just so hard. I feel like I'm paddling like mad but going around in circles.'

'You'll find a way through I'm sure, Em. And we're here to help.'

'Thanks, I know that. And your support, as always, is brilliant.'

With that two little helpers appeared. 'So, Auntie Em, we need two chocolate muffins, a fudge cake and some chocolate-dipped strawberries,' announced Lucy. The writing on the chitty recording the drinks said, 'Tee for 2', 'Kofy', and 'joos', which made Emma smile, they were still so young. She'd let Chloe work on their spelling with them later! 'That's excellent work girls, thank you.'

She didn't know where she'd be without her family. When the chips were down, they lifted her back up.

The next day a very apologetic Anne walked into Emma's shop with a huge bouquet of flowers.

'I am so sorry, Emma. I feel dreadful about all the upset I've caused.'

'Oh!' was all a surprised Em could manage at first.

'Please accept these as an apology. I shouldn't have assumed the worst about your shop, and I shouldn't have got carried away telling everyone. It was none of my business.' The woman looked genuinely dismayed.

'Well, yes . . .'

'I've not started off on the right foot at all in this village, have I.'

'Maybe not. But as long as nothing else untoward is said . . .'

'Of course it won't be. I can't believe how stupid and thoughtless I've been.'

'Well then, we may as well move on and make the best of it.' Emma took the flowers from her. 'Thank you for these.'

'Oh, I'll be recommending you for tea and cakes from now on. Have been already.' She gave a small smile. 'And thank you for being so understanding. You don't know how much this means to me.'

'Well, we can all make mistakes.' And boy, didn't she know that.

35

The following week, the dust had settled after the explosive Rock Shop showdown and Emma was concentrating on crafting a special request for a birthday gift – a chocolate shoe for a Jimmy Choo fanatic filled with artisan truffles and ganaches. It was a delicate job getting the stiletto-style shoe just perfect.

Bev was looking after the counter and café for now, whilst Em was busy. The morning seemed to fly by.

At around 11.30, Emma popped through to the shop. 'Everything okay?'

'Yeah, all good thanks. It's been fairly steady this morning, so I've managed just fine. I could do with a hand on a couple of orders that have just come in now, though.'

'Okay, that's no problem. The chocolate shoe is now moulded and is setting and I've just finished all the truffles to fill it, so I'm back in action for the shop again.'

Bev handed her two chits with orders on.

'It's funny, it's a Tuesday and there's been no sign of Mrs C today at all yet,' Bev said.

'Hmm, she's always here like clockwork. I wonder if she's away or anything? Though she never seems to go far nowadays, and she usually lets us know.'

'She might just be a little under the weather.'

'Yeah, possibly. There's a lot of summer colds about at the moment. Still, I might just pop around later if she doesn't show. Take her some chocolate brazils to cheer her up,' Em said.

The two of them got caught up with the orders, Em making milkshakes, coffees, plating up cakes, chocolate croissants and more.

In the early afternoon, Em found herself chatting with an American couple who were on vacation, touring the UK.

'We were on our way up to Scotland and had booked a night in a B&B here. It's so beautiful. The beach, the bay, and all these cute little cottages – so quaint. We just don't have places like this in the US. So much history,' the lady enthused.

'Thank you, and yes, it is very special here. It's like a hidden corner of England.'

'Exactly.' The guy was smiling.

'Yeah, and the chocolate milk is awesome too. How do you make this stuff?'

'Just pure chocolate and whole milk whisked together slowly to warm.'

'It's to die for, honestly. This your own place?'

'Yes, the business is mine.' Emma smiled. She didn't want to go into the technicalities on the property's ownership, or the heartache that was causing right now.

'Just gorgeous.'

'Thank you.'

Emma had to go then and serve at the counter, as Bev was busy in the courtyard area.

It was 4.30 before they knew it. And still no sign of Mrs C. Em was beginning to feel more than just a little concerned and the shop had emptied out.

'Bev, will you be all right here for the last half hour if I just pop across the village and check on Mrs Clark?'

'Yeah, of course.'

'I'll take her a slice of cake and a bag of her favourite brazils. She might need a bit of a pick-me-up if she's feeling out of sorts.'

'No worries.'

Emma was passing The Fisherman's Arms, heading for the pretty but unassuming row of two-up two-down stone cottages where Mrs C lived, when she heard a shout.

'Hey, Em! Wait up.' Nate was there at the back of the car park, placing empty bottles in the recycling bins.

'Hi.'

It was only the second time they'd seen each other since the night of 'the kiss'. Em had thought it was best to keep a low profile as far as Nate was concerned for a while, let her head and heart settle down.

'How's it going?'

I still feel guilty. The Chocolate Shop is up for sale. The Rock Shop's been talking me down. But other than that . . . 'Fine,' was what she actually replied. 'You?' she asked.

It was slightly awkward between them, but actually Em was glad she'd seen Nate by chance. There was evidently no ill will so it would be easier next time and thereafter. In time, they could both move on from that crazy moment.

'Yeah, I'm okay,' Nate replied. 'Keeping my head down here at work and catching some surf when I can. Life ticks on.'

'It certainly does.'

'Well, it's good to see you.'

'You too, Nate. Catch you soon. I've got to go and check on one of my elderly customers. She's usually in every Tuesday, but no show today. I just want to see if she's okay.'

'That's kind.'

'Well, yeah.' She was the kind sort of stupid girl who cheated on her boyfriend with a kiss – argh.

'See ya, then.'

'Yeah. Take care, Nate.'

She walked on and was soon making her way up Mrs C's path, where two cheery pots of colourful pink and purple petunias sat each side of the step. She pressed the doorbell and waited patiently. No answer. She knocked again, and then paused to shout through the letterbox, 'Mrs Clark? Are you there? Are you okay?'

Still no answer. Maybe she had gone out on a day trip

or something. Em was probably just being over-cautious. She could leave the cake and chocolates she'd brought on the doorstep for the old lady's return.

Em was about to go, but she just had an unnerving feeling at the back of her neck that she couldn't pin down. Something didn't seem right. She tried the door. It wasn't locked.

She poked her head around the open doorframe, calling out once more, 'Mrs Clark? It's Emma.'

There was a low murmur but Emma couldn't quite make it out. Then a frail voice, 'Oh . . . thank goodness.'

Em went down the hall and found Mrs Clark there at the bottom of the stairs, one of her legs splayed out at a horrible angle. The old lady's face was so pale.

'Oh, Mrs Clark. What have you done?' Em tried her best to stay calm.

'I tripped . . . Oooh, that hurts . . . Bugger!'

'Okay, okay. Don't try to move. It looks like you may have broken something. I'm going to call an ambulance.'

After calling 999 and giving the address and injury details, Emma found a blanket to cover Mrs C and made her a cup of sugary tea. The old lady was probably in shock and who knows how long she had been stuck like this. Em then sat with her at the bottom of the stairs, holding her hand, and helping her take sips of the warm sweet tea.

'It'll be all right. They'll get you fixed up in no time,' Emma soothed.

Every now and then the elderly lady winced with the pain, but she was trying to be so brave.

'The ambulance will soon be here. Are you warm enough? Can I get you anything else?'

'I'm fine.'

They both smiled as she was *so* apparently *not*.

Em gave the old lady's hand a warm squeeze.

'Silly old bugger, that's me. Lost my footing. Then I couldn't get to the . . . ouch . . . bloody phone, could I.'

'It's okay, easily done. And I'm here. I'll stay with you until the ambulance comes.'

Emma made a very quick call to the shop, asking Bev to close up for her and explaining the basics of the situation, not wanting to give too much detail and alarm Mrs C. She said she'd call Bev back with more news later.

'Oh no, how awful for her. Goodness, send her my love.' Bev was concerned.

'Will do.'

'And that's fine. I'll sort everything out here.'

It was about twenty minutes later when the ambulance arrived. The crew soon sorted out Mrs Clark, carefully placing her on to a stretcher and getting her some much-needed pain relief.

'We're going to take you down to the Cramlington Hospital,' they advised. Then they addressed Emma, 'Are you family?'

'No, a friend.'

'Right, well are you able to let any close family know?'

'I don't think there are any. But I'm happy to come along to the hospital myself. Would you like that, Mrs C?'

The old lady nodded, looking lost, vulnerable.

'It's the patient only in the ambulance, I'm afraid,' one of the paramedics advised.

'That's no problem. I'll follow in my car. You're in good hands, Mrs C.' Em gestured to the ambulance team. 'I'll see you very soon. Can I bring anything for you? A nightdress maybe, some toiletries?' Em had a feeling they'd be keeping her in for a while.

'Ye-es pet, whatever you think. Ooh . . .' The pain was still getting to her, bless.

With that, they wheeled her out to the ambulance and they were soon setting off, with no blue lights but at a determined speed.

Emma got a small bag of essentials together including a nightdress and slippers. It seemed odd going through someone else's belongings, but Mrs C would be glad of them for a hospital stay.

A small crowd of locals had gathered in front of the house having seen the arrival of the ambulance, asking Em for details on what had happened and wishing the old lady well. After she'd had a few friendly words with them, Emma dashed back to The Chocolate Shop to feed Alfie and then let him out for five minutes before putting him back and setting off in her car.

After a forty-minute journey, Emma reached the hospital, where she sat waiting on a plastic chair in A&E for some news. Looking around, it was as if she'd arrived in an alternative world, far removed from everyday life with its bright lights, squeaky grey lino floors, children crying, scents of disinfectant, milky tea from a machine in a polystyrene cup, and the dull tones of hushed talk from her fellows showing boredom, frustration, pain. Then there was suddenly a sense of drama as a more serious case was rushed through.

We all take our health for granted, Em mused, until boom, something goes wrong – a fall, the stealthy grip of an illness surfacing, an accident . . . Emma already knew that all too well.

Then finally some news came via a friendly nurse; Mrs Clark had been X-rayed and had fractured her hip in the fall. She was going to need surgery and a hip replacement. They were taking her down to theatre shortly and it would then be several hours until Emma or anyone else could see her. Em asked if there was any chance she could see her quickly now, pre-surgery. She imagined the old lady would be feeling vulnerable and just a word or two of comfort from a familiar face might help. The nurse agreed and led her through. Mrs C was in a cubicle but had already been moved on to a trolley, ready to go down for surgery. She still looked extremely pale.

'How are you feeling now? Have they settled the pain for you?' Emma asked kindly, taking her hand.

'Yes, pet, they've all been very good.'

'It's your hip that's broken, isn't it?'

'Yes, in two places apparently – I did a good job.' She managed a wry smile.

'You'll be okay. They'll get you all sorted out. Then you'll just have to take it easy for a while.'

The old lady nodded. The nurse reappeared with an orderly who was there to wheel the stretcher.

'We're ready to take you down to theatre now, Mrs Clark.'

Emma gave the old lady's hand a squeeze. 'I'll come back later. I'll check visiting hours and ask them to let me know how you get on in surgery, but it may be the morning before I can see you.'

'I'll be fine, pet, don't you worry. I'll be back marching up that hill to your shop again in no time.'

They both knew that was more than a white lie, but Emma kept up the bravado. 'Yes, you will be.'

The two of them were smiling through their fears, as she was wheeled away.

Emma felt shattered by the time she got back to The Chocolate Shop. She gave Alfie a big hug before letting him out, and then called Bev to update her and to ask if there was any way she could help mind the shop tomorrow morning, so that Em could visit the old lady again.

'I'll see if I can swap shifts with Ali at the surgery. Leave it with me,' Bev said. 'Oh dear, the poor love. I've been wondering how she was. And to think she was stuck at the bottom of the stairs all that time. Thank heavens you went to check.'

'I know. She was very shaken up and in a lot of pain, bless her.'

'It'll take her some time to heal after a major break like that.'

'I know. I can't see them letting her back home any time soon after the operation.'

'Aw, bless . . . Oh, I don't like to alarm you, Em, especially after the day you've had, but the landlord phoned the shop while you were out. Hate to give you bad news, but there's a viewing arranged. A couple are coming to look around the shop and flat tomorrow afternoon at three.'

Emma felt her heart sink. So this was it, it was becoming a reality. It was all about to slip away. It felt like a stopwatch had been set off and was now racing on, with her wonderful shop to be handed over at the finish line.

'Em? You okay?' The line had gone quiet.

'It's not the best news I've had all day. But I don't suppose there's anything I can do to stop it. I can't refuse to show them around.'

'Well, you could insist the estate agent or landlord does it for you.'

'Nah, I may as well bite the bullet, however much it hurts. It'll not change the outcome. Well, you never know, I may be able to spin a few off-putting negatives through the conversation.'

They both laughed.

'Ah, it sucks though, doesn't it,' Emma added.

'I know. I'm sorry, hun. Nothing like being kicked while you're down.'

* * *

Emma spoke with Max later that evening, telling him all about her sod of a day.

'Sorry, Em. That sounds tough on you. Do you think the old lady will be all right?'

'In the long term, yeah, at least I hope so. But it'll take a good while to heal at her age. She looked so frail, bless her, so vulnerable, there at the bottom of the stairs.' She was holding back tears just telling him.

'And the shop too. Is this the first viewing, then?'

'Yeah. I feel sick just thinking about it. Renting is so shit. It feels like mine after all these years, but it never has been. I knew that, but I couldn't stop my heart attaching to it, making it my home, my life.'

'Oh, Em.' Max's voice was gentle. 'Do you want me to come up and see you? I can drive up straight away.'

'Aw, thanks but it's late enough already. I'll probably be off first thing visiting Mrs C in the morning and then dashing back to do this viewing and run the shop. But what about tomorrow . . . after work? I'd love to see you then.' *To feel your arms around me.*

'I'll be there. No worries.'

'Thank you.'

'Then you can tell me all about the buyers' visit and how you spat in their hot chocolates.'

Emma had to laugh – either that or she might end up in tears.

'Okay.'

36

Emma had been to see Mrs Clark that morning, taking a large bag of chocolate brazils to keep her going, as well as some grapes and strawberries. She found the old lady on a side ward of four patients, propped up on white pillows in the hospital bed.

'Hello, Mrs Clark. How are you feeling today? How did the operation go?'

'Oh, Emma, pet. Hello. Yes, the nurse said it seems to have gone fine. Bloody uncomfortable now, though, and I'm a bit afraid to move . . .'

'No wonder. You've been through a lot.'

'Thank you so much for everything yesterday. I really don't know how I'd have managed if you hadn't turned up.'

'Ah, you're welcome. We just need to get you right now, don't we?'

'Bugger of a thing, this. I can't even get to the bathroom by myself yet.' She pointed at some crutches beside the bed. 'Got to work these things out. The nurses are helping me just now. Mind you, can't complain otherwise, the staff here are lovely, if overworked. Dashing around like bees all the time.'

'I'm sure they have plenty to keep them busy. Oh, I heard from Sheila this morning,' Emma said. 'She sends her love and is starting a rota for visits, as everyone's been asking after you in the village.'

'Aw, well that's kind of everyone. Mind, if Sheila calls in, she'll be talking me to sleep or driving me to distraction, one of the two. Never stops, that woman.'

Emma had to smile. 'I think her heart's in the right place.'

'Well yes,' Mrs C conceded. 'They say I'll be in a few days,' she continued, 'but then they're looking at getting me a respite place in a nursing home, just while the hip's healing . . . Had to tell them all about the stairs, and that I've no family to speak of. Have a cousin or two but we're not close and I haven't seen them for years, so I don't think they'll be wanting to take me to the loo or cook my supper back home.' She chuckled.

They chatted for a while, Mrs C asking about the shop, and how things were going for her. Emma didn't mention the impending sale viewing, not wanting to cast a sense of gloom.

'And how's your young man? Max . . . that's it, isn't it? He's very handsome I must say. If I were half my age, well . . .'

Emma felt herself blush.

'He's fine. I'm seeing him later, actually.' She was really looking forward to it. And she didn't have to wait until the weekend now.

'Good for you. You work too hard as it is. A little distraction now and then does no harm at all.' With that, the old lady winked, making Emma blush even more. 'He seems a real nice lad, Emma. I can tell he wants to look after you. Look at all he did last year, helping with the shop conversion, making those window seats for you. My favourite place to sit, that is.'

'Yes.' Max had been a great help last autumn, in the early days of their relationship, when he had helped add the café area to the shop.

'It's not what they say, it's what they do, tells you what they're really like. That's what my old mam used to say. Ah, there's some right charmers out there, but they never last the course.'

'I know.' Em felt a prickle of guilt about Nate, then. But that was just a blip, she reminded herself. Never to happen again.

'Ah yes, he's a keeper, Max.' The old lady's eyes were twinkling.

'I think he might well be.' Emma smiled back.

Emma arrived back at The Chocolate Shop just after twelve-thirty, ready to help with the lunchtime shift. Bev was doing a sterling job, but it was getting busy when Em arrived.

'Are you okay to stay on a while, Bev?' Em asked

hopefully. 'I'm sorry, I expect you'll be wanting to look in on your mum too.'

'Of course. I've swapped to the late-afternoon shift at the surgery. Don't start until four. So I can do a few more hours here if that helps. And I can always drop by to see Mum as I pass.'

'How's she doing?'

'Getting better, slowly but surely.'

'That's good. And thanks, Bev, you're a gem.'

They slipped into their usual roles and the time whizzed on. It was just before three when a middle-aged couple paused outside. They studied the shop front, then stood talking seriously together.

'I think your people are here,' Bev said gesturing to the front window, as Em came by with a tray of coffee and chocolate fudge cake.

'Oh, right.' Em looked up to see them staring in at her. Her heart plummeted, but all she could do was take a deep breath, serve her customers and steel herself ready for the viewing.

The couple walked in. The man had short grey hair, a whiskery beard and glasses and was smiling. The lady was tall and slim, dark – most likely dyed – hair in a bob, cool blue eyes and a tight-set mouth. They looked in their fifties. Emma wondered if they could ever love her shop as much as she did.

'Hello, we're Mr and Mrs Wilton.' They looked slightly awkward, but the gentleman did offer his hand to shake, which Emma took.

'Hi, I'm Emma. Emma Carter. So . . .' *Deep breath.* 'You're here to look around the property?'

'Yes.'

'Well then, let's start with the shop and ground-floor kitchen and move on from there.'

It was a heart-wrenching process, showing these potential owners around room by room. Seeing her life, her home, her work on display for public perusal.

There were lots of 'Ums' and 'Ahs' and 'Rights' – they weren't giving much away. But when the woman said she'd convert the shop back to a lounge area, Em had a sudden urge to slap her. Maybe she should have insisted the estate agent take the viewing after all. But part of her wanted to check out the future owners too; not that she had any control over who Mr Neil sold to, but she wanted to see if they'd at least appreciate the shop's character, her little flat's charm, *and* if they would be the sort to treasure it and look after it in the coming years. Not be ripping it out room by room to make it into an open-plan box for holiday hire, which she suspected was this couple's motivation. It seemed they had no intention of keeping it as a business or indeed living there themselves.

'Oh no, *no*,' the woman said at one point. 'We have a house over at Alnmouth. Lots of space and light there. No, this is just an investment for us; property here in Warkton is rising at such a rate and it would make such a cute *little* holiday hire,' she added coolly, with the under-tones of 'although it was fine for holidaymakers, who would actually want to *live* in a place like this?'

Mrs Wilton actually tutted at the galley-style kitchen upstairs. That was going to get ripped out straight away, apparently. Em hoped Alfie might growl at this point from his bed, but all he did was wag his tail excitedly at seeing new visitors, the traitor.

Hopefully the couple would decide there was too much to alter to make it work as a holiday cottage and go and find somewhere else, Emma mused. She couldn't help but comment that it seemed an awful lot of work they were planning. Twenty minutes later she saw them off at the shop's front door. She watched the couple walk down the hill, give a last glance back at the property, then put their heads together, deep in conversation. Em sighed heavily. She could feel pressure squeezing into a headache across her brow. There were still customers in, but as Emma reached the counter she whispered under her breath, 'Tossers' just loud enough for Bev to hear.

'Yeah, thought as much,' her friend replied with a wry smile. 'Hopefully they won't be interested in putting an offer in.'

'Fingers crossed.'

Well, it was no good moping about, she'd hear one way or another in the next few days. And if not them, then there would be someone else. All she could do was get on with her work, keep saving as much money as she could in the meanwhile in case she had to find somewhere else to rent quickly, and try and keep her options open. She'd looked seriously into her finances and sadly there was no way she'd be able to afford a deposit on a business mortgage to purchase the shop herself, so she had registered on some property rental websites but finding the ideal chocolate shop in the nearby area was proving to be like finding a needle in a haystack. In fact, the only thing she knew was that she was already in the perfect place. And it would be oh-so-hard to leave.

At least Max was coming to see her that evening, the one silver lining in all the dark grey clouds of the past few days. Maybe they could go and relax with a drink down at the pub before supper back at Emma's, and perhaps Holly and Adam might join them there. The lads seemed to get on quite well and it looked like it was going to be a lovely evening. They could sit in the beer garden and watch the boats bobbing in the harbour and just chill out and chat for a while. That sounded a plan. She'd phone Holly straight away.

When Max arrived later, Emma was in the middle of crafting a batch of creme brûlée chocolate cups. The time had flown by, what with the hospital visit this morning and the property viewing, so she was busy trying to stock up her shelves again.

'Hey, beautiful.' Max had come in by the back door and was beaming at her.

'Hi, gorgeous.'

He gave her a big hug in the middle of the shop's kitchen, lifting her up into the air.

It felt so good there in his arms, breathing in his gorgeous aftershave scent. 'Missed you,' she said.

'You too. How was Mrs C?'

'She's had major surgery on her hip last night. Very sore today, bless her. But in pretty good spirits considering.'

'That's good.'

Em was still holding a spatula in one hand, her crème brûlée ingredients ready to mix whilst her chocolate cups were cooling.

'Sorry, this has taken a little longer than anticipated,' Em explained. 'This afternoon was so busy in the shop and I had that bloody viewing to contend with. I'll just need another half hour or so to get these finished.'

'No worries. How did the viewing go, Em? Must have been hard for you.'

'Yeah, it was. It really got to me, more than I thought it would, but what the hell can I do? It's not my shop to keep. *And* this couple have no intention of running it as a shop in any way. Holiday cottage material. Needs gutting. That was the impression I was left with. Argh, it made my blood boil. They didn't seem to like it that much, from all the negative comments the woman kept spouting, so who knows, they may not even get to the offer stage.'

'Oh dear. Sorry, Em.'

'Let's move off the subject. So, tonight: I wondered about walking down to The Fisherman's for a drink before supper. Adam and Holly are keen on coming down too, just for a while. Though Holly won't be there until a bit later – her mum's taken her to Newcastle for a bit of shopping as a reward for all the hard studying she did for her A-level exams. Think she's feeling a bit nervous – it's a long wait for the results.'

'Yeah, I bet. I hated exams. Far happier building with bricks.' His gorgeous grin was back. 'In fact, if you are busy here a while, and Holly's going to be coming a bit later too, I might just give Adam a ring, see if he's finished his shift yet. We might sneak a quick half pint in before you girls join us. If you don't mind, that is?'

'Sure, you may as well. That'll give me a chance to crack on here – I'll just be half an hour.'

Emma was humming away happily when Max left five minutes later, having organised meeting up with Adam. She was looking forward to a lovely evening.

37

Max and Adam were sitting opposite each other on a bench in The Fisherman's Arms beer garden. They'd chatted about work, and Adam admitted how Holly was a bit stressed out lately. 'It's waiting for those exam results,' he commented. 'She's so keen to have done well.'

'Ah, it's understandable.'

'Yeah, I'm trying to support her, but she's the one who had to do all the studying, at the end of the day. And then,' he sounded a bit down, 'if she's got the results she needs she'll be off soon with a whole new world and future ahead of her.'

'She wants to train to be a midwife, doesn't she?'

'Yeah.'

'Good for her.'

'Yeah.' Adam's answer was brief – there seemed to be a lot more unsaid.

Nate was on shift and turned up clearing glasses at

the next table. Max nodded an acknowledgement, Nate did the same back.

'He's still here, then,' Max commented. 'Funny, Emma hasn't mentioned him at all lately. Not seen him about when I've been up here either. He used to call in the shop a bit, but I suppose I've been pretty busy and away a lot.'

Adam looked troubled, then admitted, 'Can't stand the guy.'

'Why, what's he done?' Max wondered if he'd been hitting on Holly. He seemed to like chatting the girls up from behind the bar.

There was an awkward silence.

Adam took a deep breath, 'Look, mate . . . about Nate . . . just be careful okay.'

'What do you mean? Has something been going on?'

'Ah, maybe I shouldn't say any more – but if it was me, I'd appreciate the truth.'

'What are you trying to say, Adam? Come on, mate. Spill.'

'Okay, it might be nothing. But a few weeks ago . . . that night there was a BBQ, when you were away . . . ?'

Max could feel the back of his neck prickling. He had a feeling that he *really* didn't want to hear this, yet he had to know.

'Well, the thing is . . . me and Holly were walking back up from the beach. It was late, everyone else had gone.'

'What? What happened?'

'Okay, we saw him with Emma.'

'And . . . ?'

Adam took a second, then said, 'They were kissing.'

'He was *kissing Emma*? You sure?' Max looked shocked. His hand clenched around his glass as though he might just crush it.

'Look, there may have been a drink too many involved or something. Emma did seem a bit tipsy as we left. And I hate to be the one to tell you, mate. But if it were Holly . . . well, I'd want to know.'

Adam's voice was fading in Max's head. *The bastard. The sodding bastard.*

Max stood up. Nate was still there, clearing tables. Max strode across, picked him up by the scruff of his T-shirt and raised him into the air, so they were eye to eye. Nate was dangling with several pint glasses precariously balanced in one hand. 'You little piece of scum! You leave Emma alone.' The words were forceful.

Nate stayed silent at first. He had no doubt that he deserved this. He didn't know how to begin to explain his actions with Emma. All he managed was a feeble 'Sorry mate', which came out slightly strangled as he was held in Max's grip. He waited for the punch that would inevitably follow.

Max's fists tingled, but there was a family sitting out in the garden just a few metres away from them. He placed the little piece of shit back on the ground. Jesus, any man who'd take advantage of their dead brother's girlfriend wasn't worth fighting with anyway – though it might well have given Max a great deal of satisfaction to punch his lights out.

But what hurt more . . . That massive sense of disappointment he felt wasn't with Nate, it was with Emma. And it made Max feel sick.

Max walked back over to Adam. 'Sorry, mate, but I've got to go.'

'Yeah, understood. No worries. Just shout if you need anything, okay.'

But Max was already away. The ring that was safely stowed in the jeweller's box in his pocket now felt as if it was burning a hole in his palm.

Emma looked up out of the kitchen window to see Max striding back across the courtyard. He'd only been gone about twenty minutes and she'd thought she was meeting him down there. He looked stiff, angry almost. Emma smiled. He didn't smile back.

He walked right in. Emma was washing up, having just finished the chocolates.

'Max?' There was definitely something up.

Two heartbeats of silence.

And then she knew, even before he spoke.

'I can't believe it, Em. Is it true? Ah shit, it has to be true. Adam wouldn't make something like this up.'

'What is it, Max?' She knew, but was clinging onto one last shred of hope, that there was some other reason for his anger, some other annoyance they could get back from.

'Come on, Em. Don't play the innocent. Your lying just makes it even worse. Holly and Adam *saw* you.'

Emma just nodded and bit her lip as the tears crammed her eyes. 'Yes, it's true. I did kiss Nathan. But—'

'Fuck.' He seemed to double up in pain.

'Max, please. It was just a silly, crazy moment. I think he reminded me so much of Luke . . . I'm sorry. So sorry. It didn't mean anything.'

'I thought this, *us* . . . I thought what we had was special. I thought it was love, Em. I was ready to give you everything.' He paused.

'It *is* special. I do love you, Max.'

'Well, you've got a funny way of showing it. This isn't love.'

'I had a couple of drinks, Max. I regretted it straight away. It was a huge mistake.'

'That's one thing you've got right, Em. *This* is one huge mistake.'

'Max, I'm sorry.'

The anger subsided, but instead he looked at her blankly. He appeared almost numb.

'Sorry isn't enough, is it?' She knew she had pressed the self-destruct button on their relationship.

'No, Em. I can't just ignore this.'

With that he turned and walked out of the door.

And she knew that whatever she said wouldn't bring him back.

38

There was nothing else for it than to have a good old cry. It wasn't often that Emma caved in to tears, but after the couple of days she'd just had, and now this . . . losing Max over some silly moment of madness that was all her own bloody fault.

She couldn't blame him. After all, how would she have felt seeing him kiss Siobhan now, his ex-girlfriend who he'd lived with for over two years, or hearing about that? It would devastate her. It was the loss of trust, that was what shattered everything.

Emma had gone upstairs after Max had walked out, intending to make a cup of tea, and found herself slumped on the galley kitchen floor, hugging Alfie, with big snotty tears running down her face.

She knew she could ring Bev, or Holly, for a chat – oh my, Holly and Adam had seen it all – and yes, she'd have to confess to Bev what had happened. But right now, all she wanted to do was to curl up into a ball. It was like a physical pain in her gut. Had she really lost Max forever?

He was wrong though, it *was* love. She'd just made a mistake. One mistake. She was surer of that than she was of anything. She'd ring him, explain. Not tonight. She knew he was feeling too raw, let down. But tomorrow. She'd have to try and get through to him. She felt marginally better with that thought.

She forced herself to get up off the floor and, with her mind still spinning, went for a walk with Alfie. She headed away from the village on a path that led through country fields, hoping not to bump into anyone she knew. Her eyes were still red and swollen. Walking helped her lose herself, even amongst the heartache, on a path that led through fields of golden barley swaying in a soft summer evening breeze. The countryside was beautiful where it ran down to the coast and Alfie happily scampered on, stopping here and there to sniff something of interest.

Dusk was settling with soft-pink and deep-grey hues as she got back home to The Chocolate Shop. She wondered if that couple would put in a bid, if she might get the call tomorrow, along with her one month's notice. No point worrying until it happened, she told herself, giving Alfie a gentle stroke before taking off his lead.

There were chocolates to make, brownies to bake, but she just felt totally shattered, spent. The last few weeks had been a very bumpy emotional rollercoaster. She gave in to her weariness and decided she'd set the alarm for early tomorrow and start afresh. She had an early night after forcing herself to eat a couple of cheese crackers, which was all she could stomach. And she lay thinking of Max, who was no doubt feeling rotten in his own bed forty miles away. She'd do anything to put things right between them. She had to let him know that. She couldn't lose another love, not this way.

39

The next morning, after five phone calls that went straight to answerphone, two voice messages and three unanswered texts, Em decided to give Max a break. If he wasn't ready to talk, then fair enough. She knew when to leave alone. He might just need a little time.

She settled down to work in the kitchen, getting herself organised before opening time. The brownies were made, including some new caramel swirl ones, and she was about to create a batch of Eton Mess truffles, as well as her Pimm's specials. Summer was in full flight here in Warkton, and Emma liked to reflect that in her chocolate flavours. Mind you, the weather wasn't actually playing ball today with it being overcast and drizzly, but hey ho. And every cloud had a silver lining, as it would probably mean the tourists would be looking for a nice little cosy café to spend some time in, and she'd be busy. She needed to keep busy.

Just before ten there was a call; Emma felt a lift of hope until she saw it was from Pete, Bev's husband.

'Hello?'

'Hi Emma, I've been chatting with the village committee and, I'm not sure if you've already heard, but we've got plans to put on a Summer Food Festival over the August Bank Holiday here in Warkton. A kind of celebration and a chance to showcase our local food and drink. I already have The Rock Shop and The Fisherman's Arms interested as well as The Smokery. And The Hepple Gin Company are keen to get involved too. What do you think, might it work for you? Would you consider taking a stall?'

'Wow I'm flattered, it sounds a great idea, and good for business. I might have to be careful if it's a hot day, mind, with chocolates, but I'll have a think about what will work best. The fudge would be fine. Hmm, I could maybe get a freezer rigged up so I could do some homemade chocolate ice cream in cones.' She'd been experimenting lately and was refining the perfect chocolate chunk ice cream. It might be the ideal time to showcase it.

'Mmm, I'm drooling already. Enough.'

'Hah, you're as bad as your wife.'

'We can't help being chocoholics. But that's great that you might want to be involved. We'd love you to be there. So, we're having a meeting in a few days' time to firm up plans, drum up some more publicity ideas and engage a few more stallholders, but I think the idea's proving popular already.'

'It's a brilliant idea. Summertime, lovely food, ice creams, and gin and tonics. What's not to like?'

'Exactly.'

'See you at the meeting then, it's next Thursday at the village hall, 7.30.'

'Okay, I'll be there.'

A village event was always nice to look forward to. Emma loved the sense of community here and if they put their minds to something in Warkton-by-the-Sea, everyone seemed keen to get involved to make sure it was done well.

A nagging thought came to mind: would she still be here in the village then? She hoped so. August Bank Holiday was just over five weeks away and Mr Neil had to give her a month's notice and so far, since the viewing, there had been no call from him or the estate agents – and no news was good news on that front as far as she was concerned.

But, on the Max front, no news was proving bloody awful. She'd tried to call him so many times since he'd walked out and he never answered his phone, never responded to her texts. He might just be busy at work, or not quite ready to talk as yet, she told herself, but her heart felt as if it was unravelling all over again.

After work she took Alfie out for a brisk walk down to the beach, then tried Max on his mobile once more – straight to answerphone. She held back from leaving a message this time. He would see that she had called. She then jumped in the car to get down to the hospital to visit Mrs Clark before visiting hours finished. The village 'rota' meant that Sheila had popped down through the day, and a neighbour was going to visit tomorrow.

Fifty minutes later, Emma was sitting on an orange plastic chair beside the old lady's hospital bed. The light was bright fluorescent in the ward, but apart from the chair everything else was a cool grey, the floor, the walls. Clean and clinical.

'How are you feeling today, Mrs C?'

'Just fine, pet. Other than being a bit stiff when I walk on it, I'm getting on grand. Being looked after well.' She lowered her voice, 'Shame about the food, but other than that I cannot grumble.'

'Oh . . . Well, is there anything I can bring in you might fancy?'

'Another bag of those chocolate brazils might be nice. I'm nearly through the last lot.'

'Of course.'

They chatted about the Festival event, Mrs C remembering fetes of old, with her dancing around the maypole as a little girl. Emma began to feel tired as she tried to keep the conversation going but then Mrs C paused.

'Come on now, Emma, I can see you're not yourself. What's troubling you, pet?' The old lady placed a gentle hand over hers, where it rested on the bedcovers.

'Oh, it's nothing. I'm just a bit tired, that's all. I've come to cheer you up, not spread my own doom and gloom.'

'A problem shared . . .' The old lady smiled. 'Look, I might be a crotchety old thing, but I have lived a bit. I've come across most things in life.'

'Oh, Mrs C of course you're not that.' Maybe it would help to share her troubles. 'I think Max has left me for good.' Em let out a sigh. 'And on top of that I've had a potential purchaser viewing The Chocolate Shop. Other than that, everything's hunky-dory.'

'Ah, I see. Life's full of ups and downs, pet. Let's start with your Max, then. What's happened to change things so suddenly? Last time I saw you together you looked all loved-up.'

Emma started on the whole sorry tale. Mrs C already knew about Luke and her past and she felt guilty and horrid when she got to the part about the kiss.

'I don't know how I can put it right, Mrs C. I wish I could go back and change what happened, but I can't.'

'You're right, you can't go back, pet, and we all do stupid things at times. What's done is done. There's a saying my old mam used to say, "All mistakes are lessons to be learned." You just need to find a way forward, Emma.'

'I know, and I've tried. I've said sorry and promised to never to do anything like that again, but Max just looked so damned hurt. Now he's not even taking my calls. I'm scared, Mrs C. I really love him and I've messed up big time.'

'Oh my. There, there, pet.' The old lady gave her hand a rub. 'Maybe he just needs a little time. It might be his pride that's been knocked more than anything.'

'I hope it's as simple as that.'

'And then this other stuff with the shop. Is there no way at all you can afford to take it on yourself, Emma?'

'I've looked at so many options, but no, there's no way. I can't raise enough capital as a deposit to start with, though the bank would give me a business mortgage if I could. I've been saving like mad but I'm still so far off. Oh, Mrs C, it'll break my heart to leave, but I suppose I'll have to and start over somewhere else.'

'Now that's a shame. You're a part of the village. Maybe we can try and help you find somewhere else in Warkton you could use?'

'I've thought of that too, but I need a working kitchen, space for a café, a shop to be all shelved out, and now I have the outside courtyard just right too. It'd cost so much to convert somewhere else, even if I could rent, or buy another place.' It all felt very out of reach. Like fate was about to crush everything she had achieved, and stamp on her dreams. She gathered herself. 'I'm sorry, Mrs C, I shouldn't be moaning on like this.'

'I asked you to tell me about it, remember? Anyway, it's been good to talk about something other than me and my hip. I've had Sheila here, driving me to distraction with a load of drivel about parking fees at the hospital, dog fouling in the village and Mrs Jenkins going out on a date with Mr Jones for coffee. Well why on earth shouldn't they? They're both single – and if they are over eighty, so what? Good on 'em, I say. Why the devil do I need to know about all that! I was like a sitting duck here for her barrage of tales and gossip. It's enough to send a bugger crazy.'

Emma's mouth creased into a smile. She could imagine

the pair of them bantering. It was a real love–hate relationship but everyone knew that, underneath it all, they
got along fine. The sparring was part of the fun.

Visiting time was coming to a close, the clock on the
wall showing 7.00.

'I'm going to have to go soon, Mrs C.'

'Yes, thanks for coming to see me, pet. And remember,
we all fall down sometimes, Emma, whether it's the stairs
or making a mistake, but then we get up again. It's what
you do next that matters.'

'Thank you.' She gave her elderly friend a kiss on the
cheek. 'You get well and take care. I'll be back again very
soon with those chocolate brazils, I promise.'

'You'd better.' The old lady grinned.

And Emma left with a wave, a tear in her eye, and a
glimmer of hope in her heart.

Back at the flat later that evening, there was a knock on
the courtyard door. Emma's heart surged. She raced
downstairs, to find Bev there on the step.

'Oh . . .'

'Don't look so happy to see me.' Her friend's tone was
ironic.

'I'm sorry. I just thought it might be . . .'

'Max. I know. I heard all about it from Holly. Why
didn't you ring me, hun?'

'Well, last night I was in a heap, and today I've just
kept myself busy. I've not long got back from the hospital
too. Anyway, come on in.'

'I have a bottle of wine, thought you might need it. And of course, I'll happily share it with you – just to keep you company, of course.' She lifted up the bottle of Pinot Grigio in her hand.

'Thank you.'

'It's chilled.'

'Even better.'

'So, tell me all about it then. *And*, what the hell has been happening with Nate?'

Emma groaned, then said, 'Let's get this wine open and find a cosy seat in my lounge first.'

'Before we go on upstairs, can I have a few of those Eton Mess truffles?' Bev smiled hopefully.

'Of course, go help yourself.'

Tucked up on the couch, comfy cushions behind them and Alfie snuggled in between, the full story came out.

'So there was nothing else going on with Nate, then? Just that one kiss?'

'Yes, I didn't – and don't – even fancy him. I just don't quite know how it ever got to that point. Maybe memories flooding back, how he has a look of Luke . . . it all kind of blended together and I was missing Luke so much that night. I'd had a few drinks, yeah, but I know that's no excuse. I knew what I was doing, Bev. I could have stopped it.'

'Bloody hell, and now this. Did Max fly off the handle when he found out?'

'He wasn't aggressive as such, he just seemed so hurt.

Like I'd betrayed him. And now I can't get hold of him. He's not answering any of my calls.'

'Oh dear. Holly's mortified that Adam told him. And that it's all blown up into this.'

'Hey, it's not Adam's fault. I was the one who did wrong. I didn't even realise the pair of them had been there, that they had seen. It's my own stupid bloody fault.' Em took a big swig of wine.

Bev munched thoughtfully on a truffle.

'Life, hey?' Emma said.

'It's sometimes a bitch and sometimes beautiful,' Bev stated.

'Cheers to that.'

And they clinked glasses.

40

'Hey, Em . . .' Adam caught up with Emma the next morning in the car park of The Seaview Hotel, where she'd just dropped off her delivery of turndown chocolates. 'Are you okay?'

'Ah, so, so.'

'Holly told me last night that you guys have split up.' He looked awkward.

'Yeah.'

'Oh man. Look, I'm so sorry I said anything, Em. I didn't mean to stir up any trouble. I just wanted to warn Max, as a mate, for him to keep an eye out on Nate; that was all. I never imagined he'd up and leave.'

'I know, nor did I. But I can't blame him. What I did was sooo stupid.'

'Bloody hell, I wish we hadn't seen anything that night.'

'Hey, it's not your fault. It was me and Nate that did wrong.'

'Yeah, but maybe I shouldn't have mentioned it. I've just caused a heap of trouble.'

'It's just one of those things, Adam. I don't blame you or Holly. I got myself into this mess.'

'We just feel terrible about it.'

'Hey, don't beat yourselves up . . . it's okay.'

It wasn't really; the situation was a bloody mess, but it wasn't Adam's fault.

'But it's not, is it? You two are great together. And now you're apart. I can't help thinking if I had just kept my bloody mouth shut . . .'

'It's all right. There's no hard feelings, Adam. If me and Max can work it out, well, that's up to us.'

'Do you think you might?' His face brightened.

'I really hope so – but *honestly*, I don't know. I let him down, Adam. Let down all of you.'

'I'm so sorry, Em. But if there's anything me and Holly can do, or if you just want to come out with us for some company, anything, just say.'

She didn't really fancy being the third wheel but appreciated the gesture. 'Will do, and thanks.'

Adam sighed. 'Ah, it's just such a shame.'

'I know.'

'You take care of yourself, Em.'

'I'll try.'

She looked so sad there, trying *so* hard not to. Adam felt a lump form in his throat. 'Ach, come here.' He gave her a friendly hug. 'I really hope you two can find a way back.'

'Me too. Well, I'd better go,' she said, trying hard to hold it together.

It was a full week later when Max finally answered his phone.

'Oh Max . . .' The relief was immense. But hearing his voice at last took Em by surprise and she didn't quite know how to phrase her words.

'Emma, please, I can't do this any more. Can you just leave me alone?'

Shit. That was *not* the response she had hoped for. It felt like she had been winded.

'Max, do I at least get the chance to explain? Can I come down and see you?' This was all too hard over the phone.

'I'm sorry, Em.' His tone was resolute. 'You kissing Nate . . . it's all I've been thinking about and it's killing me.'

'It didn't mean anything Max. It was just a stupid, crazy mistake. I'm so sorry.'

'Look, I believe you're sorry. But it just goes to show that what we have isn't right.'

'You're wrong, Max. We just need to move on. I swear I'll never do anything like that again. I hate that I've hurt you.'

'Okay, so maybe there's nothing going on now with you and Nate, and maybe in some mixed-up way you were missing Luke, but that still doesn't mean things are right for us.' He paused before starting again, 'Maybe I'll never match up to Luke or be enough for you, Em. Don't get me wrong, it's not that I want you to forget Luke, it's not that at all. That wouldn't be fair. He was a huge part of your life. I didn't mind you talking about him to me, that you kept his picture. That was okay. I understood that. But what I do need is for you to love me for me.'

'Oh Max . . .' How could she show him she did?

'This isn't right, Em. Not for the long term. The big stuff. Even though I'd hoped it might be.' He sounded so sad, hurt.

And his words struck a chord. Was she really over Luke, would she ever be? Did she love Max enough to give him her heart – all of it? She so wanted to make Max happy, but could she really? Would she just keep on hurting him?

Em stayed quiet for a few seconds. A few seconds too long.

'So *please*, don't call back Em. It's best we make a clean break of this.'

Best for who? Em's voice was crying out silently in her head. She felt crushed. Yet she had to respect his words, his feelings. She was the one who had messed up.

Was this it? No second chances?

'Take care, Em.' His words sounded so final.

'You too,' was all she could whisper, as her heart began to shatter all over again.

Life rolled on as it has a habit of doing. The sun still rose, the birds still sang, there were customers to serve and chocolates to make. But for Emma everything felt a struggle, like she'd lost her way.

When she had another property viewing, she led them around, showed them her life, her home, her business, somehow resigned to her fate. She knew it wouldn't be long before the right person came along, the one who wanted to make their future there in The Chocolate Shop, who'd move in and make a business out of it. This chap was on his own, looking to live upstairs and make an art gallery to showcase his and other local artists' work. He seemed pleasant enough and it sounded like it could work and be a positive thing for the village. It wasn't his fault the bloody shop was up for sale. Emma stayed coolly polite, answering his questions, whilst ripping off a few more shards of her heart.

Still, a few days later, there had been no telephone call or letter from the landlord to serve her notice and a week on, Emma heard from Sheila, as she was buying her milk and bread, that the chap had decided to go for a property in the next village – it suited him better as there was more space for a studio in an outdoor barn apparently. That woman seemed to find out everything, being the hub of local news and gossip. Oh well, Emma could breathe a sigh of relief with regards to the shop – for a short while at least.

So, she'd been given a reprieve. But her world still felt precarious. She'd left Max alone as asked, but he kept popping up in her thoughts all the time. Was he feeling as miserable as she was, she couldn't help wondering, or was he moving on?

41

A-level results day dawned, bright and sunny. By late morning, having heard no news, Emma was feeling slightly nervous for Holly, knowing her assistant's hopes and dreams rested so much on this.

Holly had told her she was heading off to the Sixth Form College that morning, along with her best friend Jess, to open the crucial white envelope. Emma wondered about texting her – she'd already sent a 'best of luck' message first thing – but she didn't want to pressure any further in case the results weren't quite what Holly had hoped for. She just hoped that it was lovely news and she was busy celebrating with her family and friends just now.

Emma was serving in the courtyard after lunchtime when a text finally came through from Holly. 'Can you meet up after work at The Fisherman's for my news?'

It seemed rather cryptic and sounded somewhat

downbeat. Emma hoped to goodness the invitation wasn't to help drown her assistant's sorrows.

'Yes of course. Hope it's good news for you. x' she messaged back.

'I'd rather tell you in person. x' came the answer.

So, it seemed she'd just have to wait to find out.

Emma set off after closing the shop. Adam had just finished work too and was already there at the bar with a couple of their friends from the village, but no one seemed to know how Holly had got on – or at least they weren't letting on that they did.

Just as Emma was ordering a half-cider for herself from Danny, the door of the bar swung open and there was Holly, looking rather dejected.

On no, bless her. Emma was already formulating her consolation talk about re-taking the exams and not giving up just yet and that sometimes your dreams just took a little longer to realise, when Holly's face switched to a huge beam. 'I did it! I got the grades I need. I'm in!'

A cheer went up throughout the pub. Shouts of 'Ah brilliant', 'Congratulations, Holly', and 'Fab – let's get the prosecco in!' rang out.

Emma looked around at all the happy faces at the bar. Yet, out of the corner of her eye, she saw Adam sigh and his brow crease, before he forced a smile and walked across to Holly to wrap her up in a big hug. 'Well done, Holly. That's really great.'

'Yeah, I'm so chuffed. I still can't believe it. Whoop!'

Emma went across then and gave her an affectionate squeeze. 'That's just wonderful, Hols. I'm so proud of you.'

'Thanks, Em. Aw, I'm going to miss you and The Chocolate Shop like crazy though.'

'We're all going to miss you too,' Emma replied.

Adam's smile seemed to drop away at her words.

'Well, come on, let's celebrate!' Em lifted the tone. 'What are you having, Hols?'

'I'll get these,' Adam interjected. 'It must be prosecco time, hey Hols? I'll get a bottle in.'

'Oh yes. Definitely time for bubbles. Thank you so much,' Holly said, grinning away.

And the celebrations began.

Later on, when the joyous hubbub had died down and Emma was putting her jacket on ready to go, a slightly tipsy Holly caught up with her at the bar. 'Hey Em, I'll come back and see you all the time. And if you're ever busy, I'll still come in and help. Like in the Christmas holidays.'

'Of course. You'll always be welcome, Holly. To help, or to just sit and chat over a hot chocolate telling me all about your student adventures.'

'Eeh, I'm nervous now.' Holly suddenly looked serious. 'It'll be a bit of a change from chocolates to babies.'

'It will indeed, but you'll be fine. Change is always a bit scary. But you go chase your dreams and give it your best shot. It'll work out great for you, I'm sure.'

'It'll be hard leaving the village,' her young assistant admitted, biting her lip.

'At first, yes. But you'll soon find your feet.' Emma tried to keep the conversation positive, knowing she might well have to do the same thing herself soon, start afresh away from the village if there was no shop left for her, but she didn't let herself dwell on that. '*And*, we'll still all be here when you come back. Students are always on holiday, as far as I can recall.'

'Hah, yes.' Holly rallied.

Emma saw that Adam was occupied, chatting away with some mates at the far end of the bar. 'So how are things with you and Adam? Did you manage to talk yet?'

'Yeah. I think we'll be okay. I told him I'll come home for weekends whenever I can. It's only an hour away, it's not like I'm going to Timbuktu.'

'Well, I'm sure it will all work out fine for you two. Just keep talking. Keep communicating.'

'We will.' A sunny smile broke out across Holly's face. 'Thanks, Em.'

'And hey, you've done brilliantly! Well done again, Holly.'

They ended the evening with a big hug.

There was another viewing of The Chocolate Shop booked for the mid-week before the Warkton Food Festival week-end. As the appointment time loomed that Wednesday, Emma felt a sense of trepidation . . . and inevitability. All it needed was that one person who felt the shop was just right for them and it would all be taken from her.

Five minutes before the due time, two lads who looked

in their late twenties appeared in the shop. The taller of the two, with dark slightly scruffy hair, came up to the counter. 'Hi, we're here to view the shop and the flat above. I'm Ben, by the way, and this is my work partner, Tom.' Ben offered his hand to shake. Tom followed suit.

'Okay, hi. I'm Emma. Nice to meet you both.' She couldn't help but warm to their friendly manner, despite the circumstances. 'Shall we start with the shop area, then, seeing as we are already here?'

'Yep.'

'Great.'

'Holly, if you can just keep an eye on the café for me for a while, that'd be great.'

'No problem, Em.' Holly smiled at the three of them. Her curiosity was evidently piqued. Why were two youngish guys interested in the shop?

'So,' Emma started, 'this is the main café and shop area. Obviously, it's running as a chocolate shop here now. So . . . what are your plans for the property?'

'Well, we have a micro-brewery over at Rothbury. The Bear's Cave.'

'Ah, yes. I've heard of that. My parents live that way.'

'Well, we're looking to expand and somewhere on the coast would be ideal.'

'Ah, okay.'

'Tom'll probably live here and keep an eye on this venture, while I continue to run the main place back inland.'

'Right.'

Emma didn't think The Fisherman's Arms would be too pleased if a new micro-brewery hit the village, but she'd heard that small local breweries, serving their own real ale, were proving very popular. Maybe there'd be room for both. And this pair obviously had a good business already if they were able to expand. It might not be such a bad thing to have in the village – but not at the expense of The Chocolate Shop and her home, she mused.

She gave them the full tour and they seemed very positive about the property, chatting to each other along the way. The downstairs kitchen would apparently be great for the fermentation tanks and brewing equipment, being a good size. Outside in the yard they'd need to make a storage shed for the casks and bottles, but they'd keep a section as a beer garden and upstairs was ideal for Tom's living quarters. It all seemed to be coming together nicely for them. The more positive they got, the more negative Emma began to feel. This was like a slow torture, having to show them around.

Alfie got made a fuss of upstairs in the galley kitchen, the canine traitor loving the attention as per usual, tail wagging happily in greeting.

There was then a hushed discussion between the lads about finances and offer prices, which Emma didn't quite catch as they lingered on the landing and she politely headed on down the stairs, the men following shortly afterwards.

'That's great,' said Ben. 'Thanks for showing us around.'
'Cheers,' added Tom.

'So, what's happening with you and your business?' Ben asked in a friendly tone. Maybe they weren't aware of her situation.

'Well, unfortunately I just rent the place. And I'm sadly not in the market to buy, much as I'd have liked to,' Emma admitted. 'So, when the new owner comes in, I'm out.'

'Ah sorry, that sucks. I feel a bit crap now,' said Ben. 'So it's not you we're dealing with?'

'Nope, but hey, it's not your fault. It's business, I realise that.' Emma sounded matter-of-fact, despite her heart breaking inside.

'Yeah, we've had our share of ups and downs too with setting up the brewery,' Tom added.

'Well, thanks so much for showing us around,' said Ben. 'Hope it all works out for you too.'

'Thank you.'

They shook hands again before the lads left the shop. Emma stood frozen in the middle of the café, watching them go. She realised it was a sense of dread and foreboding that kept her fixed there.

She turned around; Holly was stood watching her with a sad look on her face.

'Oh God, Holly. I think this might be it.'

'No . . . it can't be.' Her assistant had gone ashen. 'It can't be.'

Was this the end for The Chocolate Shop by the Sea?

42

Emma had been waiting for the call from either her landlord or the estate agent to say an offer had been made on the shop, but three days had passed now and still no news. Honestly, it was excruciating! It was the Saturday of the August Bank Holiday weekend, just after opening time. Emma looked up from loading the refrigerated counter with some just-made goodies, to see Nate stood there. They'd both been keeping a low profile since 'The Kiss' and its subsequent fallout. She still felt distinctly uncomfortable.

'Hi . . . Is it okay to have a word?' He looked serious.

They hadn't seen much of each other at all lately, both just getting on with their lives, giving each other some space and keeping it to a polite wave or brief 'hello' if they crossed paths. There must be some reason behind him coming in.

Emma looked across at Bev who was in with her. 'You okay to keep an eye on things at the mo?'

'Of course.' She gave Emma a warning smile that said *be careful*.

'Let's go out into the courtyard,' Em suggested. She knew there were no customers there as yet and it would give them a little privacy to talk. 'Can I get you a coffee or anything?'

'No, I'm fine, thanks. I won't keep you long. I know you'll be busy soon.'

They went out into the morning sunlight and sat down at the little white wrought-iron table for two – Emma's favourite spot in the garden.

'So . . . ?' Emma prompted.

'I just wanted to tell you that I'll be leaving Warkton at the end of the week.'

'Oh, okay.' She hadn't imagined him staying there in the village a long time, to be fair. But it was still quite a sudden decision.

'The work at the pub is coming to an end soon anyhow, summer's moving on and I just feel ready to go. Time for pastures new and some fresh adventures.' He smiled.

'Oh.' She was trying to make sense of her emotions. It would make life easier in some ways, yet she found herself feeling sad too. 'Crikey, well then, best of luck with everything.'

'Thanks.' He paused. 'Em, look, what I really came to say as well is that I'm sorry . . . That kiss was really stupid, inappropriate. And I hope I haven't messed things up for you and Max. Though from what I've heard from Holly lately, maybe I have. I wouldn't have wanted that.

And despite the fact he can't stand me – and in the circumstances I can't blame him – he does seem a decent bloke.'

'Yeah,' Em sighed. She watched a robin settle on the edge of one of her flower pots, thoughts of Luke, and then Max flooding her mind.

'I hope you two can patch it up.'

'Me too.'

'Anyway, it shouldn't have happened and I'm sorry. I still feel so terrible about it, like I've been disloyal to Luke. Not been much of a brother to him, have I? He'd have wanted me to look after you.' He looked downbeat.

'Hey, it takes two you know. It wasn't just your fault. And yeah, I keep thinking of it too, how we should never have let it get to that. I don't think Luke would have been too pleased with either of us.'

'Ah, it was just a crazy moment. Maybe we were both just missing him,' Nate tried to find an explanation. 'Yeah, he'll have thought we made a right balls-up of things, if he somehow could see, but you know . . . I think he might have forgiven us by now. I know it would *never* have happened if he'd still been alive. Yeah, I reckon he'd have called me an arse and given me a swift brotherly punch, but then he'd have let it go. He didn't hold a grudge for long, Luke.'

Emma smiled. 'No, he didn't.'

'And . . .' Nate continued, his tone earnest, 'I think you're wrong, Em.'

'How?'

'What you've achieved here . . .' He looked around him. 'The Chocolate Shop. How you've made a life, a good business. I think Luke would have been really proud of you.'

Emma brushed a tear from the corner of her eye. 'Aw, thank you. That's lovely of you to say so.'

'I hope we can still be mates from here on, Em. Please don't let what happened spoil that . . .'

'Of course I won't.' She patted his shoulder in a friendly gesture. It felt like a weight had been lifted. 'Thank you for coming to speak with me, Nate. All this has been troubling me so much too. *So*, pastures new then . . . and what are your plans for the future?' Em switched the conversation.

'Well, it's been great here. Warkton's a cool place. But you know me, don't like to let the grass grow under my feet. I was thinking of maybe organising a ski season in Europe over the winter months.'

'Good for you.'

'And I'm gonna spend a bit more time with the parents first.'

'That's good. They'll be pleased. They really missed you when you were abroad all that time.'

'I know. I'll go back down and stay with them for a while in Harrogate, while I'm sorting out the ski stuff and applying for posts.'

'How are they? I hope they are both fine just now? I haven't had a chance to call for a while.' Life had been pretty hectic lately.

'Yeah, they're doing good. In fact, Dad's even threatening to come out to the Alps once I get a place sorted and try his hand at skiing. Not the best idea, first time skiing in your late sixties, especially with Dad's bad back. In fact, I think Barney might be a better candidate on skis than my dad.' Barney was the family's arthritic, elderly labrador.

Emma laughed.

'Yeah, I might tell them to wait until next spring and come and do some hiking instead. More their thing. I can see A&E written all over it, otherwise.'

'That sounds a good plan. Send them my love won't you, and once this Bank Holiday weekend's over and the schools go back, I'll arrange to pop down and see them some time.'

'Well, I'd better get on. I'm sure you've got lots to do here, and I might just try and fit in a surf before I start my lunch shift at the pub.' He stood up.

Emma stood too. 'Nate?'

'Yeah?'

'I think Luke would be proud of you too.'

'You think?' He sounded so unsure then, so young.

'Yeah, it's taken guts to come and say this today, to start. And you've been brave enough to go and follow your dreams, to go and experience the world.'

'Cheers.' He seemed relieved.

'Take care, Nate. Pop in and see me before you go, yeah?'

'Of course. You take care too.'

'And stay in touch.'

'Yep. Good luck with everything here, Em. Hope it all works out.'

'Thanks.'

They shared a hug. A brotherly-sisterly lovely hug. And the world felt like it had 'righted' itself a little.

43

Bank Holiday Sunday, 7.30 a.m. It was Festival day and it was all hands on deck. By some miracle, the sun was shining as the bunting was going up. Pete and the team, using the cherry picker they'd borrowed from a local farmer, were stringing the WI's handmade flags in loops between the old-fashioned harbour lights. It was all looking very summer-fete-like and pretty as Emma headed down the hill to help set up her stall. There was chatter, as well as the seagulls' morning cries, with a few of the other stallholders already there. A sense of anticipation filled the air.

Chairs and tables from the village hall were being moved into place from the back of a trailer. Pete had a contact at the Alnwick Markets so he'd managed to borrow the metal frameworks and the stripy blue-and-white tarpaulin covers for the stalls. It was all coming together nicely.

The butcher from the next village was setting out

two large BBQ drums, ready to cook hot dogs and beefburgers and Anne had The Rock Shop's hatch open already; she'd put up her own bunting – she was so near the harbour it wasn't worth her taking a stall. Emma waved a friendly hello, and she waved back, smiling broadly. Since their clash and Anne's subsequent apology, several customers had mentioned they'd been sent up by The Rock Shop, and with Emma's new courtyard area, a further prosecco party booked in and the summer season in full swing, things had picked up nicely again.

Even Danny was up sharp, an unusual occurrence, and was perched precariously on stepladders, hanging a large handwritten sign on the side wall of The Fisherman's Arms with the help of Dave who was shouting instructions. It read 'Fish and Chip Cones – only £4.95'. The local businesses were all on board and hoping for it to be busy with happy customers and a successful day's trading.

Being the first-ever Warkton-by-the-Sea Food Festival, it felt very much like a trial run, but they had all worked so hard, it was important it went well.

Daphne, one of the ladies from the village committee, showed Emma which was going to be her stall. It had a nice position facing the harbour. Emma was pleased – they were sure to get plenty of footfall past it, as long as the anticipated visitors turned up. Em set out her trestle table ready for Holly, who had offered to run the stall, whilst she, Bev and Megan, a new girl Emma had just taken on, were working in the shop. Em would also be runner between the two, should Holly need more supplies sending down through the day.

For The Chocolate Shop's stall, Emma had had to be mindful of the warm temperatures, so none of her refrigerated items were going there; instead she had a selection of choc-dipped, plain and rum-and-raisin fudge, chocolate buttons and her seashell shapes in pretty gift bags, her puffin and seal-shaped chocolate lollipops as well as some of her chocolate bars in milk, plain, white choc-raspberry, ginger and lime and Grand Marnier. They were also going to have an ice-cream stall.

Em needed to check that the electric cable and socket she'd been promised was available, as she was going to bring down her tabletop freezer from the kitchen for the gourmet dark chocolate ice cream she had created especially – it had passed the Bev and Holly taste test with flying colours last night. There were two boxes of waffle cones at the ready and some fudge sticks made to pop in the top – The Chocolate Shop's take on the traditional 99 ice cream. Delicious, and oh so summery!

Pete came along unravelling a cable.

'Perfect, you're a mind reader,' Emma said.

'I'll just test it's all working in a minute, once it's in place,' he stated.

'Thanks, that's great. All going well, Pete?'

'Yep, so far so good. We're just hoping for a good turnout.'

'Yes, it's going to be a lovely fair day by the looks of

it. I've nearly finished setting up here, so can I give you a hand at all?'

'Well, there's a few more chairs and tables to set out for each stall, if you don't mind.'

'Of course. I'm happy to do my bit.'

'Cheers, Em.' And off he went unwinding his reel of cable between the stalls.

By mid-morning Holly had already phoned asking for some more bags of fudge. Luckily Em had plenty of extras made up and popped down to drop them off. There was a real buzz harbourside already.

All the stalls were taken. Emma spotted the Alnwick Rum stall, Hepple Gin and tonics, Lynda waved across at her from the Bamburgh Deli stall – ooh, she'd have to head over and say hello once she'd dropped the fudge with Holly – the ladies of the WI were serving fresh tea and coffee, there were Lindisfarne Oysters on ice, a fresh crab sandwich stall, and the BBQ'd sausages and burgers were smelling delicious. It looked just fabulous. Warkton had pulled together once again and put on a damned good show.

Shirley, Adam's gran, and some of the Golden Oldies group were already there, looking around. So, after dropping off the fudge and checking Holly was okay, Emma went over to say hello.

'Looks like it's all going well, Emma.' Shirley smiled. 'We've been to have a chat with young Holly and she says it's been really busy already.'

'Yes, it's going brilliantly so far and it's still early yet.'

One of the elderly gents was halfway through a chocolate ice-cream cone. 'Wonderful stuff this, lass.' He licked his lips and made a thumbs-up sign.

'Thank you,' Emma said. 'I made it myself.'

'We thought as much. It tastes just like your truffle chocolates in the shop,' he added.

'We'll call up and see you at the shop in a little while,' Shirley said. 'Think we're all ready for a sit down and a slice of cake. Well, if we can squeeze it in. There's been a lot of food sampled already.'

'Always room for cake,' smiled Dorothy.

'Well, I'd better crack on, they'll be needing me back at the shop. See you up there soon.'

'Yes, we'll catch you shortly. Try and keep us a few seats if you can.' Shirley winked.

'I'll try my best,' answered Em.

Before heading back, she quickly caught up with Lynda from the deli, who had helped support her last year by agreeing to take a selection of her chocolates for sale at her shop in Bamburgh.

'Hey, Lynda – lovely to see you here.'

'And you, Emma. It's certainly busy, isn't it. I'm so glad I decided to come along.'

'Are you keeping well?'

'Oh yes, pet, very good. And you? How's the shop doing?' She then frowned. 'I'd heard it's been put up for sale. Is that right?'

'Yes, unfortunately. I just rent, you see. Not a lot I can

do about it I'm afraid. I'm still hanging on in there until I get my notice. But if you hear about any suitable premises round your way, keep me posted.'

'What a shame. And I will do, pet.'

'Well, sorry to have to dash, but I'd better get back up to the shop.'

'Of course.' They promised to catch up properly soon.

'Have a good day.'

'You too, Em.'

Back at The Chocolate Shop it was all systems go with teas, coffees, milkshakes, bakes and cakes. The counter had a queue for orders of boxes of truffles, gift bags, and more. It was hard to keep up with it all, but they forged on. Emma's new hire, Megan, was seventeen and not long out of school. Emma knew she needed the extra help, especially with Holly about to head off to university soon. Megan had only started last Saturday and hadn't built up a lot of experience yet, so it was very much a case of 'into the frying pan'. The customers could see how busy they were, and most were happy to wait, although there was the odd disgruntled tut or sigh, but hey, they could only do their best.

In came the Golden Oldies. '*My*, we need a sit down,' Adam's gran sighed. 'It's bedlam out there now. Never seen Warkton so busy. Hear they are having trouble parking now, the public car park's full, and the high street's chock-a-block.'

'It's fabulous down there though,' Thelma added. 'All

the stalls and everything. We're loaded up with all sorts. I've got cheese, fudge, and sticks of rock for the grandchildren.'

'I've even got a mini sample of Hepple Gin for free,' chipped in Shirley. 'We're looking forward to that tonight with a drop of tonic, aren't we, Thelma? But for now, what we need is a seat and a nice cup of tea.'

'Yes, I bet.' Emma came out from behind the counter to help them. 'There's a couple just about to leave the window seat there. If you wait just one minute, I'll get it set up for you all.'

'Perfect. Thank you, Emma dear.' Shirley smiled.

'You're welcome.'

Emma had taken their order while they waited and was soon making her way back to them with a tray laden with drinks and cake. They were now all settled at their favourite window-seat table.

'How's your young man, Emma?' Dorothy asked. 'Is he here today?'

The words felt like a dart in Emma's heart, but she managed to keep smiling. She hadn't seen or heard from Max for four weeks now.

'No, he's busy today, Dot.' Emma *really* didn't want to go into any of that just now.

'Shame. Would have been very pleasant to have been served by him,' Dorothy added. 'Such a lovely lad.'

Emma kept her smile fixed and her head down whilst handing out the order. She was glad it was busy; it meant she had to keep on going. Busy was good, it kept her mind occupied and her heart shut down, keeping all those unsettling emotions at bay like a jack-in-the box.

Next, Emma had to dash back down to the harbour with a container of ice cream as Holly had rung to say she was nearly out. It was very warm outside, so she'd packed a large plastic box with ice, and nipped down in the car to get it to the freezer on the stall before it all melted.

When she got there, James and Chloe were down at the harbour too. The girls were nibbling on lurid-pink candy-floss sticks they'd got from The Rock Shop.

'Hello, you lot. Having a nice time?' Em walked over to them after delivering the ice cream.

'Yes-s.' The girls were grinning. 'The Rock Shop lady was nice this time,' said Olivia.

'That's good.'

'Want some, Auntie Em?' Lucy thrust her candy-floss stick towards her. It was licked, with pink sticky beads of wet around the edges and lightly chewed.

'Ah, no thanks, Luce, but nice of you to offer.'

'It's great here,' James commented. 'There are some really good stalls and loads of tourists about.'

'Your stand looks lovely,' Chloe added. 'And I've seen lots of people wandering about with your chocolate ice creams.'

'Good, good. What I like to hear. Yes, I've just been stocking that up for Holly. Sorry, guys, but I'm going to have to dash. It's all go back at the shop too.'

'Of course. See you soon.'

'Bye, Auntie Em.'

'Bye all. Have fun.'

And it was indeed all go for another few hours. The dishwasher was humming away, as well as new-girl Megan washing up at the kitchen sink, trying to keep up with all the used crockery. The young girl had straight blonde hair, which she'd pulled back into a ponytail for work, and pretty pale-green eyes that stood out against her milky-fair skin. She had recently moved to the village with her family, from the nearby town of Seahouses.

Megan had very much found her feet today, working hard alongside Emma and Bev. She was going to be working weekends and the week days that Bev wasn't in, giving Em that extra cover she needed, especially with Holly setting off for her new student life in Newcastle upon Tyne very soon. It seemed really odd that Holly would soon no longer be part of the team, except perhaps at holiday times. Em would miss her sunny face and temperament.

The Bank Holiday visitors were starting to drift away and the seagulls were settling to roost for the evening. Emma could hardly believe that it was almost six o'clock. The day had just flown. She decided to head down to the harbour to see how Holly had got on with the stall for the rest of the afternoon.

'Bev, you okay to hold the fort here a while? I'll just go and help Holly pack up. I'll take the car down to pick up the freezer and anything that's left.'

'Yeah, I'll be fine. It's quietened off a lot now.'

'Been a good day, though.' The till hadn't stopped pinging, which was a joyous sound for Emma after the financial woes of last year.

'Megan, thanks so much.' She caught up with her new member of staff. 'You've been such a help. I'll just fetch your pay for today, and then you may as well get away home.'

Megan had been delighted when Emma had offered her the chance to work at The Chocolate Shop after Sheila had heard the young girl was looking for a job in the village. She was a bit shyer than Holly, but polite with the customers and she seemed to be warming up to the role nicely.

'Thanks,' Megan smiled as Emma handed across her pay and a bag of fudge. 'That's great. I'm really enjoying working here already.'

'That's good. We'll see you back tomorrow then!'

She had been a little hesitant to employ the new girl at first, in case The Chocolate Shop sold quickly – especially as The Brewery Boys had seemed so keen. But if it did, she reasoned, a sale might well take a few months to go through. That thought was always there like a dark spectre, but Emma resolved to just keep moving forward, until anything happened to change that. The other way led to torment.

44

A little later at the harbour, Emma parked and walked across to find Holly at the stall.

'How's it been going? All okay?'

Holly looked up at her through red, tear-stained eyes.

'*Holly*, what on earth has happened?'

The girl took a gulp of air and then said, 'He's finished with me, Em.'

'What are you talking about . . . Who, Adam?' Em couldn't believe it. 'This can't be right, Hols. You two are such a great couple.'

'It's true. He's just been here. Came to see me. Was going to wait until later he said, but then he just blurted it out and went off in a dash.'

'Why? Has something happened? Have you two had a row?'

'No. I just don't get it. He says he still likes me, but that I need my freedom now I'm going off to uni. He says it's best for us to split up. He's adamant, Em.'

Holly slumped down dejectedly onto the stall's plastic chair.

Why did the course of love never run smooth?

'Oh, Holly. I'm sure you two can sort this out. I bet it's not because he really wants it to end. I think, in a crazy way, he might believe he's helping you. Setting you free to go off and start afresh. To go your own way.'

'I don't want to go my own way. I want to go to uni, yes, but I still want to be with Adam.' The tears plopped down her cheeks.

'Come on.' Emma put an arm around her assistant for a second or two. 'Let me help you get packed up here and we'll go back to The Chocolate Shop and you can tell me all about it. Maybe we can come up with a plan to knock some sense into that boy over a mega milkshake.'

Holly gave a small smile through the tears. 'Thanks.'

They soon had the freezer packed into the boot of Emma's car, with the seat folded down after a helping hand from Pete and one of the gents from the village committee. Three bags of fudge and two chocolate bars were all that remained of the goods for sale (brilliant!), and Holly carried them with her. All the ice cream and cones had gone – a sell-out, Holly had told her, and very popular, especially with the homemade fudge stick in the top. Back at the shop, Emma turned the sign on the door to *Closed* as the last customers left. Bev had spotted Holly's tear-stained face and looked to Em for an explanation.

'Adam,' Emma mouthed silently.

'Ah, okay,' Bev nodded back.

'Bev, we have a situation that calls for emergency chocolate measures,' Em stated. 'What would you like, Holly? A milkshake, hot chocolate, ice cream?' Em rattled off some of the young girl's favourites.

'Milkshake, please, with your chocolate sauce through it – and extra marshmallows and fudge pieces on the top?'

'No problem, I'll fetch it,' Bev offered, adding, 'then you can tell us all about it, hun.'

When they were all settled down at one of the tables, Bev and Emma with a coffee, Holly with her super-duper milkshake, Em started to explain: 'Well Bev, the thing is this, young Adam has decided that as Holly is taking herself away to Newcastle and her student life, it's best they end their relationship. To give her some freedom, apparently. That's the gist of it, isn't it Hols?'

'Yes.' She was sounding a bit weepy again. 'I've told him I don't want that. That I still want to be with him. Yes, I really want to go and do my training, make some new friends and that. But I'm not interested in looking for a new boyfriend. Why can't we just keep going and see how it works out? Why do we need to break up?'

'Ah, probably a man thing. He sets you free first, so he doesn't get hurt when you find someone else,' Bev said.

'Except it won't happen. I don't *want* anyone else. And if it's true what he says, that he still really likes me, then he's only going to hurt anyway. I know I bloody am already.' She sniffed loudly.

'Maybe he's not so sure himself, not inside.'

'I don't know, Em, he sounded pretty definite. Like that's the way it's got to be.'

'Maybe he was just trying to put a brave face on it.'

'Ah, I don't think so.'

'Well, you're not going to give up that easily are you, hun?' Bev chipped in.

'Why not go and talk to him? He might still be there at the hotel. You might catch him if you go now,' suggested Em.

'You think I could?'

''Course you can. I have a feeling you're both going to be miserable otherwise,' said Bev.

'Tell him how you feel, what you've just told us,' Emma added. 'No one knows what the future holds for sure, but if you feel that strongly, you can make it work somehow. You can still see each other, pop back at weekends. It's only an hour away, it's not like you're going to Australia or anything. Some things are worth fighting for, Holly.'

'Yes, all kinds of different relationships work out – that's if you both want it enough. Go tell him,' added Bev.

'Right. Thank you.' Holly took a sip of her mega-milkshake. A glimmer of hope re-lit her eyes. 'I'm going to find him. Right now.'

'Good for you and good luck,' said Emma.

'Go Holly!' Bev raised a high five.

With that Holly was off.

* * *

Holly spotted Adam's car in the hotel's car park. Phew, he was still there then.

She dashed into Reception to find Laura there. 'Hey, Hols.' She politely said nothing about Holly's red eyes and nose.

'Hi . . . Is he here? Adam?'

'Ah, he went out about fifteen minutes ago. Said he wouldn't be too long.'

'Oh . . . Did he mention where he was heading?'

'No, sorry, petal.' Laura had the feeling something personal was going on.

So, if he wasn't at the hotel, where was he then? Holly mused. If he was feeling anything like she'd been since their talk – as in totally crap – she reckoned he'd have needed a bit of space. So, maybe a walk?

'Thanks, I'll go find him.'

'Any message?'

'Uh . . .' *I still love you. Don't do this. Are you hurting as much as me?* 'Uhm, no.' They had to do this face to face. 'Well, you can say I was looking for him.'

'Will do.'

'Thanks.'

There was no time to waste. Something drew Holly towards the beach, the place they had walked, held hands, kissed, talked about their hopes, their dreams, their future. It was a special place for them.

She was soon heading through the track in the dunes, saw the golden sweep of the bay open out before her. There was a young family on the sands playing rounders, a man walking his dog . . . and there, further away, someone was sitting on a rock looking out to sea. She could tell from the set of the shoulders, even though they were slightly hunched, and the sandy blond hair, that it was Adam.

She found herself running.

Just a few metres away now. 'Adam!'

He turned, looked surprised. His eyes were reddened. 'Holly . . .'

Was it really over between them?

'Oh Holly . . . I'm sorry.'

Sorry he'd hurt her? Sorry it was still over? Sorry I've been a dick? Which sorry was it? 'Do you still mean it? That we're over?' Holly was almost afraid to ask.

'It all sounded fine, sensible,' Adam started. 'Give you the chance to start afresh. Go off to uni with a clean start. Make your new friends and settle in down there without being tied back here.' He paused, looked out across the sea. 'But then I saw the look on your face when I told you and I could see how much you were hurting. I didn't know any more . . . and I was hurting too.'

Holly stood listening silently, holding her breath.

'But then I felt like I had to carry it through. Oh Holly, I've been such a dickhead haven't I?'

'Uh-huh. You have.' She wasn't going to make this easy for him, but there was a curl of a smile playing on her lips.

'Argh,' he groaned, frustrated with himself.

Holly sat down on the rock beside him.

'Jeez, I've done it all wrong. And I've hurt you . . . and I can't bear the thought of not seeing you again, Holly.' He looked up into her eyes.

'I'm here now.' And that's the only place she wanted to be.

'Holly, do you think we can just wipe that conversation from earlier? Can we try again? Even when you're away? I know it might not be easy but . . .'

'We've gotta at least try, yes.'

'Oh, thank God.'

She shifted a little closer to him. 'And hey, you're a cute, gorgeous dickhead, by the way.'

'Hah,' Adam laughed.

He then leaned in, put his arms around *his* Holly, and they shared the most exquisite making-up kiss ever.

'Hey, I'd better get going,' said Bev, as she put the last of the crockery into the dishwasher at The Chocolate Shop. 'Pete's just texted; he's wanting me to help with the last of the clearing up down at the harbour. I think there's still tables and chairs to return to the village hall. It's been a good day, hasn't it?'

'Yeah.'

'And it's great that Pete's back getting involved with the village and not on the golf course quite so much. Things have been much better lately. Even Mum's feeling a bit brighter too; she popped in earlier when you were down with Holly packing up the stall and she and Dad took a stroll around the fete this afternoon.'

'That's good. I'm so pleased to hear that. Do you need an extra pair of hands with those tables and chairs?' Em offered.

'No, you're fine, thanks. I know you've still a lot to do here 'cos you'll probably need to make up some more supplies for the shop tomorrow. We're looking a bit like Old Mother Hubbard's here, after today.'

'True.'

The shop was then quiet. Em headed to the kitchen and started making some gourmet chocolate bars. Whilst she was melting the chocolate callets and getting the moulds out ready, her mind began replaying her conversation with Holly. Something nagged her inside.

Some things were worth fighting for. Some things were too important not to put right. It wasn't just Holly who was miserable. Emma had been hiding her sore, sore heart for weeks now.

So, Max may not want to see her or speak to her, but she at least had to try. As fast as she could she filled the moulds, slightly slapdash compared to her usual careful crafting, left them on the side to cool and ran upstairs.

45

'Come on, Alfie. We're off boy.'

Emma grabbed her handbag, making sure her phone and purse were in it, and the T-shirt she'd quickly scribbled on as a last-minute idea. After letting Alfie into the boot, she set off to where her heart was pulling her.

It felt right, what she *had* to do and maybe what she should have done a couple of weeks ago.

Max hadn't phoned. She had tried sending a couple more texts just this morning, but he hadn't responded. But that didn't mean it was a lost cause, not yet. He was just hurting. She couldn't just let him slip away like that, without even trying to fully explain. She felt all wrong, had done ever since that crazy kiss with Nate. She'd been having trouble sleeping, she'd been off her food. Her soul felt sore with it all.

The traffic was frustratingly slow, with all the holiday-makers filing back southward after their weekend away or day out. And then there was a tractor holding everything up. As she finally turned off at the exit, she knew she was only twenty minutes away from Max's house, and she couldn't hold back the surge of hope that raced through her.

'Not far now, Alfie,' she called over her shoulder, 'then you can have a runabout in Max's garden.'

She kept going, driving on autopilot, whilst trying to frame the words she wanted to say and testing out phrases of love and apology. Then there they were, turning off for Max's village just before the town of Hexham. Driving down country lanes, passing the first cottages of the village, the old schoolhouse now converted to a residence, the village green, the pub. The stone cottages of Max's row, his at the far end. She felt a bit light-headed.

It was now after 8.00, but she couldn't see Max's Jeep outside. Could he still be working? Visiting his parents maybe? Popped out for a takeaway dinner? Damn, she hadn't thought about him not being there. Oh well, she'd just have to sit and wait a while. She had a bottle of water in the car. She could give Alfie a drink, and then maybe take him for a stroll around the village.

She sat in the car for five minutes, then thought she might as well go and knock on the door in case Max was actually in and there was some reason why his Jeep wasn't outside. Alfie had a little run around the front garden and she knocked and rang the doorbell. No answer. She tried the door. Locked. She'd have to just be patient.

It was still light, so Em took Alfie for a wander around the village. It was an idyllic place, set in the Tyne valley.

Cream-stone cottages bordered a village green that had a big old oak tree on it. A quaint pub was set to one side of the green, and there was a church and a small village shop. She passed another dog walker with a terrier who barked repeatedly at Alfie, before they settled down and sniffed each other. The owner, a middle-aged lady, said a polite hello to Emma, adding, 'Nice evening.'

'Yes, it's lovely.'

Then they both moved on.

The sun was bleaching everything blond with that lovely soft summer evening light, it was still warm, and the gnats were out. A fat bumblebee buzzed by, then Emma watched it land on a beautiful yellow rambling-rose that was climbing a cottage wall. It was a peaceful, pretty place. Emma could see why Max liked it.

She headed back along the road to his house; damn, still no sign of any vehicle. Well she wasn't going to head home just like that after making her mind up to see him and speak with him. She'd just have to sit it out until he came back. An hour passed. She wished she'd brought a book along or something to occupy her, but she'd dashed out, not really thinking. She was feeling a bit stiff sitting there in the car. Another thirty minutes passed, and the sun was starting to set over the distant hills, softening their outlines with a dusky orange glow.

Her tummy started rumbling. Luckily, she'd fed Alfie before she'd left the shop. She didn't have a lot of cash in her purse but decided to pop to the pub for a packet of crisps and a bottle of Coke. That might just stave off the hunger pangs until Max came back. Back in the car she shared the odd crisp with the ever-hungry spaniel, and then they settled down together on the back seat. She stroked his ears, the soft fur of his back.

She must have nodded off because it was dark when she woke. She looked out. No Jeep, no Max, no lights on in the house. The car's clock read 10.20. Max must be out for the evening. Typical. She hoped it wasn't going to be a late one. One leg was dead already where she'd slept at a funny angle, and ooh yes, now it was coming back to life with a fuzz of pins and needles.

Well, she was here now, so she might as well sit it out. Em felt a bit like a private detective in a stakeout. It wasn't much fun, to be fair. It was getting chilly, so she leaned over and grabbed a blanket from the boot. A rather doggy-smelling blanket, but hey, needs must. She'd apologise to Max on that front later, but better than catching hypothermia. She found the 'Sorry' T-shirt that she'd quickly made from an old white T-shirt of hers and a permanent marker pen, before dashing off. She put the spaniel's front legs through the armholes and he wasn't bothered in the least. She'd thought it might make Max smile if she'd put it on, but at least it might now serve to keep Alfie cosy. The temperature at night cooled dramatically in Northumberland, despite it being summer. The two of them huddled together again.

It was the early hours when she next came to. Two-fifteen and still no sign of Max. No Jeep. She was sure she'd have woken anyhow if he'd come home. Even if he'd had a lift home with someone else or a taxi, he'd have had to walk right past her car. Wherever he was, he was staying all night. Emma's heart sank. Had she got this all wrong? Had he already found someone else? Was she clinging to false hope?

She dozed intermittently, hearing birds tweeting away in the half-light at around four . . . yes, the world was still carrying on . . . And still no Jeep.

The sound of a vehicle pulling up next to her car woke Emma. She blinked her eyes open. It was now light outside, but felt early; that cool, grey morning light that came just after dawn. She checked the clock – just after 6.30. *Was it him?*

There was his Jeep, parked behind her. She pulled herself up from the back seat where she had been snuggled with Alfie. There was Max getting out of his vehicle. He looked jaded. He reached her car, looked twice at it – confusion and then recognition crossing his face. Emma gathered herself and stepped out, a little wobbly, her bedhead, back-of-car hair stuck out at all angles to her head.

'Em? What on earth are you doing here?'

'I waited all night.'

'Ah . . . I'm shattered, Em. I've hardly had any sleep and I can't even think straight. Go home. We'll talk later.' Max was walking up the path to his front door, his back already to her.

'I've waited all night,' she repeated. 'Please, just let me

say what I came to say . . . You're wrong, Max. I *do* love you for you. I love your smile, your strength, the way you call me "Beautiful" in the mornings. I love the winter picnic on the beach you did for me, your thoughtfulness. I love that you like dogs, the way you work hard and the drive and ambition you have to make your business a success. I love the way I feel in your arms . . .' The tears had started crowding her eyes now and she was finding it hard to speak.

Max had stopped walking. He turned to face her, but he still had that stony, sad look on his face. 'I can't do this right now, Em. Okay? I'll call you later.'

'You promise?' She felt like she was clutching at straws.

He nodded and carried on walking, unlocked his front door and went on in.

She watched the door close. She couldn't bear to go, so she sat down on the cool dewy grass, and hugged the hoodie she had on tight around her. Right, she had to *do* something. Make him believe her. She wasn't going anywhere, and she wasn't giving up that easily. She saw a pile of red house bricks stacked at one side of the garden – he'd been intending to build a barbecue this summer and hadn't got around to it as yet. Em started arranging the bricks into letters, words, filling the grass to one side of the front garden – the lettering facing the house. He could read it when he came back out, or when he opened his bedroom curtains on the upstairs window that fronted the cottage. No doubt he was off to bed now.

Where the hell had he been all night? That thought

began to twist in her mind. Had he patched things up with his ex, Siobhan? Had he been staying over with her? Or someone else, someone new. Though 6.30 a.m. was a bit early to make your exit and come on home. Maybe they'd been 'at it' all night and he had to finally get some sleep before work. Her heart sank, a twist of jealousy wrenching it even more. No wonder he didn't want to speak to her.

But she didn't know the truth, did she? She had to give him a chance, especially if she was expecting him to give *her* a chance. She'd sit this out however long it might take. She'd give Bev a call in a while, once it was a more reasonable hour, to ask if she'd open up the shop for her. Her friend was going to be helping anyhow with it being the Bank Holiday Monday. She really should be there herself on such a busy day, but for once The Chocolate Shop could wait. She had a feeling that if she gave up now she might regret this for the rest of her life.

It was chilly outside, so Emma went back to the car and cuddled Alfie again to warm up a bit. He was still in his 'Sorry' T-shirt. Was there any chance that that might make Max smile now? Were they beyond all that? She felt so sad. In an hour or so, they'd go and camp out in the garden once more, she decided. In the meanwhile, she'd keep an eye on the house from the car and try and rest a little. She'd hardly slept, felt stiff all over and had a crick in her neck, but all that mattered was getting through to Max to explain, or at least giving it her best shot.

* * *

Time ticked by painfully slowly. Unable to drift off to sleep, Emma gave in and phoned her friend. 'Bev, hi. Look, I'm down here in Max's village.'

'Oh wow, have you two patched things up? Thank God, that's great news.'

'Well, it's not quite that simple.'

'Oh?'

'You see I'm out in the car just now . . . and he's in the house.'

'Sounds confusing.'

'It is, but I can't come home yet. We haven't had a chance to talk things over. I *so* need to talk with him, Bev.'

'Yes, of course. Do you want me to open up the shop for you?' Her friend pre-empted her question.

'Yes, please. That would be great.'

'No worries. Holly's coming in too, isn't she? We'll be fine. You do whatever you need to, hun. Don't worry how long you take either. And hey, good luck.'

'Thanks. I think I'm going to need it.'

'I'm here for you whatever happens, Em.'

'I know.'

It must have been an hour later when Emma heard a knocking noise. She stirred, confused – she must have finally dozed off.

Max appeared at her car window. 'Emma, I was about to go to bed, I'm so exhausted, and then I looked out and – and you're still here.'

She wound down the window. 'Of course, Max. I

couldn't go without speaking with you . . . without trying to explain how I feel, at least.'

'I saw your message in the bricks . . . thank you.' He held her gaze, but she wasn't sure what was there in his eyes. Sadness, lingering hurt, poignancy, love? Or was it lost love?

'I do mean it.'

The message she had written was: 'I love you for you.'

'Yeah . . .' He was nodding. 'Look, why don't you come in. Maybe it *is* time we talked.' He still sounded subdued.

Emma got up out of the car, Alfie following her.

Max screwed up his face. 'What's Alfie got on?'

'Ah, my T-shirt. It was meant as a gesture, something to make you smile . . . hopefully. But it was cold in the car, so I put him in it.'

Max did manage a small smile then. Boy, had Emma missed that smile.

They went inside, Max was heading for the kitchen. 'Do you want a tea, coffee? Something?'

'I'll have a tea. Something to warm me up.'

Max put the kettle on and organised some mugs. The pair of them then sat at his breakfast table, both looking shattered.

The question was burning in Emma's mind. Where had he been all night? But she didn't want to risk this conversation by ploughing in sounding accusatory. And his answer might change everything. She wasn't sure she was ready for that just yet.

He got up and finished making the tea, placing mugs before them both before settling down again with a yawn.

'I don't think we quite look beautiful and gorgeous this morning' she joked, trying to lighten the mood.

'Hah, speak for yourself. I'm looking as exquisite as ever, surely.' His stubble was rougher than usual and his hair, though short, was ruffled oddly. She had to stop herself from running a hand through it. 'Bit of a night, hey?'

And that was her lead in. 'Where were you?' She sounded afraid.

There was an awkward silence, then Max started, 'With Nick Knowles . . .'

That name sounded vaguely familiar. Was he a mate of Max's? Nick, Nicholas, *Nicola* – a girl? The cold fear was back. Ah, she couldn't think straight after just a few snatches of sleep in a chilly car.

Max had a wry grin spreading across his face now. '*DIY SOS* ring any bells?'

'You what?'

'Yeah, I've been helping on that TV programme. There was this disabled lad with his family over in Gateshead in desperate need of an extension to their house and some renovations, so he can get his wheelchair around and have a little independence now he's a teenager. We've made him his own room on the ground floor, with an en suite wet room and everything. It's been two all-day-and-nighters. That's why I'm so shattered.'

'Oh . . .' It was hard to take in.

'Yeah, they put a call out to any local builders. Andy, my joiner, came along too. We had the weekend off for the Bank Holiday anyhow, and I wasn't doing a lot otherwise . . .' He paused and took a sip of tea. 'It was brilliant – a bit crazy at times with so many people helping and the timescales are ridiculous – but brilliant, honestly. We all mucked in and the family and the lad are coming back this afternoon. They're just finishing off the plastering and doing some decking and landscaping in the garden this morning, so I flitted off for a couple of hours' kip.'

'Oh my word, that's amazing.' Amazing that he was doing such a lovely, kind and special thing. And *amazing* that he hadn't turned to the arms of someone else.

It was time to talk, *really* talk.

'What happened to us, Max?'

He raised an eyebrow as if to say, you know full well.

'Okay, so I know I did wrong with that crazy kiss. If I could take that back, to have never done it, I would. I never want to hurt you again, Max.'

He was looking down at the tabletop and from the set of his shoulders she knew he was still listening.

'I will regret that moment until the day I die,' she continued. 'But I can't change that it happened. And if you can't get past that, Max, if it's just too hard for you, then you have to be honest and tell me now, or we'll just end up going on hurting each other.'

He looked up at her, pain still there in his gorgeous green eyes. 'What's been hard is not having you here,

Em. Not coming up to see you, not sharing your life. Andy and the site lads have said I've been like a bear with a sore head these past few weeks. Nothing seemed right.'

'Not for me, either.' Emma's lip was trembling. 'Can we try to find a way round this?'

'I don't know Emma. I really don't know.'

She couldn't bear it. She had hurt him so much, she might never be able to make it right. Tears stung her eyes but she held them back. She'd said what she'd come to say, and here they both were, still stuck in the past, with their hurts.

'Thanks for listening.' Her voice was quiet but firm. 'I think I'd better go now.' She stood up while she still had some strength left to get out of that door, down the path and on past her brick message with her broken heart. 'Come on, Alfie.'

Max didn't stop her.

What now? Back to the shop, to Warkton? But she didn't feel able to drive just yet with her emotions all over the place, fatigue making it all the worse.

One time when she had stayed over here, she remembered, they had gone for a walk down by the river through some woods. Fresh air and a stroll might do her some good, help clear her head, prepare herself for the reality that Max wasn't coming back. But . . . at least she had tried.

She left her car where it was; she'd drive back to

Warkton in an hour or so when she'd hopefully be calmer, and she and Alfie headed out through the village, finding the path that crossed a grassy field and wound its way down to the riverside.

Ironically, it was a lovely summer's morning. Dappled light streamed through the branches of the woodland at the side of the river, bathing her in warm sunshine. Birds were tweeting away, and she spotted the grey figure of a heron, poised on tall, spindly legs, down by the water's edge. He flew off majestically as they neared and Alfie found himself a stick, which he carried for a while then brought to Emma for her to launch into the stream. Alfie adored water and was bounding in and out with it on repeat.

'Good boy, Alf.' She patted his head, which caused instantaneous tail-wagging.

Though her heart was heavy, the walk and the countryside soothed her nerves enough for her to think about turning around and heading back to her car. It was time to go back to her Chocolate Shop and her life . . . but what kind of a life might that be without the shop itself or Max?

She opened her car door after putting a damp Alfie in the hatchback. She'd go away quietly, no fuss. She didn't even pause to look at Max's house.

'Emma! Stop!' The voice was urgent. Max.

Emma stood silently. If he still wasn't going to have her back, then she didn't think she could bear any chit-chat or post-breakup analysis. It would be best if she left, right now.

'I still can't bloody sleep.'

Emma held her breath.

'Oh God, I'm saying this all wrong.' He strode down the path to her.

Emma stepped back from the car and on to the pavement.

They were face to face now. 'You – you asked me if we could try and find a way round this,' Max continued, 'if what we have is worth fighting for, yeah?'

Emma nodded, almost too afraid to speak.

'The truth is, I can't imagine a life without you now.'

'Oh, Max!' She could hardly believe it. Then found the warmth of his arms about her, pulled herself tight against his chest. To think, she might never have felt that again. They stayed like that for a while, relishing the closeness, with a huge sense of relief.

When they moved slowly apart, it was Max who spoke. 'We go forward now, not back . . . together.'

'Together,' she repeated with tears in her eyes. What a beautiful word.

'Look,' Max continued, brushing away a stray tear gently from Emma's cheek with his thumb, 'I know I can never take Luke's place, and that's okay. Honestly, I don't want to. But we can be something new. I want to be there for you, Em. If you'll let me in.' His eyes locked on hers.

'Of course, Max.'

* * *

They felt exhausted with all the emotions of their conversation, and the night they had both put in. They found comfort in Max's double bed, making love, then resting in each other's arms, the room hushed and darkened with the curtains closed. Like a cocoon of warmth and love.

Lying there, Emma still found herself feeling vulnerable after all that had happened. 'Max . . . do you still love me?'

'How could I not love you.' It was a statement, not a question.

Could it really be that simple? Where not loving someone was just unimaginable.

'I've never felt this way before, Em.' Max sounded so earnest.

Emma had. It had been that way with Luke – a simple, honest love. She realised that she had the chance to have that kind of love again with Max. After losing her fiancé in such a tragic way, she'd never thought that would ever happen. That kind of love didn't come along often and, bloody hell, she wasn't going to damn well waste it.

'Max,' she whispered in the half-light, 'I'm so sorry. I promise I'll never hurt you again. It was a horrid, stupid mistake with Nate. I think . . . he reminded me so much of Luke, I got swept up in it all. It's no excuse, I know that. And, I mean what I wrote in that message before, outside the house. I do love you. Always will.'

'I know. I love you too, Em.' He gave her a tight hug, his arms wrapped around her from behind. 'Now, can I get some sleep?'

Alfie gave a big dog sigh from the floor beside them, where he'd nestled down in Max's discarded T-shirt, still wearing his 'Sorry' top.

'Course,' she answered. And fell into a deep sleep beside Max. In fact, the best sleep she'd had in ages.

46

With the busy Bank Holiday weekend and the wonderful developments with Max, Emma hadn't had a chance to visit Mrs C at the care home in Alnwick, so she headed off straight after work on the Tuesday, to find the old lady sitting up in the residents' lounge. The TV was on in the corner but no one seemed to be following it particularly.

Mrs C's face lit up when she spotted Emma coming in.

'How are you getting on?' Emma had brought in a bunch of bright-yellow carnations for the old lady to put in her bedroom – and of course a bag of chocolate brazils. There was also a large selection box of chocolates for the other residents and nurses to share, which Emma had handed to one of the nurses on the way in.

'Ooh, how lovely. Thank you, pet.' Mrs C was smiling. 'Well, I've had some good news, Emma dear. They're letting me back home tomorrow.'

'Well, that's wonderful news. I bet you're thrilled. How

will you manage, though?' Em was a little concerned. The old lady's hip was still a long way from healed and the last Emma knew was that she was using crutches and would be for some time.

'There are carers going to come in twice a day. And they've rigged up a bed downstairs for me in the living room for now.'

'Oh, well that will make things easier for you.'

'Thank goodness I've got a downstairs loo. I'll never be able to get myself up those stairs to the bathroom as yet. Gonna have to wash at the kitchen sink. Hah, hope no one comes around the back door at that point.' She cackled with laughter. 'They'll get more than they bargained for, for sure. A sight for sore eyes, at my age, I tell you.'

Emma had to laugh too. 'I'll remember to use the front door then, Mrs C.' She grinned. 'And I'll shout loudly as I come in.'

One of the assistants came across to offer them both a cup of tea.

'Thank you, that'll be lovely. Just what I need,' Emma said. She'd taken Alfie out straight after work and then fed him, coming on here without stopping for a snack or drink herself.

'You've been so good to me, Emma.' The old lady's tone became serious. 'Visiting me often when I know you're so busy yourself. You're rushed off your feet as it is. Now then, tell me all about the Food Festival this weekend . . .'

Their tea turned up with a selection of old-fashioned biscuits: bourbons, jam sandwich and custard creams.

'Thank you, Felicity, pet,' Mrs C said warmly. 'They're all very good in here,' she said to Emma as an aside.

'Thanks,' said Emma. She took a sip of the strong but good tea and started to tell her elderly friend about all the different stalls, how well the chocolate ice cream had gone down, and her hectic day at the shop.

'I'll be there for it next year,' Mrs C nodded. 'Do you think there'll be another?'

'Yes, I think so. There was a lot of positive feedback. It took quite a bit of setting up, but the local businesses really benefited. I'd be happy to get involved again for sure.'

'Well, that's good. Bet there was lots of nice food there. We've already had our supper here. Five o'clock sharp. Fish pie tonight, not bad at all. But I still can't wait to get back to my own home. There's nothing like home, is there?'

'No, you're right.' And she thought about her Chocolate Shop and her flat, and the fact it might all be someone else's soon. Just as life was looking up once more, there was a kick to bring it all down, with the news that The Brewery Boys had put in their offer. *Oh yes*, that had happened just this morning. She'd had an off-the-record call from the girl in the estate agents, who was a friend of Laura's, to warn her. She was expecting to hear from Mr Neil to confirm he'd accepted – the final hammer blow. It seemed to be just a matter of time. But she didn't want to worry Mrs C with any of that just now.

'Emma, dear,' Mrs C interrupted her thoughts, 'I know you've already been so good to me, but would you mind popping across to see me tomorrow when I'm back at home? Maybe after work, just when you've got a minute, pet.'

'Sure.' She expected the old lady was a little anxious thinking about being back on her own again – of course she'd look in. 'That's no problem. I can check you've settled back in all right, or if there's anything you need.'

'Thank you. You're a kind girl.'

'I'll remember not to come around the back way, mind.' They both chuckled. 'Well, I'd better get back,' Emma said. 'Sorry I can't stay longer tonight, but I have lots of truffles and some chocolate muffins to make. This weekend just about wiped out my supplies.'

'Yes, of course. I'm fine. I've got Bessie and Mavis here for company, as well as the nursing staff, and *Coronation Street* will soon be on the telly. You get yourself away.'

'I'll see you tomorrow. It'll be around six o'clock time.'

'That's grand, pet. Whenever you can make it. I'll not be going anywhere. Thank you, I appreciate that.'

'Take care.'

'Bye, pet.'

Emma turned to wave as she left the residents' lounge. Mrs C and several of the other old ladies and gents waved back.

One of the nurses caught up with Emma in the corridor on her way out to thank her for the gorgeous chocolates. 'Mind, she's a character that one,' the woman added.

'Yes, I know.' Emma smiled.

'She's told us all about your Chocolate Shop. Sounds amazing. I'll have to pop along one day.'

'Aw, that's nice. And yes, do.'

'We'll miss her. Mind you, there is a downside to having her here: half the residents are now saying "bugger".'

The two of them laughed.

'Thanks for looking after her so well.'

'Hey, that's what we're here for.' The nurse gave a smile.

'Goodnight.'

'Night.'

47

The next morning, Holly called into the shop on her way to catch the bus into Alnwick.

'Hi, Em. Just a quick hello.'

'Hey, Hols. Time for a milkshake?' Emma knew that was her favourite – with chocolate sauce, whipped cream and all the trimmings. The café customers were all served for now, so she had time for a chat.

'Ooh, yes. Don't think I can resist. My bus isn't for twenty minutes yet.'

'Off anywhere nice?'

'Just to catch up with some pals from school.'

'Sounds good.' Emma smiled. 'Follow me through to the kitchen then. I'll make one of my specials up for you.' She had a feeling Holly wanted a little reassurance and some company.

'So, how's it all going?' she asked, taking out a tall glass.

'Well, I've started doing some packing. There's only

about three weeks to go, now.' Holly pulled an OMG-style grimace.

'And how are you feeling?'

'Excited . . . still a bit scared. Worried about missing Adam.' Holly described the whole heap of emotions that were buzzing within her lately.

'Aw, that's only natural. You two back on track, then?' Emma asked.

'Yeah, more than ever, actually.' Holly grinned, then blushed under her freckles. 'I think it's just going to feel a bit strange at first, being apart, that is.'

'It most likely will for a while, but it's funny how you get used to things.' Emma had seen so many changes and shifts in her rollercoaster of a life so far.

'Adam says he'll come down to see me on his days off, and I'll get back home whenever I can.'

'Well, that sounds good. If it's meant to be, Holly, you two will work it out somehow.'

'I know. And it does feel like it's meant to be.' Holly looked suddenly confident.

'Great, so you go and enjoy university and make the most of your course too.' She added a swirl of cream and some chocolate chips to the top of the drink she'd just made, and then passed Holly the milkshake.

'Yum! That looks amazing as always.' She took a sip, ending up with a frothy white moustache.

Em laughed and pointed to her own lip exaggeratedly, and then the penny dropped with Holly, who grabbed a napkin from the stack on the side and began dabbing her mouth.

'It's just too good,' she giggled.

'Hah, yes. Well, we'd better head back out to the shop in case I get any more customers in,' said Emma.

'Yeah, of course. Ooh, Mum and Dad are arranging a bit of a farewell bash. Just a few drinks at home with some family and friends, if you'd like to come along. It'll be one evening next week. I'll let you know when.'

'You try and stop me, Holly. Of course I'll come along.'

'Thanks, and thanks for everything, Em.' Her voice began to waver.

'Hey, no getting teary on me! The Chocolate Shop will still be here, and I'll be waiting to see you when you come back home.' That was fingers and toes and everything else crossed, but she didn't want to spoil the mood.

'Ooh, and I saw Bev yesterday. Did you get to see Max? Me and Adam are still feeling terrible about that. Adam feels responsible for you two splitting up.'

'Hey, it really wasn't Adam's fault. Anyway, it looks like we've patched things up.'

'Really? Aw, that's brilliant Em. Thank God for that. I can't wait to go and tell Adam, he'll be *so* relieved.'

A family came in to choose some treats to take back to their holiday cottage with them. So Em had to set to work again. Once they were all served, Holly was at the bottom of her milkshake, spooning out the last creamy contents.

'Thanks, Em. Catch you soon. And thanks for chatting.' Holly stood up from the stool she'd been on and started getting her purse out.

'Hey, no need for that. It's on me. You've been a brilliant help this last year, and you've brought a sunny smile to the place.'

'Aw, I can feel a hug coming on.'

'Come here then, you.' Em came out from the counter and gave her assistant the biggest of hugs. 'And you know you'll be welcome back here to work some hours in your holidays and the like. There'll always be a job for you.'

'That means so much. Thank you.'

Emma watched her go, silently wishing her well, wanting her to soar and find her wings in the world. She hoped to goodness she could keep her promise and that there would still be a Chocolate Shop of some sort, premises or not, for her to come back to.

After work, Emma walked around to Mrs C's house and knocked loudly at her front door.

She heard the old lady shout, 'Come on in, pet. I'm here in the lounge. I'll not get up just now, it takes me an age.'

'Of course.'

Emma found Mrs C sat up in her high-backed chair with some knitting tucked beside her. She turned down the volume on the television. 'Hello, pet. Good of you to come.'

'How are you? Good to be back home?'

'Yes, wonderful. Though it's a bit frustrating not being

able to get on as normal just yet. But I'll manage. I've been trying to do my exercises. They're a bit of a bugger, I must say, but it's good to be back. You can't beat home comforts can you?' She smiled warmly.

'You're right.'

'Have you got time for a cup of tea?'

'Yes, I'd love one – but I'll make it.'

'Well, I put everything out on a tray in the kitchen earlier, whilst I was up and about. Just in case.'

'Great. I won't be a minute.'

'There's some custard creams in the tin there too,' Mrs C called out from the living room. 'Probably a bit boring compared to all the lovely goodies in your shop.'

'Nothing wrong with a custard cream,' Em called back.

Soon after they sat nibbling their biscuits and sipping tea.

'Now then, Emma. There's something I'd like to tell you.' Mrs Clark sounded quite serious.

Emma hoped to goodness they hadn't found something else wrong with her, something more sinister.

'Well then, I've had lots of time to think about things these past few weeks. And I've come to a decision. I'd like to help you to buy The Chocolate Shop – and I'm going to give you £10,000.'

Emma's jaw actually dropped, and she splashed some tea in her lap. 'Oh, that's so kind, but you can't do that, Mrs C. That'll be all your savings.'

'Not quite. I've kept back enough to see me comfortable and I'm going to splash out on one of those stairlifts, so I can get myself back up to the bathroom and bedroom as soon as—'

'But I can't possibly take all that!'

'Yes, you can. I've thought very carefully about it. You'll make an old lady very happy if you do, Emma.'

'But . . .' Emma was lost for words.

'Look, my needs are few. I love coming up to The Chocolate Shop and what am I going to do if it's not there any more? That'd be a *real* bugger. And I have no close family of my own. You've been so good, like the daughter I never had, the way you've kept visiting and looking out for me, even when you've had so much on yourself.'

'But what about your future? What if something happens and you need more care?'

'If I end up in a home or something as I get older, they'll use the money from this house anyway. I've got some put aside in my will for the RNLI Lifeboats – Jim would have wanted that – and then there's a little there for my two cousins. I'd much rather see my money do some good now, than leave it sitting in the bank. Anyway, no more arguing. The cheque's already written. It's over there in an envelope for you on the sideboard.'

'I-I don't know what to say.'

'Yes, would be a start.' The old lady's eyes were sparkling joyfully.

Could this really be happening? Emma felt like pinching herself. Oh my, she hoped to goodness the lads' offer hadn't been accepted yet. For once, she hoped Mr Neil was being his usual greedy self and was holding out for a higher bid. Her mind started spinning. She'd ring the estate agent first thing in the morning – unfortunately it would be closed right now, or she'd have been on to them right away.

The money from Mrs C would still not be quite enough for the full deposit she knew she needed on the business loan but, by hook or by crook, she'd find a way. She was so close now. She would use all her own savings and try and get a personal loan or perhaps ask her parents to help with the last few thousand pounds she needed, on a promise to pay them back, of course.

'Oh, Mrs C, this is just so generous. Are you really sure?'

'Of course. Now, stop asking silly questions and take the cheque, for goodness' sake, girl.'

Emma walked over to the sideboard and there, leaning against a framed photo of Mrs C and her husband, was the precious white envelope, neatly addressed to Emma Carter, c/o The Chocolate Shop by the Sea, Warkton.

'Well, if I take this, you must have a share in the business.'

'Oh, I don't need to get involved with all that. It's yours – given freely.'

'Goodness. Well then, there'll at least be free tea, cake and coffee for life, as well as a constant supply of chocolate brazils.' She didn't know how she could ever repay her, but she vowed silently to look after her dear friend in the future always.

'That'll do nicely.'

'Oh my, thank you so much. I'm still in shock.'

The envelope trembling in her hand, Emma went over to give her friend a hug.

'Mind the hip now,' Mrs C said matter-of-factly.

'Oh yes, of course.'

They both had tears in their eyes. Words just weren't enough.

'I can't bloody believe it,' Emma exclaimed down the phone to Max when she got back to her flat. She had to share her news with someone immediately.

'What can't you believe?'

'Mrs C – she's only gone and given me £10,000 to help me buy the shop.' It still sounded absurd. A dream come true. A miracle.

'Wow. That's amazing, Emma.'

'I know. And no strings attached. She won't hear of me paying it back. It's a gift. Wow!'

'Bloody brilliant. Is she of sound mind?'

'Hah. Yes, she's fine. Other than her hip. Though that thought did cross my mind too. I've got the cheque and everything.' It all sounded too good to be true, but it was. It really was. 'I can ring the estate agent in the morning and I'm going to go in at the asking price. I'm sure I can top The Brewery Boys' offer that way. As far as I know, it hasn't been accepted yet.'

'Well, best of luck.' Max sounded really happy for her. 'I bet the lads went in quite a bit lower. You'll have a good chance, I think. And Mr Neil doesn't have to know it's you who's bidding just yet either. Why not go in anonymously?'

'That sounds a good idea. I'll need to confirm everything with the bank first thing for the business loan. Oh God, I *so* hope it works out. I feel really nervous now.'

Could The Chocolate Shop really be hers?

'Ring me in the morning and let me know how you get on. Go for it, Em. Good luck.'

It was so good to be able to chat with Max about stuff again, about life and work issues. And it was wonderful to be able to share this mammoth, exciting news with him.

'Oh, Em, by the way . . .'

'Yeah?'

'You know what we talked about – about how we need to spend more time together? How about a night away together this coming weekend? Do you think you can get away a little earlier on Saturday? Maybe get some help in for Sunday afternoon too?'

'Yeah, I think so. Just let me check with Bev and the girls. Leave it with me.'

Life was *soo* looking up!

48

It had been a hectic morning with phone calls being made left, right and centre. Emma had put her offer in with the estate agent the minute they had opened. Gulp! She'd put down her mobile and felt a huge sense of excitement and trepidation. Would The Brewery Boys now up their bid too? Could she still be scuppered at the last? If so, she'd have to do the right thing and hand the money back to Mrs C then, of course, she decided. It was excruciating, but all she could do was wait.

She tried to concentrate on her chocolate making, but her head was swimming and she managed to splash water into the tempered chocolate in the mixing bowl, as she took a sip from her glass. Disaster. It had 'seized' completely, so she'd have to start again. She hated waste. It cost money and time. *Right, calm down, Em,* she told herself.

This evening Luke's parents were calling by too. She was feeling a little nervous about that, after the goings-on with Nate, though she was certain nothing would have been said by Nate himself. They had phoned saying that they were coming up to Warkton to see Nathan, and to collect a few of his belongings – his camper van was apparently rather overloaded after living in it all summer – to take back down to their house in Harrogate. They thought it would be a lovely opportunity to catch up with Emma too.

So she'd offered to make them a light supper after work, as they were staying over for the night at a farmhouse B&B just a few miles outside the village.

By late afternoon, the weather wasn't playing ball – steady summer rain had set in – so her plans of having supper with Luke's parents out in the courtyard had to be abandoned. Now the shop was closed for the day, she set out the cutlery and some place mats into the window-seat table of The Chocolate Shop. There was more space and light there than up in the galley kitchen of her flat.

She'd managed to get some fresh cod down at the harbour and was preparing it as gratin with Parmesan breadcrumbs, some roasted cherry tomatoes and new potatoes. Simple, but hopefully tasty.

They arrived at seven with flowers, hugs and a bottle of white wine that would go perfectly with the fish.

'So lovely to see you, Emma,' Angela, Luke's mother, greeted her warmly. 'You're looking well. Life on the coast must suit you.'

'The Chocolate Shop is looking fantastic,' John added. 'You've done an excellent job here. Last time I saw it, it was just a shop, no tables or chairs. I bet that has really enhanced the business.'

'Yes, it certainly keeps me busy. Right, well make yourselves comfortable. I thought it would be nice to have supper down here. I'll just chill the wine a little more and fetch some glasses.'

The three of them chatted whilst the fish was baking in the oven. Angela told how they were going to get Nathan's things from the camper van in the morning and they were looking forward to having some time at home with him. Emma had asked for him to join them for supper, slightly awkward though that may have been for reasons Angela and John were totally unaware of, but he was working his very last shift at the pub that night.

Emma served the food, along with some fresh bread and butter. She asked about old Barney the dog, the cricket season (John being an avid fan), and how the wider family were. Angela said that Luke's granny, Jean, was frail but still managing to live in her own home and was doing well. She had sent on her best wishes to Emma.

'This is delicious, Emma.' John took another mouthful of cod, followed by a sip of wine.

Angela then looked across at her husband, who nodded to her, as though it was time to say something.

'Emma, there's something we want to put right.' Angela sounded rather serious.

Oh my, had they heard about the stupid kiss with Nate? Was it going to haunt her for life? Em felt herself go cold.

'When Luke died he had some savings – not a huge amount or anything . . .' Angela stalled.

John took up the conversation for her. 'Well, it's just stayed in the bank. Because you two hadn't been married, and you didn't own your own property, everything that was left came to us.'

'But that doesn't seem right any more,' Angela said, rallying. 'Luke would have wanted to help you, Emma, and Nathan has spoken to us about the business here . . . about how The Chocolate Shop has been put up for sale. We're sorry to hear that, Emma. He also mentioned that you might have to move out soon and find new premises.'

'Yes,' was all Emma could say at this point, wondering where this was going.

'Well, it's not an awful lot, just under £5,000, but we'd like you to have it, Emma. We think Luke would have wanted that.' Angela reached across to hold her hand. They had been through so many difficult times together.

Emma's eyes brimmed with tears. Was there an angel up there looking out for her? A Luke-shaped angel by any chance? 'Oh . . .'

'We don't need it, love. We have good pensions and everything we need at home,' John stated.

'But you're still starting out, Emma. You have your whole life ahead of you. I'm just sorry we hadn't thought of this earlier.' Angela smiled across at her.

'This is just wonderful. If you are both sure . . . ?'

'Of course we are.'

'Wow. Oh, Angela, John . . . a lot has happened in the past couple of days. I now have the chance to buy The Chocolate Shop myself, so I might now be able to stay here, and own it outright, which would be such a dream come true. What you're offering – it would be the final money I need for the deposit, to put it all in place.'

Angela clapped her hands together. 'Well, that's just fabulous! I'm so glad we mentioned it. It was about time Luke's money was put to some good.'

'This deserves a toast.' John lifted his glass of wine. 'To The Chocolate Shop.'

'The Chocolate Shop,' the ladies repeated.

Emma took a big slurp of wine, to hide a big fat tear that was about to plop down into her glass.

'And to you, Emma,' Luke's father added warmly, Angela nodding proudly beside him.

'To Luke . . .' Emma had to include him.

Life was feeling pretty much a rollercoaster these past few days. If it all came together, The Chocolate Shop might really be hers in a few weeks' time. How crazy-wonderful was that!

And it felt so right that Luke was going to be a part of that. It felt so special that his was the final piece of the financial jigsaw needed to buy it. As if a part of him would always be there with her too.

'Thank you so much,' she managed to say to Angela and John, her voice crowding with emotion. 'This is all a bit overwhelming.'

'For us too.' Angela now had her hankie out and John's eyes were looking extremely misty.

And they sat together a while longer, sharing tears and laughter and memories.

49

Emma had already made a tray of choc-dipped fudge, a batch of raspberry-gin truffles, some rocky road bakes and Grand Marnier chocolate bars. She was on a roll this morning; her spirits had lifted and she had everything to hope for with her Chocolate Shop by the Sea. The only fear that still lurked was The Brewery Boys being able to up their offer, or someone new appearing on the scene at the last moment with a wad of cash to spend. Money would always talk as far as The Eel was concerned. But she was determined not to dwell on that.

Ten o'clock had come around fast, Bev had just arrived and Em realised she hadn't yet had a chance to exercise Alfie. With her stocks for today now made, it was an ideal chance to slip down to the beach with him for a quarter of an hour.

'Bev, do you mind if I nip out for a quick walk with Alfie? I've not had a chance to get him out yet.'

'Of course, hun. You go. I'll be fine.' Bev had popped

her head into the kitchen where Emma was, spotting all the gorgeous goodies there. 'Ooh, I'll keep myself busy putting all your new supplies out,' she said, smiling.

'Well, don't eat them all. I know what you're like.'

'Who me?' She batted her eyelids innocently. 'As if.'

'O-kay . . . You can try *one* of the truffles, and some fudge, but that's it.'

'Argh, you're such a hard taskmaster.'

They grinned at each other.

Down on the beach, Alfie making loops in the sand chasing his own tail, Emma strolling, enjoying the sea air, the breeze on her face . . . It was going to be a warm day, the sky a bold azure, the sea skipping into the shore in silver-tipped waves.

Her mobile phone buzzed in her pocket. Maybe Bev needed her back at the shop. It might be starting to get busy. She took it out, didn't recognise the number on screen, pressed green.

'Emma Carter?'

'Yes.'

'Hi. It's Susie from the estate agents.'

Emma felt herself freeze. In that second, her hopes and dreams were there before her, dangling on a thread. Her voice went quiet. 'Yes . . . ?'

'I'm delighted to say that your offer for 5 Main Street, Warkton-by-the-Sea, has been accepted.'

'*It has?*' Emma's tone was incredulous. Things like this didn't happen to Emma. Her life had taken so many downturns she couldn't believe that finally, what she'd wanted for so long, was really happening.

'Yes, Mr Neil has confirmed that he's happy to accept. We already have your solicitor's details, so we can start putting the wheels in motion straight away.'

'That is just wonderful! Thank you *so* much.' Emma stood, gazing out to sea, hardly able to believe what was happening.

'We'll keep you updated, but the seller's solicitors will be contacting yours shortly.'

'Thank you.'

The grin started spreading widely across her face. She jumped up into the air. 'Woohoo! We've only gone and done it, Alfie!'

The dog ran to her side, looking slightly confused, then picking up on her buoyant mood, began barking loudly.

'Come on, lad.' She legged it up the beach, Alfie bounding beside her.

They ran as fast as they could, past the harbour, up the hill, Sheila catching sight of a flash of them from behind her counter, wondering what was going on in the village now.

Emma dashed into the shop just as Bev came out into the café from the kitchen with a tray of coffee and brownies. Emma stood in the middle of The Chocolate Shop, *her* Chocolate Shop, and shouted out, 'We did it! We only went and bloody did it!'

'What?!' Bev was still trying to make sense of it all. She dropped the tray down on the countertop.

'My offer's been accepted. Wow! The Chocolate Shop is going to be mine!'

Stan and Hilda were in now, as well as a couple of holidaymakers, and all four cheered loudly and clapped, caught up in the moment.

'That's fantastic, Emma.' Bev was grinning from ear to ear.

'Oh my, I still can't quite believe it. Well then, it's free drinks and cakes all round. We need to celebrate,' Emma exclaimed. She wouldn't take a penny from any of the customers there.

'Oh, Em. That is just marvellous news.' Bev delivered the order to Hilda and Stan who were smiling away, delighted. Then her friend came across and took Emma into a big hug. 'You so deserve this, hun.'

'Is it really real, Bev? Tell me this isn't a dream.'

'This isn't a dream.' She punched her lightly to prove it.

Em felt a little giddy. She still felt scared that something might happen to make it fall through. Could The Eel change his mind at the last minute? But it was already going into the hands of the solicitors . . . today. *And*, he'd got his asking price. Mr Neil probably knew he was on to a good thing. Emma had heard that the other offer from The Brewery Boys had been £5,000 below asking price, and they had been pushed to make that. She mentally wished the lads well in finding another suitable property, but this was hers, and hers to keep.

She really did feel a bit wobbly. Bev spotted her unsteadiness, grabbed a nearby chair and sat her down.

'You all right, hun?'

'Dizzy, but bloody marvellous. I feel like someone's just poured a bottle of champagne down my throat,' Em admitted.

'Hang on, I'll fetch you a cup of sweet tea. Now stay put a moment. Stan, keep an eye on her. It's all the excitement.' Bev's tone had turned schoolmarmish.

Em felt a bit better by the time Bev came back with a pot of tea and two cups. After a reviving cuppa, amidst hearty congratulations from Stan and Hilda who kept saying it was 'Marvellous news', Emma couldn't wait to share the news with Mrs Clark, whose amazing generosity had made this happen.

A few minutes later, once she felt steady again, she said, 'Bev, can you hold the fort for a little while? There's someone I need to thank.'

'Hellooo,' Emma called out, as she let herself into the front door. 'It's only me. I've brought a little thank you with me, Mrs C.'

The *little* thank you was in fact an enormous bouquet with roses, carnations and all sorts of stunning flowers, that she'd had made up especially at the florists in the next village. Emma appeared in the living room, where Mrs C sat in her comfy armchair.

'Oh my goodness. These are just delightful.' The old lady beamed. 'But there's no need.'

'Yes, there is, because we're celebrating, Mrs C. I've just heard that my offer on The Chocolate Shop has been accepted. It's really going to happen, and it's all thanks to you.' She passed the bouquet over.

'Well, it's not all down to me, lass. It's you that's got the rest of the deposit together and you'll have the mortgage to keep up . . . and the shop to make work.' Mrs C was playing her part down. 'But I'm sure you'll manage. I have every confidence in you, Emma. And thank you, these are lovely. Would you mind popping them in some water for me, pet? My best vase is in that glass cabinet over there.'

'That's no problem.' Emma headed to the kitchen and arranged them in the cut-glass vase. They looked beautiful. She brought them through and set them on the sideboard near the photograph of Mrs C and her Jim. 'Can I fetch you a cup of tea or coffee or anything?'

'Oh no dear, I've not long had something. But you help yourself if you like.'

'I'm fine too. Bev made us all one at the shop after I heard the news.'

'You'll be wanting something a bit stronger than that to celebrate with,' the old lady said, chuckling.

'Well, I'll wait until later for that. I have a shop to run today.' Emma paused. A shop that was going to be all hers. It was still all rather overwhelming. 'I still can't quite believe it and your kindness . . .'

'Well, sometimes people deserve a break in life. You've had an awful lot to deal with for someone so young, Emma, pet. Now it's your turn to have a bit of luck.'

'Thank you so much. I'll never be able to do enough to repay your kindness.'

'Yes, you will. You go and make your Chocolate Shop the best it can be. Go and make your dreams come true. That's all I want to see.'

Emma's heart was brimming. 'I will do. Of course. I won't let you down, Mrs C.'

'You'd better not.' The old lady smiled, and then gave her a wink.

50

The last few weeks had been such an emotional roller-coaster and Emma was so looking forward to her weekend chill-out with Max. The night away that he'd promised was here, and she couldn't wait to relax with him, just the two of them somewhere special, but he was keeping the destination very much under wraps. Emma had to guess what might be suitable to pack, choosing a pretty dress for an evening meal as well as some casual clothes in case they went out walking or the like. Max arrived at four o'clock as promised. Holly was ready to cover the shop for the last hour and close up. She was also going to come in tomorrow afternoon to help Bev, and Alfie was settled with Bev and Pete. Emma felt a flutter of excitement as she and Max set off in the Jeep for their romantic getaway – the chance to have some uninter-rupted time together and reconnect would be bliss.

Emma was quite surprised when he switched the indi-cator on at the top of the village and pulled into The

Seaview Hotel. Maybe he was just picking something up or had some kind of surprise arranged there first. Curious.

Max grinned at her. 'We're here.'

'What? Honestly? We could have just walked up here.' Emma really couldn't work out what was going on. She wasn't sure if this was some kind of joke. Not that the hotel wasn't lovely.

'Yep, this is it. When you already live in the best place along the coast, why go anywhere else? It'll be very special, I promise.' He got out and walked around to open the Jeep door for her.

'Okay.'

Laura was there at Reception with a big smile for them both. 'Hi, Emma, Max. Welcome to The Seaview Hotel.'

Adam then appeared, giving them both a big hug, and offering to carry up their overnight bags. 'Great to see you two back together,' he said, smiling and shook hands with Max warmly, having felt dreadful about the rift his revelation had caused to his close friends.

Max quickly signed some check-in details, and then Adam led the two of them up two flights of stairs to the very top of the hotel – the executive suite.

As he opened the door for them, Emma gasped. It was absolutely beautiful. Holly had been right when she'd gushed about it all those weeks ago. Max was just grinning away beside her, having evidently seen it already, and delighting in Em's reaction.

There was a massive bouncy-looking king-size bed,

covered in a gorgeous black-and-cream fleur-de-lys-patterned bedspread, with lots of plump cushions. A lovely cosy sitting area looked welcoming, with a beige sofa, a wide-screen TV, and a coffee table. The pictures on the walls were of the local area, with some beautiful photographic seascapes of the bay and some black-and-white images of close-ups in the dunes. There was a dining table and two smart wooden chairs – and the en suite bathroom was enormous, easily as big as Emma's whole bedroom back in the flat. It had a huge double-ended bath, and a walk-in shower, all tiled out in slate and stone. It was like something out of *House and Home* magazine.

'Wow,' was all Emma could say.

Then Adam came back to the main bedroom area and pointed out the complimentary snacks and drinks all set out for them on a lovely dark wooden cabinet. There was a posh coffee machine, kettle and teapot, with packets of scrummy local biscuits, as well as a small bottle of Alnwick Gin and some tonics on the side plus an ice bucket, and a tub of kettle chips. Em spotted her own turndown chocolates, which made her smile even wider. And, out of the bay window she could see right down the high street to the harbour.

'It's just perfect,' she said, delighted.

'Right, well I'll leave you two to it,' Adam said. 'If you need anything at all just press 0 on the phone and Reception will answer.'

As soon as Adam had closed the door behind him,

Emma couldn't resist bouncing on the huge bed and laughing out loud. It was as springy as it looked. 'Thank you,' she said to Max.

'You are *so* welcome.' And he came and joined her on the bed, the two of them bouncing until they ended up in each other's arms in the most sexy, tender embrace ever. Ending in a kiss that meant so very much.

'I'm thinking about ordering room service for later, if you'd like that,' Max said. 'We can have dinner up here – the menu sounds amazing.'

'That sounds wonderful.' She did not want to leave this room at all. Just the two of them nestled away up there. No work, no worries. The Chocolate Shop purchase all seemed to be going ahead as it should in the hands of her solicitors – so far so good. For today at least it was just about them.

She'd brought a pretty floral-patterned dress to put on that evening and she'd maybe have a shower – in the big shower made for two, she thought with a grin – and change into that later.

'There's something else.' Max looked slightly nervous as he spoke.

'Okay . . .' She hoped it was good news. She didn't want this gorgeous bubble to burst, not yet.

'Follow me.'

There was a white-painted door with a small glass window inset at the far side of the room. She had spotted it earlier, but there was so much to take in with the room, she hadn't really registered it much further. Max went first, turning the handle. The door led to a wooden-decked balcony area, right at the top of the hotel. They stepped out together. The view was stunning; they could see right across the arc of the bay and down the Northumberland coastline – the sea, the beach, the sky, the patchwork greens and golds of the summer fields.

'Oh my!' Em was lost for words after that. She couldn't think of a more perfect spot. And she had Max beside her. A tear welled in her eye. Sometimes moments in life were just so beautiful they took your breath away.

She finally found her voice again and turned. 'Max . . . it's just beaut—' Then her focus fell on the decking area itself. There was a fancy outdoor Jacuzzi, two wooden lounger chairs. She spotted an ice bucket, ready on a stand. Oh wow, he'd got a bottle of champagne organised for them. But the most jaw-dropping thing of all was that Max was no longer standing next to her. He was down on one knee, looking up at her.

He looked so gorgeous and earnest – and a little bit nervous. 'Emma, would you do me the honour of becoming my wife?'

It was so perfect, the view of the bay, being here in Warkton, being here with Max. It was almost over-whelming.

Was this really happening? Never in her wildest dreams had she thought . . .

Max was still there, waiting for her response.

Was she ready to give up her soul once more? Was she ready to take that risk?

And the answer was there in her heart. 'Yes.' Her voice was loud and clear. 'Yes!'

'Woohoo!' Max shouted out, then he spun her around in a whirl of love.

Later, they sat in the Jacuzzi with bubbles all around them from the whirlpool, bubbles popping in their flutes of champagne and bubbles of excitement surging within Emma. She could still hardly believe all this and yet here was Max beside her with the happiest grin.

They sipped champagne to celebrate their engagement. The ring he'd chosen was just stunning, a vivid green emerald with four tiny diamonds around it. He'd picked it to match the green of her eyes, he'd said. He thought she'd like something slightly unusual. And he was right. Luke had given her a beautiful, yet traditional, solitaire diamond ring. It was lovely to have something new and different. Something that was special to Max.

He turned to her, suddenly looking rather serious. 'That day, when Adam told me . . . I had the ring with me there, ready. I hadn't quite planned it out, but I was going to make it special for you that night. I thought with The Chocolate Shop at risk, if I asked you to marry me, you'd know at least that you'd always have my support. That I'd be there with you for the long run, whatever happened. And then . . .'

'Oh Max, I'm so very sorry.'

'That's why I took it so hard.'

'Oh . . .' She felt so sad that she'd hurt him so much.

'It's okay now, honestly.' He smiled at her, took her hand in the misty bubbles. 'We made our way through it, Em. No more looking back. The here and now is what matters.'

'Yes.' And she snuggled up beside him in the warm bubbles, both looking out over the glorious view of the bay.

'You've just made me the happiest man.'

She moved in to give him a very sensual kiss, full of love and silent promises never to hurt him again. To love him for him always.

Max pulled back after a lingeringly gorgeous while. 'There's something else, Em.'

Emma felt a tug inside. She hoped it was good news. All her life since what had happened to Luke she'd always waited for *the but . . . the kick . . . the hammer blow*. She couldn't help it.

'Now we're engaged, we can't go on spending all our time apart,' Max started.

'True.' She began to relax a little.

'If you're okay with this,' he continued, 'I'd like to move into your place, here at The Chocolate Shop in Warkton.'

'Really?'

'Yeah, I've been thinking about it a lot. I can rent out my house for now so we'd save money and I can help with your bills on the shop and flat too. I know you've taken out a fairly hefty mortgage to buy the place now.'

'But what about your work? You'll have to drive even further to get there.'

'It's a small price to pay to come home to you at night. I want to be with you, Em. To be together, in every way. That's what us getting engaged to be married is all about. And . . .' He looked out across the vista of the bay with the fields of golden barley ready to harvest, rolling down to the rugged dunes and the blond sand of the beach, the pewter-blue sea, and the sky above just starting to blush with the pinky-peach tones of early evening.

'It is beautiful, isn't it?' Emma felt her heart stir.

'This place has won a little piece of my heart, Em . . . The big piece is all yours of course.'

They both grinned and then took up that long, lingering kiss once more.

Later, in the early hours of the morning, Emma woke. The excitement of the last few hours was still flooding her veins, and her mind was going over the events of the day. She felt restless, drawn to go out on to the balcony. She put on the hotel's towelling robe and went out in bare feet. She could see the sea glinting silver in the bay. And then she looked up. Wow, it was stunning. A sky full of stars.

She took a deep breath.

'I'm happy, Luke,' she said softly to the night sky. 'And I'll still always love you, and I'll never forget you.'

It may have just been a coincidence, but with that, a shooting star burst into life and blazed a small trail across the sky. Watching it, Emma felt a lift of joy, and then the most incredible sense of peace.

She heard footsteps behind her and then Max stood

next to her, dressed in just a pair of boxer shorts. 'You okay?' She could feel his warmth beside her.

'Yes . . . the sky is so beautiful tonight.'

Max looked up too. 'It's amazing.'

It was as if a sparkling icing-sugar shaker had been dusted across the heavens. Looking at that expanse of stars, with Max there beside her, she had a feeling that she hadn't had for a very long time – that the future was looking bright, that life was good and so very precious.

Max stood with her, silent for a while. The two of them, side by side. Then he gently reached for her hand where the engagement ring now rested. 'You ready to come back to bed now?'

Emma took one last look at the glinting waves, the velvet sky, and turned towards her new fiancé. 'Absolutely!'

A Letter from Caroline

Thank you so much for choosing to read *The Cosy Seaside Chocolate Shop*. I hope you've had a great time in Warkton-by-the-Sea with Emma and Max. Hopefully you've been curled up with a box or bar of your favourite chocs next to you!

If you have enjoyed this book, please don't hesitate to get in touch or to leave a review. I always love hearing my readers' reactions, and it also makes a big difference in helping new readers to discover my books for the first time. You'd make an author very happy. ☺

You are welcome to pop along to my Facebook page, Twitter profile or blog page. Please share your news, views, recipe tips, and read all about your favourite chocolates too. It's lovely to make new friends, so keep in touch.

Well, the next book is calling, so it's back to the writing! Thanks again, and see you soon!

Caroline x

🅕 /CarolineRobertsAuthor
🅣 @_caroroberts
carolinerobertswriter.blogspot.co.uk

Acknowledgements

Thanks to my chocolate-making friends – June Carruthers, Louise at Cabosse in Warkworth, Kiki's Chocolates in Coldingham, The Chocolate Spa Alnwick, and Bev Stephenson of North Chocolates – for all your help, ideas and inspiration.

For my team at HarperImpulse and HarperCollins – my wonderful editor Charlotte Brabbin, and Charlotte Ledger and Kimberley Young, thanks for your support from day one. Also to all the HC staff who help with the fabulous cover designs, sales and marketing.

My lovely agent Hannah Ferguson, thanks for being there with great advice and for travelling and sharing my special moment (whilst heavily pregnant!) when I was shortlisted at The Romantic Novelists' Association Awards this year. Also to Caroline, Jo and the team at Hardman & Swainson, thank you.

For The Romantic Novelists' Association and my fabulous Border Reivers Northumberland Chapter. Thanks so much for all the years of support and friendship, and for tea, cake, prosecco and chats – essential writing fuel!

For my wonderful family and friends – a huge cheers, folks!

My readers and the book blogging community – thank you so much for getting in touch with your fantastic comments, reviews and support. It's wonderful to hear from you and I hope you have enjoyed escaping for a while in my chocolate-filled teashop kind of world.

All best wishes,
Caroline x

Bev's Raspberry-Gin Chocolate Truffles

(Makes approx. 24)

Ingredients
125ml double cream*
250g of good quality (at least 70%) dark chocolate, finely chopped
2 tablespoons raspberry gin (or why not try sloe gin, elderflower gin – whatever takes your fancy!)
125g dark, milk or white chocolate to decorate

Method
1. Bring the cream just to the boil in a small pan. Remove
   from heat and stir in the dark chocolate until melted.
2. Stir in the gin. Pour into a bowl and chill until firm (in a
   fridge for around 4 hours).
3. Scoop out a teaspoon of mixture, roll into a ball with your
   hands – this is the messy bit! – and place on to greaseproof
   paper. Repeat.
4. Melt your preferred decorating chocolate gently in a bowl
   over hot water (white or dark – both work really well).
5. Using a fork or cocktail sticks, dip the truffle balls into the
   melted chocolate to coat all over. Transfer to greaseproof
   paper to set.

*As these truffles are made with cream, store in a fridge and eat
within one week.

Perfect served with prosecco and friends!

Chocolate-dipped Strawberries

Ingredients
400g punnet of fresh strawberries
Dark (70%), milk or white chocolate for dipping (100g each
approx.)

Method
1. Prepare a tray with some greaseproof or baking paper.
2. Keep the strawberries whole with their stalks on.
3. Melt the chocolate in separate bowls. Dip the strawberries
   in, holding the stalk, so the lower half is covered. Place
   carefully on the paper and allow to cool.

*Eat and enjoy! (They can even count as one of
your five-a-day!)*

Prosecco Cocktails
(Raspberry Gin, Elderflower Gin)

Choose your favourite gin liqueur. I love Raspberry Gin for this.
(The Edinburgh Gin Company do some amazing flavours – you
can even try Rhubarb and Ginger or Pomegranate and Rose.)

<u>Method</u>
1. Add a 25ml measure to the bottom of a glass flute and fill
   with prosecco (or champagne if you're feeling decadent).
2. If you are having the Raspberry Gin flavour, pop a fresh
   raspberry into the glass to decorate!

*Hey presto! Sip and enjoy. Perfect served on a summer's day
with friends!*

Discover more baking adventures in Caroline Roberts'
heart-warming 'Cosy Teashop' series

'Oodles of charm, it's pure escapism'
Cathy Bramley

Both available to buy now!

Find out where the magic began
for Emma in the first novel in
the 'Cosy Chocolate Shop' series!

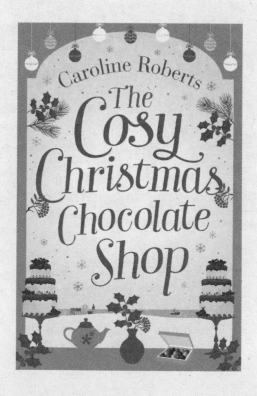

Available to buy now